THE RAGGED

Allan Massie CBE was born in Singapore in 1938. He is a journalist, columnist, sports writer and novelist. His fiction titles include *The Last Peacock*, winner of the Frederick Niven Award in 1981, *A Question of Loyalties*, winner of the Saltire Society/*Scotsman* Book of the Year, and the widely acclaimed Roman trilogy, *Augustus*, *Tiberius* and *Caesar*. His non-fiction includes *Byron's Travels* and a biography of Colette. A Fellow of the Royal Society of Literature, he has lived in the Scottish Borders, near Scott's home at Abbotsford, for the last thirty-five years.

The Ragged Lion
A Memoir

Allan Massie

First published in Great Britain in 1994 by Hutchinson Ltd.
This edition published in Great Britain in 2018 by Polygon,
an imprint of Birlinn Ltd.

Birlinn Ltd
West Newington House
10 Newington Road
Edinburgh
EH9 1QS

www.polygonbooks.co.uk

1

ISBN 978 1 84697 455 7
eBook ISBN 978 1 78885 079 7

British Library Cataloguing in Publication Data
A catalogue record for this book is available on request
from the British Library.

Typeset by 3btype.com

Printed and bound in Great Britain by Clays Ltd, St Ives plc

First, for Alison, more than ever;
then for Judy Steel

A glossary of Scots words is on page 297.

Introduction

In Naples, in 1964, I used to give English conversation lessons to a certain Contessa —. She was – it seemed to me, being then in my youth – an elderly lady, and her English was in fact extremely good, for before the First World War she had had an English, or rather Scots, governess – a Miss MacIvor from Inverness, 'where, I am told, they speak the best English, or rather the purest'. (So, perhaps, they still did in those days, for many of them were native Gaelic-speakers, and learned English as a second language.) The Contessa complained, however, that she found few opportunities these days to speak English 'seriously'; she was devoted to literature, and was prepared to pay, quite handsomely, for an hour or two of literary talk. She was indeed far better read than I, not only, as might have been expected, in Italian literature, of which I was indeed utterly ignorant, and in French, of which I had some knowledge, but also, somewhat to my shame, in English literature. Indeed, if she derived some pleasure from conversing on literary topics in English, the advantage was rather mine, not only in financial terms, but because I learned a good deal from her.

She had a particular devotion to the Waverley novels, of which I had then read only a handful, and to Scott's poetry which I had not read since prep school days, when Elizabeth Langlands (mother of the girl I later married) took us through *Marmion* and *The Lady of the Lake*. The Contessa's enthusiasm for Scott had first been fired by Miss MacIvor, who believed herself to be descended from Fergus MacIvor, the Highland chieftain in *Waverley* itself. It may seem odd to claim descent from a fictional character, but, as Graham Greene has since shown in *Monsignor Quixote*, Miss MacIvor's case was not unique.

The Contessa, in the kindest manner, used to reproach me, as a Scot with, already, pretensions to authorship myself, for my ignorance, as she saw it, of Sir Walter's work.

'Even *Peveril of the Peak*, which is not a good work, you should read,' she said. 'And *Quentin Durward* – can anything be more intelligent than his portrayal of Louis XI? But of course the greatest novels are the Scotch ones – I think it is not considered correct to say "Scotch" now, am I right?'

'There is a foolish prejudice that it should be restricted to whisky,' I said, 'but it was good enough for Sir Walter.'

'And therefore for me,' she replied, 'except that I should wish to be up-to-date, and not offend. So let us say "Scots" or "Scottish". They are sublime. His own favourite, I believe, was *Redgauntlet*. Yet for a particular reason, which I may tell you some day when we are better acquainted, I have an affection also for *Castle Dangerous*, the very last one he wrote, when he was so ill, poor man.'

'I must tell you', she said on a later occasion, 'that, besides the influence of Miss MacIvor, and my real admiration for Scott's novels and poetry, I have another peculiar reason for my interest in Sir Walter. You see,' – she paused, and, if I remember, blushed – 'his younger son, Charles, when he was attached to the British Embassy here, was a particular friend of my great-grandmother. In fact . . .

But there, for the time being, she broke off.

On my next visit, she said:

'You will find this hard to believe, but I possess what is a manuscript of Sir Walter's. It is not one of the novels, rather a sort of memoir, most peculiar. I should like you to read it. I think you would find it interesting.'

So a day was fixed, and a time appointed in the late afternoon, and I was settled at a rococo table in the library of her apartment in the family *palazzo*, before a pile of yellowing manuscript. The hand was not Scott's – even I could tell that, for it was manifestly Italian.

'Yes, of course,' she said, 'it is a copy which I believe Charles Scott presented to my great-grandmother, but read it – you will find it of interest.'

I obeyed, and indeed found it of some interest. Now, as it happened, I had not then read any biography of Scott, not even a popular one such as Hesketh Pearson's (which is, by the way, admirable); nor had I read his *Journal*; nor did I have any knowledge of the bibliography of Scott's works, nor of the state of Scott scholarship. In short, it never occurred to me that I was reading something which had never been published. No doubt it should have done so; but I was young, somewhat frivolous and, in any case, had lunched rather well. I may even have fallen asleep over my reading.

I had to leave Naples very soon afterwards, for pressing reasons of no concern now, and, though we exchanged letters for a few years, gradually lost touch with the Contessa. In time I returned to Scotland and slowly made myself into what I am today: a professional author, novelist, journalist, hack, what have you. Over the years I also repaired the deficiencies in my reading of Scott, which the Contessa had deplored, and came to admire him more and more deeply, concluding that he was not only incomparably the greatest Scottish writer – and that his only rival among English novelists is Dickens – but that he was also, if not the greatest Scotsman, which is perhaps a meaningless term, the most thoroughly Scottish of our great men: and I came to agree with Hesketh Pearson who called him 'the noblest man of letters in history', and wrote that 'he was the only person within my knowledge whose greatness as a writer was matched by his goodness as a man'.

My reverence and affection – no, love – for Scott were enhanced when in 1982 we moved from Edinburgh to the Borders, taking a house in the Yarrow Valley, some half-dozen miles from his beloved Abbotsford. No one, I believe, can come to understand Scott who does not also know Abbotsford, and for the opportunities given me to get to know the house and imbibe its atmosphere, I am profoundly grateful to its present custodians, his great-great-great-granddaughters, Mrs Patricia Maxwell-Scott and Dame Jean Maxwell-Scott.

Then in 1988 Judy Steel, who was then Director of the Borders Festival, asked me to write a play about Scott. *The Minstrel and the Shirra* ('Shirra' being the Selkirk word for Sheriff, and Scott having been, of course, Sheriff of Selkirkshire) was produced at the Borders Festival the following year, having its first performance appropriately in the Little Theatre made from the old game-larder at Bowhill, one of the seats of the Duke of Buccleuch, chief of the Clan Scott, and then in a revised (and improved) version at the 1991 Edinburgh International Festival, when Robert Paterson gave an uncannily convincing representation of Scott; he later repeated this at a special performance in the library of Abbotsford itself, on what was for me a singularly moving occasion.

Now, throughout this period I had given little thought to the manuscript which I had perused in somewhat cursory and inadequate fashion in the Contessa's library a quarter of a century back. Certainly, my memory of it was dim, and, if I thought about it at all, I suppose I assumed that it had been used by Lockhart as material for his monumental biography of his father-in-law.

Then I received a letter from the Contessa. Though over ninety, she still maintained a lively interest in art and literature, and somehow had learned of *The Minstrel and the Shirra*. She expressed her delight that at last, as it seemed, I had acquired a proper admiration for Sir Walter, and then continued:

'You will remember that I showed you the manuscript, or rather copy of a manuscript, which Charles Scott gave to my great-grandmother, though I do not think you read it with the due attention it deserved. Nevertheless, now that you have *reformed*, I intend to leave it to you in my will. It ought to return to Scotland. Moreover, my husband's nephews, my only surviving family connection, are *camorriste*, or at least in league with the *Camorra*.* They have no pride of family, and think of nothing but making money. I have no time for them, and it grieves me to think of how they dishonour their ancestors. My great-grandmother would be horrified if she could see them. Charles Scott entrusted the manuscript to her as to someone he loved and respected, and it should be passed on to someone who will feel the same emotions for it. Besides, it ought now to be published. It never has been, you know. I believe that when you read it, I omitted to give you also the note which Charles Scott himself wrote concerning it. You will find it of the *greatest* interest. By the way, I read your novel about Vichy France – *A Question of Loyalties*. Have I the title right? Not bad, not in Sir Walter's class, naturally, but not bad for this awful century of ours . . .'

---

* *Camorra, camorriste*: The Neapolitan Mafia.

I replied at once. We exchanged a couple of letters. Then she died. There were the usual legal delays. Then eventually in the autumn of 1993 the manuscript arrived.

This time I read it eagerly, and with a growing astonishment. How, I wondered, could I have been so obtuse in 1964? How could it not have been published? Then it struck me that it must have made a deeper impression on me than I had supposed, for certain passages in *The Minstrel and the Shirra* echoed others here of which I had retained no conscious memory.

The question of its authenticity at once arises. Since the manuscript exists only (as I have said) in a copy made by an Italian copyist – though the paper is of the right date – the matter can be resolved only by internal evidence. Certain passages resemble parts of the *Journal* very closely – often indeed almost word for word; others bear an equally striking resemblance to sentences or paragraphs in Lockhart's biography. It could therefore be a fabrication made chiefly from these sources. If so, one must wonder what can have been the point of it, since no attempt appears to have been made to profit from it at any time in the last century and a half.

For my part, I am impressed by the Contessa's assurance that Charles Scott gave it to her great-grandmother, all the more because I suspect that she believed there was more than affection between them (something at which Charles Scott hints in the last page of his Notes – if indeed they are his – which are here printed as an *Afterword*). When she said he 'was a particular friend of my great-grandmother. In fact . . .' and then broke off, I think she was on the brink of suggesting that there had been an affair, and that she might herself be a descendant of Sir Walter. Modesty, pride of family, stopped her short; which is why I have chosen to conceal her name.

Yet it must be admitted that there is no record of any other copy of this 'memoir'. There is none in the Library at Abbotsford where any such would certainly have been uncovered by either the former Librarian, the immensely erudite Dr Corson, or by his equally learned successor, Dr Douglas Gifford, in the all-but-impossible possibility that Dr Corson might have overlooked such a document. Nor can any record of one be traced in the National Library of Scotland, nor in the Library of any university in the United Kingdom or the United States of America, nor in any private collection. There is therefore room for scepticism.

For my part I find the style and matter convincing. It is not Scott at his best, but then, if it was for the most part written, as Charles Scott avers, in the last year or two of his life, when his health was broken and his intellectual faculties were decaying, that could not be expected. After all, neither *Count Robert of Paris* nor *Castle Dangerous*, his last two novels, is Scott at his best; though, having read, and accepted, the memoir, I now understand the Contessa's respect and admiration for the latter.

I believe that this is what happened. The manuscript was abandoned, as Charles Scott – let us suppose the author of the note is indeed Charles Scott – reports, in the Casa Bernini in Rome, where Scott had lodged during his few weeks in the city, and was then handed over to Charles as he passed through Rome on his way back to his post in Naples after Sir Walter's funeral. He had at least one copy made – perhaps two – his intentions remain a little unclear. One copy, or more probably the original manuscript, was sent to Lockhart, who made considerable use of it in compiling his great biography. This would account for the resemblances between Lockhart and the memoir; that is to say, Lockhart drew on the memoir rather than some presumed fabricator – but who? – on

Lockhart. As for the resemblances to the *Journal*, they may be easily dismissed: either Scott used the *Journal* as a source for the memoir, as Lockhart and all subsequent biographers have used it; or, writing about the same events in a different form, he almost automatically from time to time employed the same words. That is natural enough: we have all done so writing letters to different people about the one event.

Having used the manuscript, and drawn from it what he wanted, Lockhart then destroyed it. (It is possible, of course, that he merely lost it, but I doubt that; Lockhart was careful with his papers.) I realize this may seem a monstrous charge to bring against a dead man. But there was, of course, an unhappy, and recent, precedent: the burning of Byron's memoirs by those who believed they were caring for his reputation (not realizing that in doing so they destroyed their own). Lockhart had a great reverence for his father-in-law, nowhere more clearly indicated than in the pious death-scene he composed for him, which most modern critics judge a fabrication: an account of Scott's death as it should have been rather than as other evidence suggests it more probably was. There are passages in the memoir which must have pained Lockhart – which must pain any lover of Scott – for they indicate the deep distress and confusion of mind to which, from time to time, he was subjected in his last years. It is likely that Lockhart thought they would do Sir Walter no credit. I consider him mistaken if he indeed thought so. They seem to me to show Scott struggling with the utmost nobility and courage against the horrors to which his weary brain and spirit were subjected. It seems to me also that the contrast between such moments and the many passages of lucid and even sunny authority testifies very fully to his remarkable qualities. But, if Lockhart thought otherwise, and acted accordingly, I impugn his judgement, not his motives.

Charles Scott, I believe, knew his brother-in-law well, and assessed him correctly, when he wrote that, having taken what was useful to him from the memoir, he would 'out of a wish to protect my father's good name of which he is the very jealous guardian' destroy the manuscript; and I agree with Charles in thinking that view of it 'quite mistaken'.

I have only a few notes to add to this already over-long Introduction, but the first of them supplies an additional, personal, reason for my confidence of its authenticity. The reader will find that some curious scenes of a supernatural sort are set in Hastie's Close, off the Cowgate, in the Old Town of Edinburgh. It so happens that while I was engaged in editing the manuscript – no easy task, for we have to consider an Italian copyist, with perhaps an uncertain command of English, transcribing a manuscript which Charles Scott who knew his father's hand well had difficulty in reading – so that frequently I have had to hazard a guess at what Scott meant to write (those scholars engaged now on the preparation of the Edinburgh Edition of the Waverley Novels will, I am certain, extend their sympathy to me); it so happens, as I say, that while engaged in this task, I got into conversation with some friends one evening in Edinburgh concerning manifestations of the supernatural in the Old Town; one of those present, a young writer named Saul . . . asked whether I knew anything of Hastie's Close.

'No,' I replied (indeed lied) cautiously.

He then recounted an experience he had had there, which I shall not repeat, it being his story, not mine (and in any case I have forgotten the details); but the gist of it was that he had been made intensely aware of the presence of evil.

'Let us go there at once,' I said; which we did, but unfortunately the sound of rock music from a nearby night-club was sufficient to obliterate any supernatural resonances there might be.

Nevertheless the coincidence was sufficiently remarkable to be persuasive – I mean, the coincidence between what he described and what Sir Walter experienced or imagined.

I might note one other curious coincidence. At one point the author of the memoir – that is to say, Sir Walter – in discussing his medievalism remarks that future scholars would come to know far more about the Middle Ages than he did, but that he had done things – such as taking part in cavalry manoeuvres, building a castellated house, etc – of which later scholars were likely to be personally ignorant. This point is also made by A. N. Wilson in his admirable and enthusiastic study *The Laird of Abbotsford*; and since Mr Wilson cannot possibly have seen the memoir when he wrote his book, he is to be congratulated on his percipience.

Three final points: I owe a debt to all those who have encouraged me in this task, or who over the years have contributed to my knowledge of Scott, and enthusiasm for his life and work. There are a great many, but they must certainly include the Contessa —; Mrs Patricia Maxwell-Scott and Dame Jean Maxwell-Scott; Judy Steel; Robert and Elizabeth Langlands; Robert Paterson; Professor David Daiches, Paul H. Scott, Owen Dudley Edwards; Dr Eric Anderson, Dr David Hewitt, A.N. Wilson, Euan Cameron, and Giles Gordon.

Second, I take issue with Charles Scott, whose speculations are otherwise of the greatest interest, on one point. He observes that his father sometimes spoke in his last months of returning to poetry, and writes: 'The examples of verse here – often perhaps carelessly and perfunctorily thrown off – may not represent him at his finest' (an opinion from which I do not dissent) 'but they are sufficiently so to suggest, to me at least, that he would not have made the return in vain.' I fear that filial loyalty may have impaired Charles's critical judgement, and I would expect most readers to agree with me rather than with him.

Finally, while I was engaged on the work, a Cabinet Minister (for such men do – whether you like it or not – exist) expressed his enthusiasm for Scott, and suggested to me that a revival must be due. I expect the great Edinburgh Edition of the novels to provoke that, but if this work, which you are about to read, does anything to encourage it, then the hours of painful scrutiny of a flowery hand and of close examination of sometimes less than wholly coherent English, or Scots (either carelessly written in the first place, as was often Sir Walter's wont, for he relied much on his copyists and on James Ballantyne as proofreader, or simply misunderstood or illtranscribed), will have been more than worthwhile. If this book persuades anyone to turn to Scott's novels, both I and that intelligent reader will be well rewarded.

Allan Massie

Editorial Note: I have, for the convenience of the reader, given a title to each chapter (there is none in the manuscript), and, where appropriate, added a date which refers either to the events narrated or described in the chapter, or, more speculatively, to the year in which I have judged it may have been written. (*A.M.*)

I

Reflections, 1826

His Majesty, whom I believe, despite a wealth of testimony *ad adversum* (as we say in Scots Law) to be a good man – or at least a man whose inclination is to virtue, though the winds of life, fortune, fate, what have you, have all too frequently blawn his weathercock in a clean contrair direction – has now fallen prey, they tell me, to delusions. He has taken to relating with a heist of detail, how he led his regiment of Hussars – the 10th, as I recall – in a desperate charge at Waterloo. Then he will turn to the Duke and invite him to confirm the tale of his exploits. The Duke, being both courtier and ironist – without which latter attribute it were impossible for any honest man to be a courtier – then inclines his head, and remarks: 'I have frequently heard Your Majesty say so.' Now some will see in this only matter for comedy; moralists, an example of the degeneracy of princes. But, gazing out across the night sky of this divided city of Edinburgh, with the lum-hats rattling in what James Hogg would call 'a warlock-bearing wind', I see neither of these things. There is the possibility, I observe, that His Majesty with whom in my time I have cracked many a jest, kens fine what he is doing, and there is the possibility that what some call his 'delusion' is but a species of romance. For the distinction between what is and what is not is one that has puzzled philosophers at least since Plato, and when Dr Johnson sought to refute Bishop Berkeley's questioning of the reality of matter by giving a dunt with his foot to a stone, the refutation only holds good if you first accept the reality of the boot on the good Doctor's foot. These are strange thoughts for a man such as I perhaps, but then I have set so many beings skipping into a semblance of life from my study here or that at my beloved Abbotsford, that I may be forgiven in my night watches for questioning the nature of reality.

This would astonish my friends, for they regard me, I think – and believe I do not flatter myself – as a steady long-headed man. I see myself in that light also – some of the time. And why not? I have never been carried away by my renown, which I do not think ill-deserved, and for that reason may congratulate myself on the possession of a bottom of common sense. When I assure folk that in the great scale of things, literary fame and literary achievement are not worth a docken, I speak sincerely. On the other hand, when the characters of my imagination rise before me, I find it easier to converse with Jeannie Deans than I have ever done with Lady Scott. And where would that strange thing fit in Horatio's philosophy? Or in any notion of reality?

I am known too as a sociable man, a welcoming host and not unwelcome guest; but my happiest hours have been spent alone on a braeside with a book and a bannock and my dog. How would the fine ladies who smile to receive me in their drawing-rooms feel to hear that? What would any of us feel if our secret thoughts were spoken?

I have been thinking, often, of late, of a friend of my youth, Richard Heber. He was a man of great cultivation, charm of manner and address, who talked sense and sound morality. He had wit and gaiety, and passed everywhere, or generally, as a good man.

He shared my antiquarian interests and I dedicated one of the verse epistles in *Marmion* to him. He rose in the world, well-esteemed, and became Member of Parliament for the University of Oxford. And this man, of whom only good was thought, was detected in unnatural practices – with stable-boys, as it was said – and so, exile, disgraced, to Boulogne, then Naples, I suppose, where his vice is said to be freely practised, an object of contempt, ridicule and disgust. But to himself? Is he, I wonder, the same man in his own mind? I cannot believe otherwise. I have never been subject to that temptation, but the thought of Heber now makes me think it a mercy that our secret thoughts are hidden from each other. If at our social table we could see what passes in each bosom around we would seek dens and caverns to shun human society. Lord keep us from all temptation for we cannot be our own shepherd.

I write that sentence easily; and then I think of Heber in one of the rambles we took in our youth and of how we arrived at the inn at Grasmere, and of how he joked with the ostler – a comely lad, as I noticed even then – to take good care of his horse, or he would be obliged to chastise him; and then a look passed between them which I interpreted as an expression of good humour and mutual regard. And now I find myself pondering the significance of that exchange of words and glances. I remember the dinner that followed, with Wordsworth, though not the conversation, though I suppose Wordsworth spoke of his poetry, and its excellence – a habitual subject with him and one for which I do not reproach him, for his poetry is excellent and there were few enough ready to say so, so that he felt it behoved him to supply for himself the praise he considered his due. I remember this, as I say, and the excellence of the saddle of mutton we consumed, but none of it is as clear in my mind as that exchange between Heber and the boy. Yet even here

I pause, for that memory was buried for years, and has only come forth in its clarity since I heard of poor Heber's disgrace.

These are strange thoughts for a ruined man, and perhaps perplex me now to divert me from my task: my novel *Woodstock* – a tale of Cavaliers and Roundheads which it is sair wark to set in motion.

I made my early books out of my own being; now I make them out of other books. 'Hard pounding, gentlemen,' as the Duke said at Waterloo.

I have ever been a puzzle to myself, and if I divert myself now from my task, it may be on account of a consciousness that I have not long left to me to settle my accounts – not those accounts with which I am indeed deeply and properly concerned, my arrangements with my creditors, but the more profound and essential accounts with – I hardly know what – my soul? my Maker?

What I cannot now deny to myself is what in the days when I trusted myself to my imagination I dared not contemplate, for fear that examination would stifle what was most vital in me; but which, now that is moribund, I can no longer shrink from facing: the thorough and primitive duality of man. I employ the word 'primitive', not as my friend Francis Jeffrey and his troop of Whig reviewers might employ it: to denote a condition from which the progress of civilization has set us free; but rather as something inescapable, something that is of our necessary and enduring essence. Two natures – again, I think of poor Heber – appear to me to contend in the field of our very consciousness; so that if we – no, I – can be said to be either, it is only because unavoidably I am at root, and rootedly, both. When Christ prayed that this cup should pass from his lips, and knew that it could not do so, he spoke for all suffering humanity as surely as when he hung on the cross.

I caught my face in the glass on my return from the Court this evening, and saw in it what I feared to see: the madness of Lear, though it is not my daughters but my debts and my dreams that have brought me to my present pass. I make a fine show still in the public view – *fier comme un Ecossais* – but, alone, I call for cataracts to howl.

I made a fine show this morning even. I was accosted at the Court by little Mr Thomson of the Bank of Scotland.

'Ahem, Sir Walter,' says the shilpit cratur, then takes a pinch of snuff.

'Ahem, Sir Walter,' he tries again, 'the Bank of Scotland,' he says, 'the Bank of Scotland' – pronouncing the name with the same reverence that my friend and gamekeeper Tom Purdie used to bring to talk of 'fush' – 'the Bank of Scotland is not altogether happy with the arrangements for the settlement of your affairs that have been proposed . . . not altogether happy.'

Pinch of snuff.

'Proposed and agreed, Mr Thomson . . .'

'Nevertheless, Sir Walter, nevertheless, the Bank is of the opinion, having taken close cognizance of the proposed arrangements that they are insufficient, not wholly conversant with requirements, if you follow me, Sir Walter.'

'Mr Thomson,' I said, 'I do not follow you.'

'The security', he says, 'is deemed insufficient, conseedering the huge sum in question. In short, the Bank is determined, having taken, as I say, full cognizance of all matters relevant and material, that the marriage settlement which secures the property and heritage rights of Abbotsford for your son, Major Scott, should be reduced. That is to say, reduced.'

Pinch of snuff.

'Mr Thomson,' I said, speaking – I hope – calmly, 'the Bank must understand this. I am prepared to meet my obligations. I am ready to work myself to the grave to do so. But if the Bank presses me harder than the law requires, then I shall avail myself of the shield of the law, and allow myself to be declared bankrupt, with the security for my dependents that would ensure . . .'

'Oh crivvens, Sir Walter,' he says, startled out of gentility, 'you'd never do that, Sir Walter.'

'And why not, Mr Thomson?'

'The shame, Sir Walter, the shame, you'd never surely expose yourself to the shame of a public sequestration . . .'

'Mr Thomson, the Bank should understand this. I am ashamed of my debts, but not of their public recognition. The shame lies in the condition, in that fact, not in its acknowlegement. Perhaps you will be so kind as to report this to the Bank, and assure them that they have not taken, as you put it, full cognizance of the circumstances, which, you may remind them, include an agreement with which all interested parties have already concurred.'

So he hummed and he hawed, and shifted from foot to foot, and dabbed some more snuff up his nose, and assured me that he would convey my response to the Bank and trusted that he would be able to persuade them, etc, etc . . .

And I trust he will. But it smacks of sharp practice, and I'll have none of it.

Well, things maun be as they may, but if they press me over hard, they will learn that the Scotts were aye fiercest in the roughest fight. *Agere et pati Romanum est*: of all schools commend me to the Stoicks.

So, here I stand, Walter Scott, Baronet, of Abbotsford in the County of Selkirkshire, near widower and certain debtor, fifty-five, given to attacks of giddiness, and with my future as bright or grim as the Fife coast on a day of November haar. But in my heart I am still the lame bairn that made up stories for himself in the dark to keep the bogles off; and in doing so invited them in and made them dance.

> Oh merrily sang the fiddler's tune
> To the company filled with mirth
> But as merrily sounded the fiddle's note
> When the dance was that of death.

It occurs to me that if His Majesty really believes that he led the charge of his Hussars at Waterloo, he is a better man for the desire his lie expresses.

2

Childhood and Youth, 1771–87

Every Scotsman has his pedigree. It is indeed often our only possession, along with our pride and our poverty. I was not lacking in pride of pedigree, though that is scarcely a matter that affects a child. Indeed it is as age creeps upon one, and one feels one's own faculties decay, that interest in ancestry commonly grows strong, awoken in many cases, I am sure, by observation of one's own descendants. But childhood is a state, not a narrative. Though time may often hang more heavily on a child than on the grown man, the child is yet in a singular fashion free of time, for the future is at once unimaginable and without limits. Perhaps this is what Wordsworth means when he tells us that 'heaven lies about us in our infancy'.

But my own infancy was marked, and therefore interrupted, by illness. I was born in a foetid wynd in the Old Town of Edinburgh, where the houses leaned so close across to each other that – it was said – a man could stretch out his hand and shake that of his neighbour on the other side of the alley. Brothers and sisters died around me – six, I think – and I myself contracted a species of paralysis which, leaving me lame, has certainly influenced the course of my life. But for it, I am certain I should have been a soldier, for all my life, till recently, at least, my heart has been stirred by tales of martial deeds and set alight by the sound of martial music. Now tales of gallantry are more like to set the ready tears of old age flowing.

There is something to be said for childhood illness. It throws the sufferer back on himself. I early became a voracious reader, and stored my mind with legends, history and song; tales of chivalry were most to my taste and did much to form my temperament.

It happened too that I was sent to Bath to take the waters, which the doctors believed might alleviate my condition. It gave me, young as I was, experience of a softer, more polite way of life and social intercourse than was to be found in our ruder Edinburgh. It was not wasted on me, and as a consequence I have never indulged in the folly of contemning our southern neighbours. On the contrary, I have loved England ever since, second only to Scotland, and curiously this love was never shaken by what I learned of the long and heroic resistance which throughout more than two centuries my ancestral compatriots conducted against the threat of English dominance. It has seemed to me all my life that in the circumstances of the time, considering the natural tendency of warlike kings to try to add to their dominions, the threat was as natural as the resistance; and no matter for either praise or blame. But I do not know if I would have quickly come to this conclusion if I had not enjoyed that sojourn in the genteel society of Bath, which I felt, deeply, even as a young child.

I passed other years of my infancy at my grandfather's farm of Sandyknowe, in the shadow of Smailholm Tower. This grandfather, Robert Scott, was long remembered as a notable judge of sheep and cattle: a good peaceable man, whom I recall but dimly for he died when I was less than four years old. (That was before my visit to Bath.) In my memory, he wore the same expression that I catch in my shaving-glass, and I have known this give me a jolt when I have seen a certain tender expression cross my face, at a sudden remembered thought; it is the way he looked on me as a bairn.

Sandyknowe stands on a ridge above the Tweed, a few miles from Dryburgh Abbey where in time I shall be laid to rest, being entitled to a grave there on account of my familial connection with the house of Haliburton. I have been known to say that if I am a poet – which Francis Jeffrey has taken leave to doubt – it was childhood there that made me one, for from Sandyknowe the world opened before me as a broad, wind-blown country, with a prospect of a long twenty mile past the three-headed Eildons and on to the line of the blue and distant Cheviots. It was impossible to gaze on that, or to know the ruined splendor of our Border abbeys, without acquiring a sense of the past crowding upon me: in my dreams I saw our Merse forayers setting forth to harry the lands across the Border; I saw English armies marching up the old road that the Romans had built, and in their shadowy rear the legions themselves. Life at Sandyknowe was pastoral: the ewe-milkers carried me up the crags above the farm and I knew every sheep in the flock by name. Yet even on a summer evening, when the sun slipped behind the Eildons, shedding a soft yellow-gold on the gentle landscape, I knew how often this Arcadian mood had been cruelly broken in the past.

Moreover, a dead man filled my imagination. This was my great-grandfather, also Walter, who was known throughout Teviotdale as Beardie. His own father, Walter too, had walked in quiet paths, for he was a member of that pacific body of Christians known as Quakers, to whom I attempted to do some justice in that novel which is my own favourite among my works, if only because I put more of myself in that book than in any other, or indeed perhaps all of the others together – I mean *Redgauntlet*. But Beardie, it may be in rebellion against his father's tranquil ways – a rebellion shared, it would seem, by an elder brother, who was killed in a duel – was of a different temper. He became a fierce Jacobite, who fought with Dundee and was out in the '15, and was thought fortunate to have escaped a hanging. Thereafter, he never shaved his beard, having taken a vow not to do so till the exiled line of Stuart Kings was restored.

I shall say somewhat more of my remoter ancestors, though I believe this is not to the modern taste. Well, the waur for the modern taste, say I, for a man who has no care for his ancestors has little reason to care for his posterity either. He is trapped in the narrow dark of his own time, like a prisoner sunk in a slit-dungeon. They were not great men, though formidable and not to be trifled with. I am a collateral connection of the Scotts of Buccleuch, and have enjoyed the friendship of three Dukes who bear that noble title, but my branch of the family had put out its shoots from the trunk before the Scotts of Buccleuch commenced their great ascent in the peerage, and I own Scott of Harden as the chief of my sept. In my ancestry I number that hero of the ballads, Auld Wat of Harden, who married Mary Scott, the Flower of Yarrow. Those were the raiding days, and the tradition is well-attested that when the larder grew scanty she would place a dish of spurs on the table as a sign to her husband and sons that it was time to go riding again. I have had cause to smile at this story, for my dear Charlotte, having learned my fondness for it, as a result, I fear, of that frequent repetition to which wives are compelled to submit, learned to turn it to her advantage: 'Scott,' she would say, 'I must have a new dress;

so you must write a new novel.' A melancholy digression that memory is for me now.

Auld Wat's son William married the daughter of Sir Gideon Murray of Elibank, an ill-favoured lass known as 'Mucklemou'd Meg'. It was a case of 'tak the lass or feel the rope around your neck', and being a prudent man he took the lass, who proved as demanding a wife as those not favoured by nature often are, feeling as they do a need to assert themselves that more fortunate ladies may be free of. Their third son became Laird of Raeburn and married a MacDougal of Makerstoun, which family has some claim to be the oldest in Scotland. (That was the Quaker, Beardie's father.)

My own father, Walter Scott, broke the mould and removed to Edinburgh, where he was apprenticed to the law, and became a Writer to the Signet. He married Miss Anne Rutherford, the eldest daughter of the Professor of Medicine at the University; her grandfather had been minister of Yarrow, and her mother was a Swinton of that Ilk, and a descendant of Ben Jonson's friend, the poetic Earl of Stirling.

So, altogether, I had a fit pedigree for either warrior or Border minstrel.

My father was a good man, uncommonly handsome in youth, whose cast of mind made him a narrow one, but always affectionate. He was conscientious in his profession, to which he was devoted, with a high reverence for the Law, but – unlike many lawyers, I fear – had more care for his clients than for his own fortune. He was a devout Presbyterian who passed many of his leisure hours in the study of theology in which he was consequently deeply versed. His religion was Calvinism of the dourest kind, and the Sabbath was observed with the most rigid propriety in our household. He abstained from secular employment on the Lord's day, and his bairns were compelled to abstain likewise from all reading but that of the Scriptures. He had nothing of the spirit of that Border worthy, who was reputed to have interrupted his reading of the Good Book with the words, 'Had it no' been the Lord's will, this neist verse wad hae been better left oot, but since it is His will, I'll just read it to you lichtly.' Yet because my father was a man of infinite kindness, and neither prig nor hypocrite, this Sabbath restriction was less irksome than it might otherwise have been.

My mother was less devout, but not one to cross her husband; or rather her devotion took a different, perhaps more practical, form, since it expressed itself principally in good works and charity. It was she who encouraged me in my taste for poetry; her head was stored with the ballads and more recent, formal verses also, for she was peculiarly fond of Pope. In her youth she could remember talking with a man who had fought at Dunbar in the Civil Wars and could recall Cromwell's Ironsides marching up the High Street of Edinburgh, singing psalms. I was her favourite child, on account, I have always supposed, of my ill-health, for she feared that I would follow my six siblings to a child's grave; she called me 'Wattie, my lamb', to the day of her death, when I was middle-aged, a father myself, and had won some repute for my verses; and I am not ashamed to recall her tenderness now. Indeed I would be ashamed to forget it, or omit mention of it.

With her I read Homer's *Iliad* in Pope's translation, and from her I acquired my passion for Shakespeare, which has never deserted me, and which is not the least of my debt to her. Debts to parents are what can never be repaid, and the consciousness of this grows as one sees them sink into the decrepitude of age. I owe much to her friends, my aunts Janet and Christian, and Miss Alison Rutherford of Fairnilee (later Mrs Cockburn and author of an affecting version of *The Flowers of the Forest*) and Mrs Anne Murray Keith; all of whom spent many hours talking with the sickly child, or reading to him. Not the least of my debts to these ladies is to the language they spoke, Mrs Keith in particular speaking the old court-Scots of Holyrood, which has now quite died away, though I have attempted, with what success I know not, to preserve it in some of my fictions. There is nothing that can have a more profound influence on a child with any gift for composition than hearing language that is rich and precise; and I do not believe I would have become the writer I am if I had not enjoyed this experience in childhood.

I began Latin at my first school, a private academy kept by a Mr Fraser, but made little progress, for Fraser, though a worthy man, was but a grammarian, and plaguey dull. Yet he ground something of the elements of the tongue into me. We had by this time left College Wynd, without regret save on my part, for it excited my youthful imagination to know that that noisome alley stood on the site of the house of Kirk o' Fields, where in the winter of 1566 Lord Darnley had been murdered. Our new quarters were in the recently built George Square and they were not only more healthy but provided evidence of my father's advancement in his profession.

I then proceeded to the High School of Edinburgh, which in those days was kept by Dr Adam, a considerable scholar, and capable of imparting his enthusiasm to his students, though in other respects a man of unfortunate judgement, which would lead him into political affiliations generally thought disgraceful at the time of the Revolution in France. With him, I read the standard Latin authors, following Caesar's campaigns with what I think must have been an intelligent interest, and feeling the melancholy beauty of Virgil. I was never an exact scholar, for I cared more to draw the meaning from the work, the essence as you might say, than for the niceties of grammar and syntax. Yet I got enough to be able still to read Latin for my own pleasure, and for that I am very grateful.

My father, eager for my success, provided me with a tutor to supplement the teaching of the High School. This was a certain Mr James Mitchell, a virtuous man who later became minister at Montrose. He was a stiff scholar, too, and equally rigid in his religious and political persuasion, which was of the Calvinist and Whig mode. I was soon accustomed to disputing with him, for my political opinions were already clean opposite: I was a Cavalier and he a Roundhead and Covenanter. I admired the gallant Montrose; he the dark and politic Argyll. I took my politics of those days, not from any general principle, but on the same ground that Charles II did his religion: my conviction that the Cavalier creed was the more gentlemanlike of the two. Thought and experience – I may say in justice to myself – have confirmed much of my youthful prejudice. I believe in the value of tradition and accustomed ways of thought as of life, and I have learned to distrust all political abstraction and the theorists that delight in it.

I would not wish to suggest that life was all study. Indeed, though I read so widely and with such zest, I could never credit myself with being either studious or scholarly. I roved as I pleased, and read without method. My memory was of the best, but it retained only what pleased it. I have always relished the reply of an old Borderer when complimented by his minister on the strength of this faculty in him: 'I hae nae command of it,' he said. 'It retains what hits its fancy, and I misdoubt me, sir, that gin ye were to preach twae hour, I wadna be able to recall a word o' what you had been saying when you were finished.'

Edinburgh was an unruly and rowdy city in those days, as I believe the young – if they have a mind to it – can find most places to be. One feature of our lives in which we took the greatest pleasure was the strife in which we regularly –and in other respects irregularly – engaged with the lads of the neighbouring quarter: the Crosscauseway, Potterrow and Bristo Square. These encounters were known to us as 'bickers' and since the neighbouring quarter was inhabited by a poorer sort of folk, they partook somewhat of the struggles between the Patricians and Plebeians in Ancient Rome. They were fought with stones and sticks, and with much grappling and wrestling when we came to close quarters. Sometimes they would last for a whole evening, and, though there was ferocity, they were enjoyed on both sides, and a certain respect grew between the antagonists. One such stands out in my memory, for he was ever foremost in the opposing army: a tall, finely made blue-eyed boy, with long fair hair – the very image, it strikes me now – of a youthful Goth. This lad was ever first in the charge and last in the retreat – the Achilles or Ajax of the Crosscauseway. We never knew his name, but called him 'Green-breeks', from the breeches he wore, which indeed with a ragged shirt in some coarse material formed his only garment, for he fought barefoot and bare-armed.

One evening, when the battle was at its fiercest, Green-breeks got himself separated from his cohorts, and had laid hands on our standard, when one of our army, who had – deplorably and I know not how – got possession of a hunting-knife or small hanger, struck out at him, and laid his head open. He fell insensible to the ground, and the noise of battle was stilled by our horror of what we saw and what we feared. To our common shame, both armies melted away, leaving poor Green-breeks, his bright hair blood-boltered, to the charge of the watchman who soon appeared on the scene.

Meanwhile, the bloody hanger was thrown into one of the Meadows ditches, and the boy who had wielded it slunk away in renewed shame and terror. Green-breeks was carried to the Infirmary, where his wound was tended, and where he remained for a few days. He was questioned closely, but, with true nobility, declined to give any account of how he had come by his wound or to offer any identification of his assailant. When we learned of this, our hearts were touched by his gallantry, and we took up a collection for him, which he disdained to accept, saying he would not sell his blood; he would take, he said, only some snuff for his grandmother, if we would be so obliging as to obtain it, for she was devoted to snuff and could ill afford it.

I have often thought of Green-breeks and wondered what became of him. My younger brother, Mr Thomas Scott, who had also kept a warm memory of the lad, once proposed him as the subject of a novel, suggesting that he might be carried to Canada and involved in adventures with the colonists there. But nothing was made of it. Years later, when we dared to inform my father of this event, he reproached us, saying he wished he had been told at the time for he would have made it his business to help a boy of such spirit and nobility to establish himself in life. At the time, of course, on account of the sword, we were ashamed and afraid to speak, a circumstance which I now recall without surprise – for such feelings were natural to us at our age – but yet also with a degree of self-contempt.

It is at odd moments – sometimes in dreams – that the image of the young Goth returns to me. I cannot believe that he will have dwindled into a mean or humdrum way of life. I never spoke to him, save on that occasion when he refused our proferred recompense and asked for snuff 'for the auld woman', but he has haunted my imagination strangely. When I met the young Lord

Byron I could not but think of Green-breeks, for he had the same impetuosity, courage, and fire. But of that perhaps more later.

I left the High School in the spring of 1783, and passed six months at my aunt's in Kelso, where I attended the local Grammar School for a few hours a day, and formed a friendship with James Ballantyne, with whom I have ever since been so closely connected. My aunt's house stood on the bank of the glittering and resolute Tweed, and there under a spreading plane-tree in her garden I first read Percy's *Reliques of Ancient Poetry*. I read throughout the summer day, dinner forgotten, till towards dusk anxiety grew and I was fetched back into the house.

It is to this period of my life also that I trace the awakening of that feeling of delight in the natural beauty of the earth which has never deserted me, and to which I cling fast even now. The neighbourhood of Kelso – the most beautiful, if not the most Romantic, village in Scotland – is well calculated to arouse that feeling, for the landscape is not only lovely in itself, but rich in historical and legendary lore and associations, which to me are necessary for the complete enjoyment of natural beauty. This enjoyment is intensified when the associations belong also to one's own immediate inheritance:

'How shall we sing the Lord's song in a strange land?' as the Israelites asked, exiled, by the waters of Babylon . . .

Or, in a piece of doggerel, that has stuck in my mind since I first happened upon it:

> The streams of the southland are grand to the ee,
> But the streams o' the southland are no' part of me . . .

That autumn I put away the black bonnet, the bright waistcoat and the brown corduroy breeches of the High School boy, and matriculated at the town's college otherwise known as the University of Edinburgh. (If James VI and I had had his way it would have been known as King James's College, for on his return visit to Edinburgh in 1618 he was so impressed by the manner of the Latin addresses to him that he proposed to bestow this royal recognition. But he went south again, and the thing or intention was, I suppose, forgotten.) I attended the class in Humanity which was ill conducted and where I made accordingly little progress. I also frequented Dr Dalzell's Greek class, but since I was commencing *ab initio* while most of my fellow scholars had already mastered the basic grammar, I found myself all at sea, and covered my confusion by declaring that I saw no merit in Greek since Homer was in any case inferior to Ariosto, through whose works I had picked my way while at Kelso. This impudence aroused the contempt of Dr Dalzell, who therefore had little time for me. I sympathize with his impatience, and regret my attitude all the more, for I discovered later that he shared many of my prejudices. He used to maintain that Presbyterianism had killed Classical Scholarship in Scotland – 'smoored it wi' theology', he said; and the celebrated English divine, the Revd Sydney Smith, once told me that Dalzell had complained to him that 'If it had not been for that confounded Solemn League and Covenant, we would have made as good longs and shorts as England . . .' Maybe so; certes, our best Classical Scholars in that seventeenth century so deformed by a narrow religious fanaticism were Cavaliers and subsequently Jacobites. But there's 'nae yeese greeting ower a spiled hairst' as farmers say.

That I derived little benefit from the College was not entirely my fault, however, for I suffered renewed ill-health during the first years of my attendance, and was confined to bed and a lowering vegetable diet:

> In my lone chamber lying,
> I span imaginary tops,
> I dreamed of knightly deeds,
> And eek of mutton chops.

My most prolonged spell in bed came during my second year of apprenticeship to my father's law firm, though it was not – I think – a mere nervous reaction to the drudgery of my office work, my dislike for which I in any case endeavoured – with success, I believe – to conceal from my father, whose own reverence for the Law was such that my sentiments must have distressed him.

The vegetable diet – coupled with the command that I must not even speak, which was a considerable deprivation for one of my conversational bent – affected me with a species of nervousness which I had never known before, and of which I am glad to say I have been free ever since, at least till these last months. I would start upon even slight alarms – I experienced a want of decision in even small matters – I was acutely sensible to what at other times would have been mere trifling inconvenience. All this I associated with my restricted diet, and have never been able to rid myself of the conviction that the association was just, though reason tries to persuade me that the condition may have been the result of the disease rather than the prescribed cure.

It was about this time, during an intermittence in my illness, that I had my one meeting with Robert Burns. It was at an evening at Professor Ferguson's house at Sciennes. Being but a lad, I was naturally silent and anxious to observe rather than participate; but it happened that Burns's eye was caught by a print, and that he was moved by the verse attached. He read it aloud, and asked the company if any knew its provenance. By a lucky chance I recalled that the lines came from an almost forgotten poem by Langhorne, with the unpromising title 'The Justice of the Peace'. I imparted this information, in a whisper, to my neighbour, who passed it on to Burns, indicating that I was the source. He thanked me with a graciousness which I am still happy to recall.

What impressed me was his eye. It was large and of a dark cast, and glowed (I say literally *glowed*) when he spoke with feeling or interest. I never saw such an eye in a human head, though I have seen the most distinguished men in my time. It was a penetrating gaze, which seemed to draw on deep reserves, on a profound well of intellect and emotion.

With that illness childhood passed away. I rose from my bed, taller, robust, despite the vegetable diet. I was ready for any adventure, though bound by my father's wish, to the desk of my apprenticeship. Yet my mind ran free. I do not think I can ever have had the temerity to describe myself as well-educated, for there was no pattern in my extensive reading. I read for pleasure and my own peculiar enlightenment. There have been times when I could have wished to have had a more perfectly formed mind, but in general I have had the sense to put these thoughts behind me. My education made me what I am, and a more regular one might have stifled these impulses which have made me minstrel, poet, novelist. I went where the wind blew me, but with a certain native prudence I kenned the airt from which it came.

3

Tamlane, Fairies and Superstition: Reflections, 1826

All day in the Court the old rhyme ran in my head:

> I quit my body when I please,
>   Or unto it repair;
> We can inhabit, at our ease,
>   In either earth or air.

As I made my way down the Mound, with a sharp wind throwing the haar from the Firth in my face, I found my hand cramped on the head of my stick, and a pain – heart? – heartache? – I do not know – caught me behind the breastbone. For a moment the hum of the town was strangely still, as if I had been carried from it . . .

> There came a wind out of the north,
>   A sharp wind and a snell;
> And a dead sleep came over me,
>   And frae my horse I fell.

We belong to a rational age. I hear that on all sides, and would think myself a credulous fool if I doubted it. But then I think myself equally credulous for accepting the dictum. Superstition is foolishness we have gotten ourselves beyond; yet, in the mirk light, in the owl-time, in solitude, can any man of imagination not feel other worlds pressing about him? Can he be certain that reality yields itself only to the intellect?

James Hogg tells me – swears to me – that his grandfather, old Will o' the Phaup, saw the fairies dance at Carterhaugh, less than a mile from the Duke's seat of Bowhill. In that meadow, between Yarrow and Ettrick, I have had an old woman indicate to me the electrical rings which she assured me were the trace of fairy revels.

'Just there, shirra,' she said, 'just there, they put the stands of milk, and of watter, in whilk young Tamlane was dunkit, tae restore him to mortal man . . .' Then she led me a few yards further, and remarked how no grass grew where the stands had been placed, and gestured to a thicket of alder and hawthorn, where, she said, Miles Cross (a corruption, as I think, of Mary's Cross) had stood, beside which Janet in the Ballad had waited for the arrival of the Fairy host.

When I got one version of that Ballad from old Mistress Hogg, James's worthy mother, she said to me:

'But you'll nae prent that, shirra, for it wadna please the gude neighbours to see the words written doon . . .'

The 'good neighbours' is the term which the old folk of Selkirkshire still apply to the fairies. It is no doubt intended to propitiate them, in the same manner as in some parts of Scotland, the Devil is referred to as 'the good man'. This, however, can have another signification, for the 'gudeman' in our Scotch tongue is the name given to the tenant of a farm or piece of land; and so Satan or Lucifer is taken to be the tenant of the infernal regions. It used also to be the custom to leave a portion of a field unploughed, which was known as the 'gudeman's croft'. This was almost certainly an act of propitiation.

There are parts of my own life which I prefer to leave unexamined – and some might term that a species of moral 'gudeman's croft'. Again, of course, there is a reasonable explanation, which satisfies . . . reason: that I consider the habit of self-examination pernicious and debilitating.

When I wrote in the *Minstrelsy* a long introduction to the ballad of Tamlane – as in subsequent writings on Witchcraft and Demonology – I adopted the robust sceptical tone proper to an educated man of this generation; and I do not doubt that I was right. The cruelties that have been perpetrated on account of the widespread belief in these matters are abominable, and it is good that we have got beyond such nonsense.

Yet I had a lurcher bitch once that would not pass a wood where a man had hanged himself. Reason told me the wood was not altered by that action; the dog's reluctance, which must have been occasioned by something imperceptible to me, contradicted reason:

> I quit my body when I please,
>   Or unto it repair;
> We can inhabit, at our ease,
>   In either earth or air.

It is not difficult to formulate an exegesis of the belief, formerly almost universally held, in the presence and power of fairies, elves, goblins and other sprites. They may be considered the residual deities of the old religion that flourished before Christianity opened men's eyes to truth.

Another more recent memory comes upon me. It so happened that one night I found myself in the Cowgate, that sad street once the abode of the great nobility of Scotland; the great Cardinal Beaton, murdered in his castle of St Andrews by John Knox and other fanatical reformers, who included the black-hearted Sir James Balfour, had his Edinburgh palace there. The street is now sadly decayed and given over to the poorer sort of folk. It runs parallel, I must explain to those ignorant of Edinburgh, to the High Street, but at a lower level. Memories hang about it, of both revelry and dark deeds. I have heard it called a secret street of blood. Now I had been drinking in a tavern, but not so deep as to dull my senses. Indeed they were rather at that point when they seemed more alert than usual, when the eye picks out with unaccustomed clarity relations between buildings and the sky to which it is habitually blind. For some reason that escapes me I turned off up the steps that lead to a noisome close that goes by the name of Hastie's, and, being in a contemplative frame of mind, and, as I say, alert to the relation of objects, I leaned against a wall and lit a cheroot. My mood was placid and I even made verses in my head, as has often been my wont in such a condition – verses that on the occasion of which I speak have quite fled from me. As I rested there, at peace with man and the world, I felt even in that dead night a chill wind strike against my cheek, and there came upon me a sudden fear. Music started around me, but music such as I have rarely heard, a thin dancing fiddle that played a tune with no melody, and yet seemed to summon the listeners to a dance. A cloud slid over the moon, and I was assailed by a consciousness of a circumvallent evil. The houses were dark and still; no sound came from them, and I knew that the fiddle was played by no earthly being. I say 'I knew', because at that moment I had no doubt. I would have fled. I count myself a man of at least ordinary courage; yet I would have fled. But my feet would not respond to my will. Then the threat offered by the music died away. Its tone altered. I heard in it a softer invitation, and involuntarily my feet now mounted the steps in the direction in which the fiddle seemed to beckon. I looked up and, at the top of the steps, I saw three figures: the first, the fiddler, in sharp profile, with long hair over his shoulders; the second, an old dame crouched on a stool and smoking a pipe; and the third, myself, Walter Scott. The old woman turned to him, and took his hand, and indicated with her pipe at a fourth figure now emerging from the gloom: a slim girl, barefoot and with her head thrown back as if she was laughing. Yet no sound came but that of the mocking and inviting fiddle.

Then there was silence. A universal darkness covered all. I do not know if my will had rebelled. I only recall the inclination which I had experienced, and the feeling of sadness and loss which now suffused me.

> And was I called to Elfland, cuddy,
> Where the white lilies bloom
> Or to that mirk, mirk land, cuddy,
> The shades ayont the tomb.

My fear fled with the vision and the dying of the fiddle. I shook myself like a spaniel emerging from the Tweed.

'Weel, this is unco strange,' I said, 'is it no, Walter Scott, o' the Faculty of Advocates?'

But however reason re-asserts itself, such things cannot be forgotten.

There is a house in the West Bow, uninhabited for more than a hundred and fifty years because it was the dwelling-place of Major Weir, known as 'Angelical Thomas' on account of his fervour in preaching, till he confessed his dealings with the Devil, and was burnt at the stake, refusing the consolations of religion and crying out, 'I have lived like a beast. Let me die like a beast.'

> Will o' Wisp before them went,
> Sent forth a twinkling light;
> And soon she saw the Fairy bands
> All riding in her sight.
>
> And first gaed by the black black steed,
> And then gaed by the brown;
> But fast she gript the milk-white steed,
> And pu'd the rider down . . .

You have to be a man of determined narrow rationality to find such stuff merely fanciful; and if you are such a man, go and stand in Hastie's Close on a night twixt moon and mirk.

4

First and Second Love, 1791–1826

There are men who make love, love affairs, and the pursuit of women the main business of life. It has never been my way, and, truth to tell, I consider it a more proper mode of conduct for a Frenchman than a Scot. There is something demeaning, even unmanly, about it. Of course there are others – Byron, I fancy, was one of them – who are themselves so frequently, even incessantly, the objects of pursuit – women's prey – that they can scarcely be blamed for succumbing more often than may be thought decorous or moral. I am thankful that I have belonged to neither type, for when one considers how many hours must be passed in the whole weary rigmarole of seduction, or being seduced, it can be no wonder that the poor wretches are so often not only exhausted, but unfitted for, and denied, many of the more varied and even vigorous pleasures of existence. Old Baret in Elizabeth's reign describes such carpet-knights as 'those which serve abominable and filthy idleness'; to see a French fop enter a drawing-room has ever been enough to turn my stomach, usually a robust organ.

Conversely, however, the man who knows not love may be compared to a miser of the emotions. It is true that I have never been a great hand at depicting the tender passion in my novels, and this may fairly be accounted a deficiency. Yet when I read a book such as *Les Liaisons Dangereuses* by Monsieur Laclos – though I can admire the skill of its execution – my ain deficiency is one which I do not regret but rather thole happily.

And yet, and yet, if I cannot summon up the complacency of Sir Andrew and say 'I was adored once too', I can turn it round and confess that I have adored.

It began in the kirk, Greyfriars Kirk, on a wet Sunday in I forget which month of the year 1791. Looking across the pews, during a sermon that was even longer and more soporific than young men of sense usually discover sermons to be, I caught sight of a profile of such perfection that . . . that what? – that in the language of cheap romance, I was smitten. It was a young girl of no more than fifteen or sixteen. When she turned towards me I saw that the full face was worthy of the profile, but it was nevertheless the profile that ensnared me. She had large blue eyes, soft dark chestnut ringlets that framed the profile exquisitely, a complexion of cream and roses which turned more rosy as she caught my eye upon her, a generous mouth, and lips inviting the madness of kissing. Ever since, I have never been able to mock the young who declare their belief in that phenomenon 'love at first sight'. Indeed I would rather agree with Marlowe that 'whoever loved, that loved not at first sight?'

As we left the kirk, the rain – cold, sleety, Edinburgh rain blown slanting on the wind – had come on, and I was delighted to see that she was without an umbrella. I unfurled mine like a warship hoisting sail in pursuit, and was by her side, gallant as any cavalier. She accepted the protection I offered with a smile of the utmost sweetness, and then before we could engage in conversation – which was perhaps just as well since my tongue was tied as tight as a sailor's knot – her mother, umbrellaed, hove into sight.

As it happened she knew me – 'young Mr Scott,' says she, 'how kind of you', not adding the words that flew into my mind 'to a damsel in distress'. I recognized her, too, as Lady Jane Belsches of Fettercairn, an acquaintance of my parents – perhaps her husband was one of my father's clients, but of that I cannot at this distance of time be certain. The mother's arrival freed my tongue. I was able to talk of common everyday matters, attempting to do so in a manner that might show off what I had of wit and intelligence without exposing me to the charge of coxcombery. I escorted them home, was invited in to take a dish of tea, accepted willingly. Conversation ensued – again memory tells me nothing of what was said; but I was conscious that even in my state of immediate and utter besotment, I did not acquit myself too badly. When I dared – that is to say, when Lady Jane's glance was abstracted – I shot a look at the girl, whom I had discovered to be called Williamina. That look was intended to convey to her that I had constituted myself her knight, that the gesture with the umbrella meant at least as much as Sir Walter Raleigh laying his cloak on the puddle before Queen Elizabeth. She responded to this evidence of my passion with a demure lowering of those cornflower eyes, an action which intensified, if that were possible, my emotion, for it suggested to me that she was not wholly indifferent. Then, with a tact which I can still admire, I took my leave while my presence was yet welcome, a gesture of civility which was rewarded by an assurance from Lady Jane that she hoped I should feel free to call on them again. Free to call upon them again? I should have felt free to scale the wall of the tenement which they inhabited.

Our acquaintance ripened. To attempt to recall the conversation of two young people falling in love would be absurd at such a distance of time. No doubt for the most part like the generality of lovers we spoke a mixture of nonsense, reticence, and the occasional expression revealing something of our deepest feelings, from which, no doubt, with a like characteristic modesty, we retired with a blush and a stammer.

Certainly, however, we grew closer together, so much so that my father, honest man, thought it proper to speak to Sir John about the matter. He was, and it is to his credit, fully aware of the difference in rank, for not only was Sir John a baronet, but Lady Jane was the daughter of the Earl of Leven and Melville. Some may think this paternal intervention harsh. Nevertheless I see now – and, I believe, felt even then – that his warning proceeded from his certainty of what was in my own best interests, for he could not believe that Williamina's parents would consent to what at that period in my life and our family's history must have been judged by the world to be a misalliance; he did not wish to expose me to the charge of being a fortune-hunter; and he hoped – I am certain – that by nipping the affair in the bud, he would save me from pain, disappointment, and the censure of the world. That such intervention must cause me immediate pain may not have occurred to the worthy man, whose virtues did not extend to a great degree of sensitivity in matters of the heart. Yet even if it had occurred to him, he would not have refrained from performing what he considered to be his duty.

Curiously, perhaps, Sir John did not appear to be perturbed. He thanked my father for his care for the interests of all concerned, but assured him that he had formed a great respect for 'the young man', as he called me, and was therefore not disposed to bring matters to a halt. It would be presumptuous in me to suggest that he had discerned gifts or qualities in my character of which I had not as yet given any sign to the world in general. It may rather be that he enjoyed my company, for he certainly responded to my youthful enthusiasm, and frequently urged me on to wilder flights of conversational fancy and anecdote. But I think it most probable that he assumed that the affair, like the bonfires gardeners make of autumn leaves, would, unlike the bush that summoned Moses to the service of the Almighty, consume itself in its own good time.

Be that as it may, for three years I was in a dream of love. My friends were accustomed to toast my devotion to the 'Lady of the Green Mantle' as we agreed, in chivalric fashion, to term her. My hopes ran high, especially when, in the spring of 1796, I paid a prolonged visit to the family seat at Fettercairn. I was on the verge of proposing marriage, though in truth my material circumstances did not yet warrant such a step, at least in connection with such a bride. And then all evaporated. In the autumn, Williamina's engagement was announced to the banker Sir William Forbes of Pitsligo, who had been a friend of mine in College and in the Edinburgh Volunteer Light Horse.

I do not know what determined her. She had an affection for Sir William, but then she had an affection for me also. Perhaps there was something wild and uncertain in me which alarmed her – I was already translating German poetry, not, I would propose, an activity alarming in itself, but one suggestive of a strain in my nature which she may have found disconcerting. A man is bound to seek explanations for the preference shown to a rival in love, and it is unlikely that he will hit on the true one. Perhaps Lady Jane persuaded her. I do not know, for, though she had always stood my friend, there is a profound gulf fixed between the enjoyment of the company of a young man and his acceptability as a son-in-law. Certainly Sir William had more to offer in material terms, and no wise mother will disregard such a consideration.

Yet the truth may simply be that the truth is never ascertainable in such matters. Who can determine, who can track, the vagaries of the heart? It is one reason why I have fought shy of any profound attempt at the delineation of the tender passion in my novels: that I do not believe in answers, or am at least aware of my inability to discern them.

I was desolate, heart-broken for two years. Then my heart was handsomely pieced together. Nevertheless the crack will be with me till my dying day. It is like an old plate, good enough to use for the family breakfast table, but banished when guests are present. Some of my friends were anxious, as friends are on such occasions, for my sanity. It was reported to me that one said to another, 'I shudder at the violence of his most irritable and ungovernable mind.' His fears were groundless or at least exaggerated. The truth is that melancholy, by which I mean love-melancholy, is not so deeply seated in a robust and elastic mind as the sentimental school of novelists would have us suppose. It gives, it yields, to the busy hum of life. I wrote verses to Williamina, and that eased my pain.

> The violet in her greenwood bower,
>   Where birchen boughs with hazels mingle,
> May boast itself the fairest flower
>   In glen, or copse, or forest dingle.
>
> Though fair her gems of azure hue
>   Beneath the dewdrop's weight declining
> I've seen an eye of lovelier blue,
>   More sweet through watery lustre shining

The summer sun that dew shall dry,
   Ere yet the day be passed its morrow;
Nor longer in my false love's eye
   Remained the tear of parting sorrow . . .

It was false itself to call her my 'false love', but poets maun be permitted their lies, and convention insists that any lost love has played the poet false.

There is another convention: that the poet can rid himself of a sentiment by putting it in verse. Alas, that too is false. It so happens that as a young lover I carved Williamina's name on the turf at the castle-gate in St Andrews, and returning there, half a lifetime later, when the poor lass was already in the grave, I sat on a nearby gravestone, and wondered why the name should still agitate my heart. Then, not long syne, with Williamina sixteen, seventeen, years dead, I met old Lady Jane at a reception in Edinburgh; and it was as if the tomb opened and the very grave surrendered its dead, for I fairly softened myself, like a daft old fool, with recalling stories and fond memories, and jests and smiles and all the pleasures and pains of our long-departed social intercourse, till I was fit for nothing but shedding tears and repeating sad verses the whole night long. Sad work, sad work. The very grave yawning, Eurydice sought for, and time rolls back these thirty years to add to my perplexities.

But youth is resilient. 'Men have died from time to time and worms have eaten them, but not for love,' as brave Rosalind has it. The cracked plate made a show of sorts. Some half-dozen months after Williamina wed Sir William, I made a tour of the English lakes with my friend Adam Ferguson (son of the philosopher) and my brother John. Something of the elder Ferguson's philosophy had rubbed off on young Adam, and it may be by extension on me. No matter how it happened, but my spirits were buoyant as they have usually been when engaged on travel. In the little watering-place of Gilsland, pretty as a miniature of Highland scenery, I came upon a young lady, pretty as a miniature herself. She was brown and tawny where Williamina was pink and fair. She had more than a suspicion of a foreign accent, light as a robin, whereas Williamina spoke with an equal lightness, but slowly, with the thoughtfulness of that north-east corner of Scotland, hard-won from nature, from which she hailed. This young lady was the daughter of a French refugee, a royalist and a Huguenot from Lyon. Her name was Charlotte Charpentier, and her guardian in this country – the father being dead – was Lord Downshire. We exchanged glances, and she did not lower her eyes in any pretended bashfulness. We fell into conversation, and discovered that we agreed well, though there were few subjects beyond pleasantries on which we found that we cared to converse. (How often in the years to come I have heard her say, 'Scott, I do not think thoughtful people can ever be truly happy.' Sometimes, to amuse me, or attract more attention for the company, she would exaggerate the foreignness of her accent and drop the h from happy.) Our first encounter took place at a ball at which I wore my uniform of the Edinburgh Volunteer Light Horse. It delighted her to see men in full regimentals. I knew from earliest conversations that our very differences, allied to her good sense and lively humour, made it possible that we should live contentedly together. I proposed; she accepted me without any missish demur or pretence that my offer had so taken her by surprise that she would require to think about it. Her guardian's consent was obtained; my father, alas in poor health with death staring him in the face, approved the thought that his gangrel loon was on the point of settling down, and the deed was accomplished. We were married in St Mary's Church, Carlisle, on Christmas Eve 1797, and I have never regretted it.

Years later, consulted by my friend Lady Abercorn about the proposed engagement of one of her children, and the advantages of a love-match as opposed to an arranged marriage, I wrote:

> Mrs Scott's match and mine was of our own making, and proceeded from the most sincere affection on both sides, which has rather increased than diminished during twelve years of marriage. But it was something short of love in all its forms, which I suspect people only feel once in all their lives, folk who have been nearly drowned in bathing rarely venturing a second time out of their depth . . .

My poor Charlotte. I owe much happiness to her, and I do not believe I ever caused her great pain. Perhaps that is as much as any husband can hope to say, and more than most can truthfully claim. She did not enter my dreams. She had no interest in what I wrote, and indeed I can conceive nothing more destructive of domestic happiness for an author than a bluestocking of a wife who subjects all his scribblings to the sort of criticism that belongs properly to the reviews. We understood each other, I believe, or at the very least she understood as much of me as I cared to have understood.

When she lay on her deathbed, those brown sparkling eyes, which once caused one of our sons to tell her that what he admired most in her was 'her laughing philosophy', now dulled with pain and with the laudanum they had given her to try to alleviate her suffering, she yet raised her head from the pillow, and with a smile and a sigh, said reproachfully, 'you all 'ave such melancholy faces'.

I trust that when my time comes to depart I may equal her Roman stoicism, a stoicism which could surprise only those whose sole knowledge of her was as a bright social being.

I have never admired the uxorious man, for there are parts of a man's life which should properly remain separate from a woman's; and the uxorious man diminishes himself and denies a large part of his nature, but I contemn the bad, the careless, and the selfish husband utterly, and I trust I may acquit myself of this charge.

Indeed I may go further. The time may come in this disjointed memoir, written to staunch the pain of these hours of grievous fortune, when I choose to talk, as I have ever shrunk from talking, about the works that have proceeded from my imagination; but I shall say this now. Critics have complained that my heroines are for the most part dull. So they are, I fear, plaguey dull. It is strange, for I have lived much of my life among fine ladies, ladies of quality; and am no great hand at depicting them in my novels. The reason is plain, though perhaps hidden from my critics. It is that I do not hear them talk. They do not speak to my imagination, and when a character fails to do that, the words lie leaden on the page. Yet when I happen on an old crone like Madge Wildfire or Meg Merrilees, my prose takes wing. Perhaps my father was right when he said I was born to be a strolling pedlar. That was in the time of my youth when I spent whole days, even weeks, wandering the hills, with no purpose but movement and the making of strange acquaintances. 'Whaur's Wattie?' they would speir at home. 'Somewhere atween the Tweed and the Pentlands.' The accusation of being a strolling pedlar did not and does not, displease me, for what, when all is said and done, is a minstrel and story-teller but a species of pedlar?

And then Jeannie Deans: her douce scrupulous Presbyterian voice conceals its warm humanity aneath a dour rectitude. When I was writing *The Heart of Midlothian*, her voice dinged in my lugs. Oh, Jeannie, you are worth a clutch of my fine ladies.

If Charlotte had known Jeannie, she would have admired her character, but she would not have been comfortable with it, and Williamina – Williamina would have shaken that bonny head and wondered at the strange airt my imagination led me in. But then, if I had married Williamina, would it have remained active, or would I have directed myself with more determination towards my career in the Law? Married to her, might I have become Lord President of the Court of Session? Strange are the ways of Providence, that bitter disappointment and heartbreak can drive a man to fulfil himself in other ways.

5

On Mortality, 1826

When I cast back over the past in this manner, my pen runs with its old easy gait. I have ever been a rapid writer, rarely pausing in my execution, a habit or attribute that I credit to my practice of telling myself stories in the hour before I rise from my bed, so that the day's work is half-formed before ever I settle myself at my desk. When I have gone most flowingly at my task, the words have run like the Tweed in spate, for it has aye been as if I was remembering rather than inventing.

But now, in these dark watches, as the wind rattles the lums, and the moon scuds along the roof-tops, and I wait, sleepless, for another dawn that promises nothing but more toil, my thoughts move with an old man's nervous and hesitating step. There is something gruesome about the dawn sky in a city: oh to be on the braes above Abbotsford, and hear the laverock and the whaups. But I am unjust; the fault, dear Brutus, lies not in the stars, or in the city sky, but in myself.

I look mortality in the face.

> I dreamed last night I walked with death
> Upon a barren strand

The wind blew chill, and cold his breath;
I felt his fleshless hand.

I have never said, like medieval folk, '*timor mortis conturbat me*', for I have seen too many good Christian deaths to fear the hour when we are led like little children into the dark. What disturbs me and keeps me from my bed, or from sleep when I venture there, is something both more awful and less absolute than death. It is easy to say 'Be absolute for death. Or life or death shall thereby be the sweeter.' It is an undiscovered country, and if no traveller returns from its bourn, why then ... but these are foolish night thoughts. It is Lear's cry, 'Let me not be mad, sweet heaven,' that rings in my ears.

How the world would wonder, and many laugh, if they could see me in this dark wood: Sir Walter Scott, Baronet, of Abbotsford, Sheriff of Selkirkshire, known – I do not flatter myself – for robust sanity, a man fixed in his own mind, and therefore in the eyes of others, for courage in adversity. Courage in adversity: that's the thing to keep a hold of. But I think of Bothwell chained in that dungeon in that Danish castle, the name of which I forget. I have always prided myself on my memory. It is on account of its excellence that I have aye been able to work so fast. Where other men have been delayed in their labours by the necessity of consulting books to mak siccar of their references, I have drawn them up from what seemed to me an inexhaustible well. And now the springs have begun to run dry. That frightens me.

I spent years once preparing a complete edition of Swift, solid labour, for though I admire the manner of his writing beyond measure, and though the matter often pleased me on account of his power of invention and his gift for the unexpected yoking together of otherwise discordant ideas, it was still hard pounding because his misanthropy revolted me: and now all that comes to mind, or rather the first thing that comes to mind when I think of him, is that he was a poor devil who feared he would die from the top, his mind gone; and that his fears were confirmed.

I have always accounted myself a good Christian – saving always the reservation that I would not make a parade of Christian virtues. 'When you pray, do not pray as the Pharisees do . . .' I have ever abhorred enthusiasm, and indeed when I abandoned the Established Church of Scotland to adhere to the Episcopal Kirk, I gave it as my reason that as an Episcopalian, I did not have to gang to the kirk sae often. There were other reasons, which I may call historical-political, and I have sympathy too with Charles II who became a Roman Catholic because he said it was the most gentlemanly religion, which is what I thought of Episcopalianism. I was dismayed by the unction of so many of our Presbyterian preachers, and their insistence that they belonged to the Elect, and that even the Moderates among them accounted themselves the unco gude. But now, last night, I fell on my knees, with some difficulty on account of my rheumatism, and tried to pray, but the words would not come. The words would not come to me, who has never been short of words. My poor Charlotte once met Dr Wilson who operated on my tongue when I was a bairn, and said to him, 'Why, Dr Wilson, you must be accounted the cleverest surgeon in all Britain, for you set Scott's tongue going then, and it has never stopped since.'

Yet when I tried to pray, there were no words.

Is it a judgement on my folly? Yet the Lord is said to have a tenderness for fools.

I wonder when I am dead, where this journal will be found? In a chest in some obscure lodging-house, where I have hung up my scutcheon, and have died, perhaps like the great Duke of Buckingham, in the worst inn's worst room? Or will it be discovered in the library at Abbotsford, and will folk then laugh indulgently at these moments when I approach the yawning jaws of despair. *Facilis descensus Averni*, but the way up is hard, for you must first find and pluck the golden bough.

A glass of toddy and a cheroot may steady me.

When I die, will folk shake their head and say, 'puir gentleman, puir gentleman, naebody's enemy but his ain. What a peety he took thon foolish title.'

'Lead us not into temptation', but I ran towards it, waiting for no leader.

In 1659, the Earl of Traquair, Lord Treasurer in King Charles's Privy Council in the 1630s, was found begging in the streets of Edinburgh without even the means of pay for the cobbling of his boots. The great financier of the Covenant, Sir William Dick of Braid, died in a debtors' prison in England.

Is it any wonder that such thoughts oppress me? It was easy – and manly and admirable – to say, when they confronted me with the debts that had been accumulated in I know not what sort of fashion posterity will decide, 'My own right hand shall save me'. But if I fail? What awaits me then?

And if my memory is failing, how can I succeed?

These are night thoughts that will vanish with the dawn.

The happiness of so many hangs on my labours – my family, my dependants at Abbotsford, even my poor dogs.

That is another thought that oppresses me.

If only I could sleep. If I cannot sleep, if only I could pray. Perhaps if I could pray, I could sleep.

The rose that blooms at Glastonbury
Flowers on Christmas Day,
A sign to Christian men, they say,
That if we think on Glastonbury,
Sorrow and sin will pass away.

The old carol pleases me.

The rose that blooms at Glastonbury
Springs from the Cross of shame,
A sign to Christian men, they claim,
That if we think on Glastonbury
We have our share in Christ's own name.

I mind an old man I came upon dying in a poor cottage in Liddesdale who said to me, 'Shirra, shirra, I hae lang been yare tae meet my Maker, but I would fain have been blithe tae see another lambing and the broom yalla on the braeside.'

My heart went out to him, but there were still wreaths of snow by the dykes of the sheep fold, and he slipped away between the rising of the moon and cockcrow, babbling like Falstaff of what he could never have again.

Shall I go like him, easy but regretful, or like Bothwell screaming as the demons assailed him?

When thou from hence away art past,
  – Every nighte and alle,
To Whinny-muir thou com'st at last;
  And Christe receive thy saule . . .

That verse, from a dirge, sung by the lower ranks of Roman Catholics in the north of England, while watching a body prior to interment, has haunted me – the whole dirge has haunted me – since I first heard it. I included it in my *Minstrelsy*, and Mr Frank, the executor of the late Mr Ritson who had discovered it in a manuscript of the Cotton Library, containing an account of Cleveland in Yorkshire in the reign of Queen Elizabeth, was kind enough to send me the following note:

> When any dieth, certaine women sing a song to the dead bodie, recyting the journey that the partye deceased must goe; and they are of beliefe (such is their fondnesse) that once in their lives, it is good to give a pair of shoes to a poore man, for as much as, after this life, they are to pass barefoote through a great launde, full of thorns and furzen, except by the meryte of the almes aforesaid they have redeemed the forfeyte; for, at the edge of the launde, an oulde man shall meet them with the same shoes that were given to the partye when he was lyving; and, after he hath shodde them, dismisseth him to go through thick and thin, without scratch or scalle . . .

I suppose it is a memory of the parable of the Good Samaritan.

Well, when Tom Purdie came up before me in my capacity as Shirra, on a poaching charge, and I dismissed him and made him my gamekeeper, he subsequently becoming of all men the one in whom I reposed most love, trust, and confidence, I bought him a pair of boots when he entered my service. So perhaps I too may pass 'through thick and thin, without scratch or scalle'.

Yet there are thorns and furzen enough in this world, and in my present predicament I feel not only barefoote, but naked as Lear, Kent, and the Fool to the storms of the world.

Lord, let me not be mad, sweet heaven, and Christe receive my saule; and let me see the broom yellow on the hillside above Abbotsford.

6

Border Memories and First Poetic Success, 1797–1808

I have ever felt myself a Borderer. The melancholy romance of the House of Douglas moved me from my earliest childhood. It rose in splendour with the Good Lord James, the companion of Bruce; it ended piteously with the eighth Earl, after many years of exile in England, returning full of longing to see his native land once more, having vowed that upon St Mary Magdalen's day he would lay his offering on the altar at Lochmaben. But those Border lords who had profited from the downfall of his house united to oppose him, and he was seized by a son of Kirkpatrick of Closeburn, who had been one of his own vassals. 'Carry me to the king,' said Douglas, 'for you may well profit from my misfortune; thy father was true to me while I was true to myself.'

This noble speech so moved the young man that instead he offered to escort the Douglas back to England. Weary of exile, and perhaps of life, the aged Earl refused, and, by the intercession of the young Kirkpatrick, who had been touched by the decay of greatness, he was permitted to end his days, in monastic seclusion, in the abbey of Lindores.

When it is considered that between the rise and fall of the Black

Douglases, the family experienced the extremities of fortune, endured the grisly and brutal murder of the gallant youth who was the sixth Earl, taken by treachery and summarily beheaded with his younger brother in the courtyard of Edinburgh Castle, and also the murder of the eighth Earl by the king's own hand at Stirling, is it any wonder that my youthful imagination was enflamed?

> Edinburgh castle, towne and tower,
>> God grant ye sink for sin.
> And that for the black denner
>> Yerl Douglas gat therein . . .

The lines ran in my head for days after the first hearing of them, and now, in old age, I cannot think on that sudden brutality, when the black bull's head was laid on the festive board and the two youths, and their friend Malcolm Fleming of Cumbernauld, were dragged to the headman's block, without tears pricking my eyes.

No one can deny the savagery of life on the Borders as the Middle Ages drew to a close and chivalry slipped behind a cloud. Consider for example the depredations of the English armies during the Rough Wooing conducted by the Earl of Hertford (later Duke of Somerset) in 1547, when the burning abbeys, keeps and farmhouses shed a lurid light from valley to valley. It was no wonder that, when they were able, the Scotch Borderers took an equally savage revenge. A French officer, by name Beaugé, serving in the army which the Regent, Marie de Guise, had called to her support, has left a description, which recalls the atrocities of the late war in the Peninsula. The castle of Ferniehurst, three mile out of Jedburgh, and the seat of the Kers, was for a time held by the

English whose commander, Beaugé says, was guilty of such excesses of lust and cruelty as would have 'made to tremble the most savage Moor in Africa . . .' The castle was assaulted, and the commander surrendered himself to the Frenchman, imploring him to save him from the vengeance of the Borderers. One of them, however, recognizing in him the violator of his wife, swiftly advanced, and with a single sweep of his broadsword, carried the Englishman's head four paces from his trunk. Immediately a hundred Scots rushed to dip their hands in the blood of the oppressor. Other prisoners were put to death, and when this task was completed, the Scots, poor as they were, purchased the unfortunate wretches who had had the prudence to surrender themselves to the French. 'I myself,' says Beaugé, with what I can only call military sang-froid, 'sold them a prisoner for a small horse. They laid him on the ground, galloped over him with their lances at rest, and wounded him as they passed. When slain, they cut his body into gobbets, and bore the mangled pieces on the points of their spears. I cannot', the polite Frenchman who had sold the poor wretch remarks, 'greatly praise the Scottish for this practice. But the truth is, that the English had tyrannized over the Borders in the most cruel and barbarous fashion; and I think it was but fair to repay them, according to the proverb, in their own coin . . .'

Savage times, which we are well rid of, and yet, strangely attractive to the imagination of youth.

I was much taken, I recall, with the story of Johnnie Armstrong, the great bandit chief, who marched out to meet James V, with all the pomp of assumed equality, as one monarch come to debate with another. The king would have none of it, and Johnnie and his thirty-six men were hanged on growing trees at Carlanrig Chapel, ten miles above Hawick on the Langholm road. When I was a bairn, it was still the crack of the countryside that the trees on whilk they were hangit withered away. Well, Johnnie may have been no better than a Sicilian bandit of our own day, but in the language of the ballads, he was indeed equal to the king – as he claimed to be:

> To seek het water beneath cauld ice,
>> Surely it is a great folie –
> I hae asked grace of a graceless face,
>> But there is nane for my men and me.

That was speaking to a king, indeed, and like a king.

The ballads enflamed me. I conceived – how or just when I cannot recall – the ambition of making a collection of them, and I believed that this might prove a fit offering to lay on the altar of my country, once proud and independent, now in danger of losing its memory of itself, and so its consciousness, in the benevolent embrace of a large polity, which also, and properly, required of me my devotion. The ambition, I am sure, grew slowly. It was the fruit of numerous excursions through the Borderland, mostly in the company of my friend, Robert Shortreed, then Sheriff-substitute of Roxburgh-shire. At first, I confess, I had little thought of scholarship. We were land-loupers, intoxicated with the sense of freedom, the queerness and the fun. But in this way I came to know, what I could never have learned, had I stuck to my last in Edinburgh – as so many of my lawyer-friends did – all sorts of ranks and conditions of men. I learned to talk as easily with a travelling tinker as with a minister of the kirk – often more easily, to tell the truth, for I have aye had the uncomfortable notion that a homily might be in preparation and have felt uncomfortable among the professionally virtuous, from which charge I am happy to acquit many clergymen of my acquaintance.

When we first travelled through Liddesdale, there was no road that could bear a wheeled carriage. I mind once, coming to a farm, keepit by an Elliot, for they are mostly members of that wild clan there. We were as ever invited to bide the night, but the gudeman seemed in strangely low spirits, and what was more remarkable was that when the festive board was set, it was lacking in certain accustomed elements of festivity. In short, there was but milk to drink, and the only ale was Adam's. The meal was partaken of for the most part in a gloomy silence, for the low spirits of our host depressed those of the company. When the board was cleared, he said, to a young scholar, perhaps a nephew resident during the university vacation and studying for the Ministry, 'Weel, Eben, there's nocht else for it, so we'll juist hae to hae you read us a chapter of the Gude Buik.' Nothing loth, young master Eben began to read, choosing with what seemed to me an absence of tact which boded ill for his success in his future profession, to regale us with an account of the wandering of the Children of Israel in the desert. When he arrived at the passage where Moses strikes the rock and the waters gush forth, our host gave an audible sigh that turned to a groan. His head sank, and the young man read on. All of a sudden the Gudeman Elliot raised his hand and said 'Whisht!' There followed a prolonged silence, till, unmistakably, came the clip-clop of horses' hooves. 'The Lord be praised,' he cries, 'it's the keg at last. Now we can offer hospitality to the shirra here' (meaning Bob Shortreed) 'and the young advocate-loon' (meaning myself) 'of whilk we needna be affrontit.' Then there was a great bustle. The keg of brandy brought from smugglers on the Solway was borne in, broached, quaichs filled and downed, and filled again, amid such hilarity as you might find when the gates of a prison have been opened and the unfortunate long-incarcerated wretches have been released, while the young aspirant preacher was left in the middle of a chapter, even of a verse, on the other side of Jordan.

It all went to the making of me. He travels furthest, I sometimes think, that doesna ken his destination and aiblins has no care for it. We are driven on by impulses beyond our understanding, which, when we look back as from a hilltop we have climbed, seem to have led us there as straight and smooth as if by a turnpike road.

It was in the course of my search for ballads that I first encountered James Hogg. Hogg is a remarkable man, though less remarkable than he thinks himself, a criticism that could doubtless be levelled with equal justice at the majority of men. Our lives have been strangely intertwined; we may even be the same age, though, since Hogg's age, to my knowledge, has altered according to the company he is in, or according to the mood of the moment, I cannot be sure of this. He was born and raised, the child of a poor family, in the parish of Ettrick, and he commonly – in my view mistakenly – is referred to – and has even been known to describe himself – as being uneducated. It is true he has neither Latin nor Greek, and his knowledge of history is defective, which is not surprising, for I do not believe he attended the parish school beyond the age of nine. Yet, since he grew up with the music of the ballads and the words of the Bible continually about him, he has acquired a sounder bottom of education than many who have gone through the common mill of schooling. As to the History, he accepts for instance the extreme and prejudiced view of the Covenanting tradition, even of those fanatics called the Cameronians. Indeed I recall an exchange between us when he published his novel, *The Brownie of Bodsbeck* set in the reign of Charles II.

'I like it ill, Hogg,' I said, 'very ill. It is a false and unfair picture of the times.'

'Na, na, Shirra,' said he, with some degree of impudence, 'it is the picture I hae been brocht up tae believe in since ever I was weanit. And there's naething in it that isna true, which, Shirra, is mair as you can say of your *Auld Mortality*.'

In fact, the novel is the old tissue of Covenanting fabrications and lies. As I remarked to the Duke of Buccleuch, 'Hogg has slandered Claverhouse to please the Cameronians, who do not read novels, and therefore will not be pleased.'

Hogg has tried me sorely, financially and in other ways, but I am fond of him, and feel myself in some curious fashion responsible for his well-being.

Another thought strikes me. Hogg has no sense of history because he grew up in the narrow valley of the Ettrick, where past and present coalesce; my upbringing under the shadow of Smailholm Tower made it inevitable that I should see history as a great march or procession, from the day when the Roman legions first forced their way through the passes of the Cheviots to the present.

Of course, difference of rank and my own fuller (though imperfect) education must contribute also to our different attitudes, mine critical, Hogg's credulous.

Hogg was, however, a great help to me in my work of collecting the Ballads, though it was necessary to take some care in scrutinizing his offerings, for he was not above attempting to pass off a production of his own as an authentic ancient ballad, and indeed I discovered him in this deception more than once. Certainly, in the same context, I must confess that a like charge has been levelled at me; and indeed I did not scruple to add verses where the sense seemed to require them, or emend others which appeared defective. I feel no shame in such a confession, though once when I was speaking of the pleasure of making verses, a kind friend – such friends are always to be found – remarked, 'Mak them Scott? Indeed I rather think you steal the maist of them.' I did not contravert that charge either. The truth is I can scarcely see a verse but I itch to make it my own. I think no worse of myself for that, and therefore, doubtless, should forgive poor Hogg for yielding to the same desire to scratch the itch. It was indeed ever in this manner that our Border minstrels worked. When they got themselves a verse, they added and emended and omitted and embellished, till each had made it his own, a thing different and yet aye the same, a thing personal and yet held in common. No, borrowing and emending verses that have been handed down to us sits easy on my conscience. I can forgive myself that, and a man should be almost as ready to forgive himself as to forgive others.

And some of the verses I added to traditional ballads seem to me as good as anything you may find in the original:

> Oh I hae dreamed a dreary dream
>   Ayont the Isle of Syke
> I saw a dead man win a fight,
>   And I think that man was I . . .

Old Mistress Hogg, James's mother, was of even greater assistance than her son, for her head was richly stored with old verses, although in many cases it was but fragments of the whole ballad which she could recollect. Nevertheless I owe much to her, and was therefore not disturbed, but rather amused, by the reproof she delivered when the *Minstrelsy* appeared in print.

'Shirra, Shirra,' she said, shaking her head and puffing at her clay pipe, 'ye hae spiled them awethegither. The sangs were made for singing and no for prenting – and furthermair, Shirra, they're nouther richt spelled nor richt setten doon.'

'Maybe so, Mistress Hogg,' I replied, 'but I owe many of them to you, and whatever the faults or deficiencies of my edition, it ensures that they will never be forgotten. It ensures their survival or preservation, and that is something which, with the progress of civilization, could not otherwise be guaranteed.'

She was not, I fear, convinced, but then, living in the upper reaches of Ettrick, she could remain in happy ignorance of the progress of civilization, and retain the conviction that she inhabited an unchanging world.

'Ye hae broken the charm, Shirra,' she said, but I owe to her many verses of 'The Outlaw Murray' and all sixty-odd verses of 'Auld Maitland': no inconsiderable debt.

I had many other coadjutors. There was Willie Laidlaw, from Blackhouses in Yarrow, who has long been my factor, amanuensis, and the Lord knows what else besides, at Abbotsford; a man of the rarest virtue, combining humility and unselfishness with an extraordinary competence in all the affairs of life.

Even more remarkable was John Leyden, a shepherd's son from the village of Denholm in Teviotdale. It was Richard Heber who discovered him for me, browsing in Archibald Constable's bookshop in the High Street of Edinburgh, Leyden, with that uncommon perseverance and acumen which were among his principal characteristics, then having fought his way to the university. A large, awkward, raw-boned fellow whose first appearance was somewhat appalling to persons of low animal spirits, Leyden was perhaps the purest and finest scholar it has been my privilege to know. Among his endearing traits was a refusal to learn to speak polite or genteel English, on the grounds that he feared it would spoil his Scots. His appetite for other languages, however, was inordinate, and it was a sore day for me when he departed as an assistant-surgeon to the distant and deadly shore of India, whence, alas, he was never to return. Leyden, like Hogg, was a true poet himself, though curiously he expressed himself more easily in verse in the pure English which he refused to speak than in the Scots to which he was devoted.

Finally, in this record of tribute to those who assisted me in the compilation and publication of the *Minstrelsy*, I must mention my boyhood and lifelong friend James Ballantyne, who undertook the printing of the volumes, a far greater and more arduous task than anything which he had previously attempted.

I was fortunate to have so many eager to assist me in a work which I conceived as a patriotic duty.

The *Minstrelsy* made me, for I had gotten myself a reputation. The year after its publication Mrs Scott and I removed from our cottage at Lasswade, and took up residence at the house of Ashiestiel overlooking the Tweed upstream from Yair. This was done partly at the insistence of the Lord-Lieutenant of Selkirkshire, who thought it wrong that the Sheriff should not have a residence in the Forest, as indeed I was bound to do by statute which decrees that a sheriff must bide for part of the year at least in his shrievalty. But I was happy to comply, though disappointed that I could only lease, and not buy, Ashiestiel. Nevertheless it was a house that pleased me, situated as it is in the most beautiful and Romantic stretch of the valley of the most beautiful and Romantic of rivers, my beloved Tweed.

Around the time that we took up our residence there, Harriet,

Countess of Dalkeith, urged me to compose a long poem of my own, stipulating only that it should be set in the period when the ballads themselves were being made. The idea would have attracted me, even if it had come from some source other than that of the House of Buccleuch, to which I owed fealty, and to which I was already bound by ties of friendship.

I had been struck by the manner in which Coleridge had composed his 'Christabel', and first essayed something in that metre, but it proved insufficiently rapid for either my talent or purposes. Octosyllabics appeared to me to be the thing, for they allowed me a dancing lightness, they gave scope to whatever facility I might have in rhyming, and they also permitted a certain conversational ease.

The poem was intended to illustrate the customs and manners which formerly prevailed on the Borders of England and Scotland, and in this sense may be considered a natural successor to the ballads collected in the *Minstrelsy*. I adopted the plan of the ancient metrical romance as allowing a greater latitude than might be considered proper in a regular poem, and the device of putting the romance in the mouth of an aged Minstrel, to be considered the last of his race, who, as he is supposed to have survived the Revolution of 1688, may be thought to have caught something of the refinement of modern poetry without losing the simplicity or naivety of his original model. The tale itself is set more than a hundred years earlier, about the middle of the sixteenth century, when most of the personages portrayed actually lived.

I proceeded, as I have ever done, more by instinct, happy or otherwise, than by deliberate ratiocination. It has ever been my belief that any considerable work of art – though it is not for me to say whether the *Lay* can be so regarded – derives less from the intellect, though that must exercise a controlling and shaping power, than from some deep well on which the maker draws, ignorant though he must be of the springs which feed it. If the *Lay* has any peculiar merit, I believe it rests in something which I find difficult to describe, if only because I fancy there was a certain novelty in my method; and it is ever hard to find the right words for what has not been done before. The *Lay* is not precisely an imitation of earlier times, for the reader, or auditor, must always be conscious that the Minstrel is a creation of the present day, that he is observed by the author who is a man of our own time, and who acts as both a filter and a commentator. It is perhaps presumptuous or pretentious in me to call this a species of double-vision; and yet I do not know how else I might describe it.

I wrote the *Lay* fast, with all the ardour of a huntsman in pursuit of a noble quarry. I was doing something new to me, and also delightful. I have never pretended an indifference to the material rewards to be expected from a work of literature, and indeed I should be ashamed to proclaim such indifference. There is good sense in Johnson's observation that 'no man but a blockhead ever wrote except for money', for writing is hard labour; but it is also delight, and I have – till recently at least, alas – felt powerfully that joy in composition, which is one of the purest of passions that can move the heart, and which draws the painter to his palette, the musician to his instrument, the dancer to the dance, and the poor struggling author to his writing-table.

The *Lay* pleased me, and a work which gives no pleasure to its author is unlikely to please the public. Indeed, there is a great impertinence, it has always seemed to me, displayed by those authors who contemn their own productions, which they are nevertheless ready to lay before the public. It is like a man who makes a joke, or tells a humorous anecdote, at which he does not laugh himself; it is as if he says, 'This may be good enough to amuse you, or please you, but, forgive me, I am made of finer stuff. To say this is not to proclaim that one is altogether delighted by one's own productions, or blind to their faults; on the contrary, it is merely to say, 'This is the best that I have contrived to do with this material; I am not ashamed to offer it to you. Make of it what you will.'

Again, the author who deprecates his own work is like the hostess of an inn who lays on the table food that is inferior to that which she will herself consume in the kitchen. (Alas, in my travels, I have met too many of whom I fear that may have been true.) But there is a nicety in our refined age which encourages many authors to practise a sort of mock-modesty, which is itself corrupting, for it may lead them in time to offer work to the public which in truth is of a quality which really demands modesty. My own work has been of variable worth, but with my hand on my heart I may say that it has always been the best I could do with that material at that time.

I was fortunate that the *Lay* pleased. It pleased Lady Dalkeith who had requested it; and since it was natural for me to honour the house of Buccleuch, that was my first reward. It pleased some of the great ones of the world; both Mr Pitt and Mr Fox spoke in praise of it, and perhaps Fox's praise meant more to me, for I was opposed to his politics and an adherent of Pitt. It pleased some of those whom I could now term my fellow-poets. Jeffrey in his *Edinburgh Review* offered a degree of commendation which he denied many of my later poetic efforts, though even at this early stage he uttered a warning – 'Mr Scott must either sacrifice his Border prejudices or offend his readers in other parts of the Empire' – a warning which I was happy to ignore. Best of all, it pleased the general public. I have no time for the author who writes for a precious few. Once, when my daughter Anne condemned something as 'vulgar', I reproved the poor lass, more harshly than she deserved perhaps, and told her that what was called 'vulgar' was what appealed to the generality of mankind, and that nothing truly great or good has been uncommon.

So I was launched on a new career to supplement my lawyerhood. (The first edition of the *Lay* brought me £169 6s in royalties, and when a second was called for I sold the copyright to messrs Longman for £500 and another £100 to buy a horse.) But it was never my intention to become only an author. I held fast to my father's dictum that authorship was a good staff but an ill crutch. Moreover, though I say this with hesitation, since it may offend some of my friends, a man who is only an author is in general a puir cratur. I would make an exception of a pure poet like Wordsworth, or even of Pope, who was handicapped by his crippled state. But Johnson, whom I revere, observed that 'every man thinks the worse of himself for not having been a soldier', and Johnson, that noble, struggling soul, was the last man to adopt the airs and pretensions of fellows who think themselves superior to the common run of mankind because they possess the facility to string one sentence on another. I have ever entertained the suspicion that Shakespeare himself thought more highly of the skill he showed as a man of affairs in the management of his theatre than he did of his literary productions, which, no doubt, with the happy ignorance of genius, he cobbled together to set the box-office ticking. And Johnson too, I recall, was filled with enthusiastic pride when his brewer friend, Mr Thrale, made him executor of his will.

So, although I was now established as an author, thoughts of authorship occupied but a small part of my mind and time. I had my law business, of which more later, and at Ashiestiel I threw myself with ardour into the life of a country gentleman. I did my literary work before the feck of the household had left their beds, and then spent ten hours a day out of doors, engaged either in riding, fishing, shooting (though in later years I have grown more tender and come to dislike the killing of birds and beasts except for the larder), or in supervising the planting of trees and laying out of the policies, which soon became an abiding and overwhelming passion. As this grew upon me, I became ever more strongly aware that I held Ashiestiel only on a lease, and I began to look about me for a property I could call my ain. There is an old saying that as soon as a Scotsman gets his head above water, he begins to think of land. I contemplated buying the property of Broadmeadows in Yarrow, a house in a bonny situation, but one which offered insufficient scope for development. My uncle had died and left me the property of Rosebank in Kelso, but that being in Roxburghshire was without my shrievalty. I therefore sold it, and resolved to employ the capital I realized in purchasing my ain place, as soon as I happened on somewhere suitable.

Meanwhile I engaged in a new venture, though one which I felt bound, on account of my position in the legal profession, to keep secret. I invested funds in James Ballantyne's printing business, for I could see many advantages in this; the unfortunate author frequently being like the poor man at the end of the line who gets the thinnest gruel. But again, more of this at a later date, if I survive to continue this memoir.

There was only one dissentient from the chorus of praise directed at the *Lay*.

Charlotte read the first canto and shook her head:

'Scott, Scott,' she said, 'why is your mind always on these boring old knights and minstrels?'

Well, as Tom Purdie says, 'A fond wife is near aye richt, Shirra, and that's some consolation whan ye're warsted, as a man commonly is, in a matrimonial argument.'

Oh Tom, how grateful I have often been for your robust good sense.

7

On Death, Wordsworth and Shakespeare, 1826–7

As I limped, weary, down the Mound from Parliament House in the dying of the afternoon, I was accosted by Sir John Sinclair – Cavalier Jackasso, as I call him – who vies with the Earl of Buchan for the title of the greatest fool in Scotland. Opening on the matter with his habitual pomposity, he finished by offering the suggestion that it would be no great trouble for him to arrange a match between me and the Dowager Duchess of Roxburghe.

'It would be a great thing, Scott, a great thing for you,' he said, 'it would elevate you in Society, and solve your financial problems, for I happen to know that her widow's jointure is a handsome one.'

It was all I could do to refrain from striking him with my walking-stick; such impudence, such tastelessness, with my poor Charlotte not long in the grave.

But I contented myself with the reply that if I was to marry again, which seemed to me in the highest degree improbable, I remained capable of choosing my own wife. I now see, however, that I have fallen low indeed, if I have become an object of pity and concern to such as the Cavalier; I wonder how many others are girding themselves up to make new arrangements for me. I'll have none of it.

I ate a solitary supper of salted herring and boiled potatoes, in an acute misery; a fit of low spirits which nothing can cure but work. I took a dram of whisky after, and that failed to enliven me. I smoked a cheroot though I am inclined to think the tobacco makes my fits of giddiness worse. Yet there is some solace in the activity of smoking, the Lord knows how or why. It is a sad business when a man is reduced to finding comfort in what he formerly took for granted, and yet how else should it be? I sit hunched at my desk, with the manuscript of *Woodstock* before me; and I can do nothing. I see nothing before me but toil which no longer delights. Let me consider my blessings: that I have been fortunate much of my life, and that, unlike the generality of mankind, I have been permitted to find profound satisfaction in my labours. No more: yet as Corporal Nym said, 'Things must be as they may', and there is no arguing with fate. If it is my destiny to die in misery, then it has been my good fortune to live most of my life abundantly. But still, what paltry things we are – lords of nature, as we term ourselves. Why, consider that something of inconceivably minute origin, the pressure of a bone, or the inflammation of a particle of the brain takes place, and the emblem of the Deity, man made in God's image, destroys himself, or, worse, someone else. We hold our health and our reason – aye, our reason – on terms slighter than one would desire were it in their choice to hold an Irish cabin or a black-house in the Hebrides.

I sleep badly. Last night, I woke with a sharp cramp, which disturbed a dream in which the figure of Green-breeks appeared before me, in his youthful Gothic splendour as if time had rolled back upon itself. I have a notion that in the dream we conversed, as I have often wished we had been able to do, and as we never found occasion to: but I repeat myself, for I have already recorded the impression he made, indelibly, upon me. Be it so; it is, if not the privilege, then at least the affliction and penalty of age and failing powers, that we find ourselves going over old ground, casting on pools where we have already determined no fish are lurking.

Young Cadell, who has a scheme to publish a complete edition of my novels, which he describes, without irony, as the *magnum opus*, has been urging me on.

'Sir Walter,' he said, 'believe me, you are a magician still.'

It was kind and gentlemanly of him to say so, but the wand is broken.

> Broke the wand, and broke the spell,
> In fancy's realm no more to dwell.
> The king of beasts condemned to be
> Caged in sad perplexity;
> Or like the hind that makes his way,
> Heavy-legged at end of day,
> Homeward to an ashy hearth,
> A vacant hut, by cheerless path,
> Condemned to solitude and gloom
> And endless toil before the tomb
> Opens to receive him in,
> Sick of life's resounding din.

That last line is vile, but I am too weary to mend it.

When I was last at Abbotsford, they had to hold me upright on an old pony, I that used to be accounted the rashest and most reckless rider in the countryside.

* * *

An hour later: only an hour. I fell asleep in my chair, my cheroot in my mouth and woke to find ash scattered over my dressing-gown. Then, seeking solace, I have been reading Wordsworth's *Immortality Ode*. There is the true magic there, which makes my own efforts at versifying seem like the mewling of an infant.

> The thought of our past years in me doth breed Perpetual benediction ...

And yet, when I last saw Wordsworth, though he was as assured of his own merit, indeed genius, as ever, I knew that his wand too was broken, though not his health. The gates of wonder have closed on him, and he is like a man held in an image of himself which he can no longer sustain. We are permitted only brief moments when we seem to see beyond the common light of day. 'Our birth', he says, 'is but a sleep and a forgetting.' I know that feeling; there are such strange moments of illumination scattered through the ballads. 'I do not think thoughtful people can ever be truly 'appy', as poor Charlotte used to say; so be it, yet they are granted those rare and precious occasions when they can say with St Paul: 'Then I saw through a glass darkly, but now face to face'.

I have never thought of myself as a visionary, for I have ever held that I was rooted in common sense, of the earth earthly; and yet

> He slept the summer day in green,
>   He woke to find the corn gold;
> The milk-white stag was briefly seen,
>   Ere wreaths of snow obscured the fold.

It is natural for a man to brood on death and what lies beyond the grave, natural and profitless.

As I work also, intermittently and without zest, on my life of Napoleon, it occurs to me to wonder what thoughts ran through his head as he lay dying. They say his last words were '*tête de l'armée*', as if he still dwelt on military glory. Well, I have ever responded to the trumpet's sound, but now, such glory seems but a trumpery ambition. The Duke of Wellington, a wiser and more humane man than his great adversary, told me once that a battle lost was only a degree more terrible than a battle won. There must come a moment in the life of any generous-hearted soldier when the thought of war and slaughter revolts him; and yet they say that when Napoleon was asked which had been his greatest battle, he replied 'Borodino – it was so far from home'. On the retreat from Moscow the French army cried out in horror at the stench of the unburied corpses as they retraced their path across that fatal field.

Even so, war displaying man at his extremity is a thing to wonder at. When Napoleon's Guard was retreating from Waterloo, after their Emperor had fled back towards Paris, instead of dying on the field as a true hero would have chosen to do, they were called on to surrender. '*La garde meurt, mais ne se rend pas*' was the reply, and when I first heard that gallantry, my eyes brimmed with tears.

Honest Sam Johnson, who held the Christian faith with as devout determination as any man could, confessed himself terrified of death; but, if Wordsworth is right when he calls 'birth but a sleep and a forgetting', is death then a remembering? As in dreams perhaps? Did my dream of Green-breeks last night denote that that brave youth is dead?

This habit of introspection is new to me, and cannot be healthy.

I have aye held that a man is better, and wiser, not to subject himself to overmuch examination. A healthy man is naturally blithe; are our spirits then determined merely by the condition of the liver?

I have loved Shakespeare all my life, but in these last days, the plays I turn to most readily are *Antony and Cleopatra* and the two parts of *Henry IV*. The former is a strange choice for a man who would never have believed the world well lost for love, or have imagined himself in Antony's position, or indeed put any of his imaginary creations in such a state. But the end is magnificent: 'the soldier's pole is broken' – like my wand, and 'there is nothing left remarkable beneath the visiting moon'. The strength of that epithet 'visiting' – as for *Henry IV* – the conversations between Falstaff and Mr Justice Shallow (who is near to being as great an idiot as the Earl of Buchan or Sir John Sinclair) – why, there is the stuff of sad mortality in them. 'We have heard the chimes at midnight.' And Falstaff's 'tush, man, mortal men, mortal men . . .'. there is all the blithe indifference to death of the healthy man in that observation, even if it is the deaths of others that he is contemplating.

Dawn pricks the sky – another night without sleep. I dare not read *Lear*. It comes too close. Sometimes I think I might take to dram-drinking in a regular fashion, though I have always despised drunkards, while loving conviviality as well as any man.

Wordsworth again – how his lines run in my poor head:

> Full soon thy soul shall have her earthly freight,
>   And custom lie upon thee with a weight,
> Heavy as frost, and deep almost as life . . .

There is the true magic there again. When he is in full flow, he strikes that note more truly than any man since Shakespeare.

But then his vanity always amused me also. Hogg once visited him in the Lakes and, seeking to make agreeable conversation, remarked that there could rarely have been such a constellation of poets . . . (I think Southey was with them, or perhaps Coleridge). Wordsworth was offended. 'Constellation, what means the fellow?' There is something of Pope's portrait of Addison in that remark. 'Bear, like the Turk, no brother near his throne . . .' Jamie was offended in his turn by Wordsworth's implicit denial of his right to call himself a poet; so when the great man proposed that they carry their excursion further to view another of his beloved lakes, Jamie replied, 'na, na, I dinna want to see ony mair dubs. Let's awa to the public and hae a drap of whusky.' I rather think Jamie drank alone that night.

There are three hours yet till I must be at the Court. If I throw off this lethargy, and set myself to my task, I can do aiblins six sheets of *Woodstock*, a tale of Cavaliers and Roundheads. But what, I ask myself, have I to do with either? Nevertheless, the thing must, and shall, be done.

'Whaur are you gaein', my bonnie boy,
  Now give me answer true.'
'I'm blithe to see the warld, mother,
  And that is answer true.'

'The warld, I fear, is false, laddie,
  A place of dule and shame.'
'I ken the warld is false, mother,
  A place of dule and shame.

'But man maun mak his way, mother,
　　Through briar and through thorn.'
'Aye, man maun mak his way, laddie,
　　Though he rue that he was born.'

Woodstock . . . Chapter XX: 'The affectionate relatives were united as those who, suffering under great adversity, still feel the happiness of sharing it in common.'

8

A Life in the Law, 1787–

My father's love and reverence for the Law derived from his consciousness of our own lawless Border background. He was no great historian, but he knew that we had risen from an almost savage society, in which custom dictated manners, while no strong realization of legality controlled conduct. Accordingly, he saw the Law as the bridge by which social man has crossed from barbarity to civilization. Only the Law could order relations between men to their common advantage.

He was a modest, economical man, whose mind was so constructed that – beyond the weighty and elevated matter of theology in the study of which he occupied what would otherwise have been his hours of leisure – he valued little beyond the family save the just application of the Law, and he regarded successes gained in other fields as necessarily inferior to those which might be sought in his profession.

His social tact was exemplary. Though he was a devout Whig and Presbyterian – but no prig – one of the few whom I have known profess Whiggish principles without making himself into a prig – he had clients, men who trusted him, who belonged to the other party, and some of them had been adherents of the Prince and 'out'

– as the saying went – in the Forty-five. With such my father was careful never to offend. They were, in his view, 'unfortunate gentlemen'. He respected their convictions which he did not share, and did not speak of the Prince as the 'Pretender' or of the Rising as the 'Rebellion'. When giving the loyal toast, if such were present, he contented himself with drinking to 'the King', leaving it to the company to determine whether they had raised their glasses to George or Charles.

His reverence for the Law was such that he gave his services even to those of whom he might profoundly disapprove. I mind one gentleman who came to the house, rather than to my father's place of business, arriving by night with his cloak pulled around the lower part of his face. When he left, he sent a boy down into the street to see that the road was clear before he dared take his departure. No sooner had he gone, than my father took the glass from which his client had been drinking, and hurled it into the fireplace.

'No member of my family or household,' he said, 'shall drink from a cup that has touched the lips of Mr Murray of Broughton'; for his mysterious client had been none other than that wretched gentleman who had been the Prince's secretary and then betrayed his fellow-Jacobites to save his own neck and estates. But, though he deplored his conduct, I believe my father served him as well and conscientiously as his more worthy clients.

My early years in the Law were passed in drudgery – the drudgery of copying endless legal documents – in my father's office. There had never been any question but that I was set for a legal career. My elder brothers had received commissions in the Army and Navy respectively. My own lameness, as I have said, precluded any such career for me; and I would have been a vilely ungrateful young fellow if I had denied my father his dearest wish that I should enter his profession. Even the drudgery of copying had its rewards; I was paid at threepence a folio sheet which enabled me to buy books and attend theatres. Moreover, the habit of solid industry stood me in good stead in later years. On one occasion I recall that I wrote some ten thousand words without intermission. Besides I loved my father, and I felt the natural pride and pleasure of rendering myself useful to him.

It was his ambition, however, that I should enter into the more lofty and dignified branch of the profession. He was proud to be a Writer to the Signet; but he was determined that I should become a member of the Faculty of Advocates. 'To live to see you plead a case, with a rich mastery of the law, is my fondest desire, Wattie,' he would say; and it was a desire which I was in no way loth to satisfy. Accordingly, at the age of seventeen I began my Law classes at the college.

Let me do justice to the only years in my life in which I applied myself to learning with stern, and undeviating industry. I set myself to learn the Law thoroughly, and I have never regretted it. My closest friend in these years was William Clerk, son of Sir John Clerk of Eldin, and we devised a course of study together, in which we subjected each other to daily interrogations – a method which I do not hesitate to recommend to any student, no matter what his subject. We examined each other daily in all points of Law, and in the summer I would walk from our home in George Square, down over the Mound and up the West End of Princes Street, to collect him from his father's house, that we might pursue our mutual examination on the way to College.

It was a proud day, for both of us, and for my father too, when on the 11th July 1792, we passed our final trials, and were admitted to the Faculty and could assume the advocate's gown. Then we mingled with the throng in Parliament House, till after an hour I said to Clerk, in the accent of a Highland lass at a hiring-fair, 'weel, hinny, we hae stood by the Tron for mair nor an hour, and deil a ane has speired our price.'

After the hard work of study, my early years as an advocate were a time of abundant leisure. This is a common experience. The young advocate walks, or stalks, the floor of Parliament House, hoping to have a solicitor or attorney pluck him by the sleeve and offer him a brief, and is usually doomed to disappointment. Some work came my way, courtesy of my father and some of his friends, but for the most part I passed the day in idle conversation, and amused myself with observing the idiosyncrasies of the Senators of the College of Justice, many of whom, with my natural facility for impersonation, I could mimic in such a manner as to divert my equally briefless friends.

There was old Lord Eskgrove, for instance, who seemed to mutter into a long jutting chin – a jaw as deformed as that of any Hapsburg, and who never sentenced a wretch to death without concluding: 'Whatever your relig-ious persua-shon may be, there is an abundance of rever-end gentle-men who will be most happy to guide you on the way to yeternal life'. It is a misfortune, or a deficiency, of our legal system that many men attain the Bench, when their faculties, if not yet positively decaying, are, at the very least, inferior to their earlier condition. The French order things differently, for with them the judiciary is a separate branch of the Law into which young men can enter. Yet I do not know that this answers better. An advocate acquires a deeper experience as a result of the social intercourse he enjoys, and thus comes to possess a more profound knowledge of life and human nature, than may perhaps be attained by one who settles into a magistracy early in life.

The truth is that all systems devised by mankind are defective in certain respects; perfection is not to be found this side of the grave.

Then we are to consider that a judge may excel in some areas of the Law, and fail in others. The late Lord Braxfield affords a good example. No one had a more profound or subtle understanding of the complexities of feudal law; and to hear Braxfield disentangle a complicated matter of inheritance or land-law was an education in itself, affording evidence of the greatest refinement of intellect which could be imagined. Yet this same Braxfield was also a brute, lacking the ordinary decencies of humanity. 'Aye, ye're a verra clever chiel,' I recall him saying to one prisoner in the dock, 'but you'd be nane the waur o' a hanging.' I was unfortunate enough to attend the first Trials for Sedition which he conducted with a disregard for the humane virtues which caused him to be dubbed 'the Scotch Jeffreys', the reference being to that lawyer of equal brilliance and equal inhumanity, who disgraced the Law of England by his conduct of the Bloody Assizes after Monmouth's rebellion.

Now I knew that most of those brought up before Braxfield were light-minded fellows, and that their intoxication with the horrid theories of the Revolutionaries in France threatened the stability of the social order; I never doubted that Henry Dundas (Lord Melville), the effectual Regent of Scotland, was wise to bring them to trial. But there was a relish in the manner in which Braxfield conducted himself in Court which disgusted me. 'Jesus Christ was a reformer too,' cried one poor wretch from the dock. 'Muckle he made o' that,' sneered His Lordship, 'he was hangit.'

But I run ahead of myself. My early years at the bar were in general unremunerative. I often found myself, in Sheriff Courts, defending poor men who were unable to pay a fee. I did so partly because they required a defender, and partly because I deemed that the practice of advocacy, even if immediately unrewarded, would serve me in good stead in the future. Not all my penniless clients failed to reward me. A housebreaker at Jedburgh, whom my best efforts had failed to save from conviction, thanked me, and apologizing for his inability to pay me, said he would substitute in recompense two pieces of advice, which might do me a good turn in the future.

'Nivver trouble yoursel to keep a muckle great mastiff o' a watchdog,' he said, 'for the like o thon are nae trouble to us. But instead keep a wee yelpin' snappin' terrier indoors, and we're like to gie ye a wide berth. An' nivver trouble yoursel' wi thae newfangled locks, for we can aye pick or brak them, but trust to ane o' thae auld heavy yins wi' an auld rusty key, and your hame'll stand secure.'

Aye, as I remember telling Lord Meadowbank:

> Yelpin' terrier, rusty key,
> Was Walter Scott's best Jeddart fee.

Early in my career I defended a scoundrel accused of poaching, with somewhat more success. Leaving the Court, I told him in an undertone that in my opinion he was fortunate to have been acquitted.

'Aye, aye,' said he, 'I'm o' the same opeenion mysel', and to show my gratitude, sir, if you juist gie me your direction, I'll see you hae a fush frae the Duke's pool for your denner.'

Among the more amusing of my early cases was one which took me for the first time to Galloway (and thus gave me the scenery twenty years later for *Guy Mannering*). The minister of the parish of Girthon was accused of loose behaviour, specifically that he had been 'toying with a sweetie-wife at a penny wedding' whereat he had also sung certain dubious, or more than dubious, songs. The case subsequently went before the General Assembly of the Kirk, where I argued manfully that there was a distinction to be drawn between a man who was *ebrius* and one who was *ebriosus*, which is to say, between a man who happened to be drunk and another who was habitually so; and my client, I claimed, with considerable pertinacity, though with no inner assurance, fell into the former category. His clerical brethren did not agree. I lost the case, but my argument greatly amused my friends and did something to raise my standing in Parliament House. For months afterwards at our convivial suppers, we debated the distinction between *ebrius* and *ebriosus*, concluding for the most part that we belonged to the former class, but that, if we were to prolong our sessions into the next day, we might be accused of having descended, or risen (as some asserted) to the second.

I arrived at the Bar towards the end of the period of heroic drinking among the judges. Braxfield rarely sat on the bench without a bottle of claret to hand. There was a story that still ran the rounds of a celebrated judge of the previous generation, whose servant refused to admit a client to his lodging on the grounds that his Lordship was at his dinner. The client, or his attorney, demurred, declaring that he knew his Lordship never dined till four and it was now but half-three.

'Aye,' said the servant, 'ye speak troth; but ye hinna understood me. It's yesterday's denner that he's aye sitting at.'

In the country, of course, old habits died still harder. I recall a supper given by a hard-drinking, indeed sodden, Selkirk attorney (certainly *ebriosus*, rather than *ebrius*), to myself, and two brothers of the Bar, George Cranstoun and Will Erskine. Since in my youth I had a head like a rock, I alone of the three of us matched our host, glass for glass, bottle for bottle. So, when the time came for us to take our leave, he let the other two mount their horses, with all the difficulty common on such occasions, and ride off without a word. But he embraced me with the enthusiasm of one who has found a friend after his own heart, and announced, 'I'll tell you this, Maister Walter, thon lad Cranstoun's a clever chiel, and he may weel reach the tap o' our profession; but tak my word for't – it'll no be by drinking.' Well, Cranstoun, clever but odd, like all his family, did in time ascend to the Bench; and indeed it was not by drinking.

I confess that I was never a great advocate. There was something in the business which displeased me. When I was young, and embarking on my career as a poet, my friend Charles Kerr of Abbotrule urged me not to neglect the Law. 'With your strong sense,' he wrote, 'and your ripening general knowledge, that you must rise to the top of the tree in the Parliament House in due season I hold as certain as that Murray died Lord Mansfield. But don't let many an Ovid, or rather many a Burns (which is better) be lost in you. I rather think men of business have produced as good poetry in their by-hours as the professed regulars; and I don't see why a Lord President Scott should not be a famous poet (in the vacation time), when we have seen a President Montesquieu step so nobly beyond the trammels in the *Esprit des Lois*.'

This was kind of him and generous; and I agreed with his judgement of the poets; but it was not to be. After my father's death, my appetite for success at the Bar slackened, for my greatest pleasure in achievement there would have been his pleasure. My profession and I came to stand nearly upon the footing which honest Slender consoled himself on having established with Mistress Anne Page: 'There was no great love between us at the beginning, and it pleased heaven to decrease it upon further acquaintance.' Nevertheless the Law was my career and I would have been a neglectful husband and father had I cut myself loose and followed the profession (if it may be so-called) of letters exclusively.

I was happy therefore, in 1799, on the death of Andrew Plummer of Middlestead, Sheriff-deputy of Selkirkshire, to succeed him in that post – on the recommendation, I am proud to say, of Lord Melville and the Duke of Buccleuch – which appointment reduced my reliance on my earnings at the Bar. Indeed with what I got there, my wife's independent income, my share of my father's estate, and my stipend as Sheriff-deputy, I had near £1,000 a year; and I believe my friend Jeffrey, an advocate of far greater pertinacity and finer acumen than myself, was not making a quarter of that after ten years at the Bar. Then in 1806 I was also appointed Clerk to the Court of Session, a well-salaried post that relieved me of both financial anxieties and the drudgery of the Bar. It afforded me also some entertainment, and the occasion to observe the contrarities and perplexities of mankind as they are revealed in the highest Court in Scotland.

As to my position as Sheriff I carried out my duties, I trust, with both diligence and humanity. I delighted in the opportunity it gave me – indeed the obligation it imposed upon me – to live for at least half the year in my beloved Borders; and in short it seemed to me that at the age of thirty-five I was one of the most happily circumstanced of men. I had obtained – as I thought – financial security. I divided my time agreeably between Edinburgh and the Borders; I had a happy home, a loving wife, and a growing family in whom I delighted.

As a sheriff I exerted myself very frequently to try to persuade litigants to abandon their case, and settle the matter amicably out of Court. Truth to tell, the greater number of cases that came before the Sheriff Court of Selkirkshire should have got no further than argy-bargy ower the garden wall.

Indeed, though a man of law myself, I have ever thought there was something sickening in seeing poor devils drawn into great expenses upon trifles by interested attorneys. Yet too cheap or easy an access to litigation has its own evils, for the proneness or propensity of the lower class to gratify spite or the desire for revenge in this manner would be a sad and injurious business – were they able to thole the expense. I have aye done my utmost to check the desire to go to law, or for one man, as the saying goes, 'to have the law on' another. But I trust that whenever a case presented itself, I have dealt with it on its merits, and since in my time I found against both James Hogg and the Duke of Buccleuch (through his gamekeeper), I think I can fairly acquit myself of any charge of partiality.

My duties as Clerk to the Court of Session retaining me in Edinburgh during the Law Terms, most of the Sheriff Court cases were of necessity heard in the first instance by my Substitute, who for the first quarter-century of my tenure of office was my friend Mr Charles Erskine, writer in Melrose; when he died, to my great regret, in January 1825, I appointed in his place my kinsman William Scott, younger of Raeburn. I had also another Substitute in reserve on whose services I could call if ever Erskine was unavailable or indisposed; this was the worthy Mr William Borrowman, surgeon in Selkirk.

I have therefore been well served. It has been my custom to require my Substitutes to deliver to me a clear statement of the case, which I would then consider, and respond to in a written judgement. Nevertheless, my presence was frequently required: to hear debates in the actions, to take evidence, to examine ground in dispute, or to conduct criminal trials. Fortunately, there have been few of the last sort, though in such I have ever tried to temper a proper and necessary severity with a degree of mercy. There were naturally those in the country who would have been better out of it. I recall once, when I was driving up Yarrow, a man running up to the carriage and exclaiming that Will Watherston was murdering Davie Brunton in the Broadmeadows woods. I presumed the man was exaggerating, but in any case, after a moment's reflection, said: 'If Will Watherston murder Davie Brunton and be hanged for the deed, it is the most fortunate thing that can happen to the parish'; and told my coachman to drive on.

Hogg was with me on that occasion, and it became one of his favourite stories. Alas, Will Watherston did no more than give Davie Brunton a good dunt on the head, and the pair lived to trouble the parish for a good many years.

9

A Strange Encounter and Thoughts on the Nature of Civilization, 1826–7

Tonight, coming away from a dinner of the Friday Club, which I myself was responsible for founding half a lifetime ago, I found myself in the mood for solitude and shook free of my fellows to wander the night-streets on my own. If they wondered at my unaccustomed lack of sociability – or rather at my abrupt willingness to divorce myself from their society, for till this fit came over me, I had been merry enough, and had tackled the game pie, claret and whisky with as good a will as any, while not being remiss in contributing what I could to the merriment of the conversation – why then, I could not have explained myself; and must have answered them with some offhand jest.

I had been alone for some quarter of an hour perhaps, and had made my way up the Canongate, before I admitted to myself where I was heading, and so turned by Moray House, through a close, down some steps, and headed for the Cowgate. It was not my expectation that the scene which I had visioned in Hastie's Close would repeat itself. If I had been certain that it would I might have directed my steps elsewhere, or clung close to my companions of the night. Yet, as soon as I confessed my purpose to myself, I knew an eagerness which has long been foreign to me.

I advanced in some trepidation. Mist hung around the rooftops, and the silence and solitude seemed unnatural.

> Oh loth to hear the sound of pipe,
>   Of fiddle or of drum,
> But yet some dancing spirit seems
>   To beckon me to come.

The close was deserted. I mounted the steps to where I had seen the figures, and the world retreated from me. I felt the hollow chill of absence. I leaned against the damp wall, and listened, listened for the music that had led me on and was now denied me. Then it was as if a hand, chill and wringing wet as a grave-cloth, was pressed upon my brow. Fingers explored my cheeks, and my mouth was dry. This impression too vanished from me, and I could only suppose I had imagined it. Still I waited, as if I had been promised a tryst, and like a lover torn between jealousy, hope and despair, refused to accept that it was denied me.

Then, just at the moment when I was about to depart, feeling, with a reluctance for which I cannot account, cheated, and conscious too that I had made a fool of myself, I began to shiver. The shivering was uncontrollable, like one in the grip of fever. I was at the same time burning hot and icy cold, though how these two sensations could be simultaneously experienced is more than I can rationally comprehend. Yet it was so. And then my ears were assailed by the sound of weeping. It was a woman, I think, though could not be certain. The creature's distress was acute, but her – I am sure the voice was female – lamentation failed to express itself in words ... I have heard such keening in a Highland cottage where a corpse lay awaiting burial, but there was an intensity, an urgency, to the grief that now disclosed itself to me, that made such wailing lamentation seem contrived and artificial. It was as if whoever wept wept now, not only for herself, not even only for me, but for all the race of men. That is fanciful, and there is no one to whom I could confess it. I was filled with pity, but that emotion was soon succeeded by fear, as a consciousness of a surrounding evil pressed hard upon me. Then, while I still shook and sweated and shivered, and listened rapt to that unearthly, and yet all too human, pain and sorrow, there was silence all of a sudden, the poor creature being cut off in midstream. I knew a momentary relief, but this was shattered by what followed: a mocking laughter as if of a troop of devils.

I do not think I fainted, but I have no clear recollection of how I got myself away, of what resolution it took to compel my feet to move, or of how, leaning heavily as I must have done, on my stick, I made what I can think of only as my escape.

Now, back in my lodgings, in my dressing-gown, with a cheroot alight, and a glass of toddy to hand, my puzzlement remains as extreme as the impulse which drove me thither is obscure. I have looked through some old books recounting Edinburgh crimes and legends, and can find nothing to explain it, no story of terrible murder or dark deeds committed there: and I am certain that if I had knocked on the door of one of the inhabitants of the close, they would have been deaf to what I heard.

And yet I heard it. I did not imagine it. I am certain of that. There was evil in the air:

> Oh I will show you where the white lilies grow
> On the banks of Italie ...

I had been moderate in my consumption of wine and whisky, as I generally am now, for I am nervous of the fits of giddiness which are like to overtake me. There is no one to whom I can recount this experience, for my old friends would look pityingly at me and, no doubt, depart shaking their heads and muttering sadly that I am no longer the man I was. I could not speak of it even to Lockhart, my dear son-in-law, in whom I have come to repose more confidence than in any other man. He is of too rational and sensible a cast of mind; and he too would be pained by what he would, I am sure, regard as evidence of a tendency to some nervous indisposition, even crisis. James Hogg would be bluff and consoling.

'Aye, Shirra,' he would say, 'there's nae doot in my opeenion that you hae been assailed, marked oot and assailed, by some emissary o the deil. I mind fine the same thing happening to me masel . . .' for it is one of Hogg's amiable characteristics that no awful thing can happen to any of his acquaintance, but he has had an experience to match or surpass it. Besides, I cannot share his certainty – I mean, the certainty that he would have – that the Devil exists, or could conceivably take any interest in such as me.

I remember though – the memory creeping back to me like mist rising from the Tweed in late November afternoons – that as I leaned against that wet wall, I tried to pray, and no words came.

It is foolish to perplex myself with this matter, and yet I cannot rid myself of it. If it was indeed my imagination playing a vile trick on my mind, then my fear is all the greater. It is poor Swift again, dying from the top.

But why was I so determined to go there, my determination being, I now realize, all the stronger for my refusal for so long to confess my purpose to myself?

I have no fear of death. I believe I can say that with complete honesty. I trust in the Lord, without making any public profession of my faith, and I trust also that I shall be raised redeemed into life everlasting, though as to what form this will take, I confess myself devoid even of any capacity for intelligent speculation.

If there is truly any evil – spirit, I suppose I must say – that lurks there, it is folly to expose myself to it; yet it is the sort of folly that acts upon one like a drug. Even as I sit at my desk, my cheroot drawing bonnily, I am conscious of a powerful temptation to return – and then what? Face it out? There is no sense in such thoughts.

I have often been questioned, of course, about my attitude to the supernatural, and I have generally managed to fob my questioners off with some easy or evasive answer: to the effect, for instance, that such beliefs in demons, brownies, ghosts and bogles, are natural in a primitive state of society, but must, in equally natural fashion, evaporate with the progress of civilization. I have, though I rarely care to speak of my own works, remarked that in what I must consider the best piece of fiction in this vein which I have written – the story of Wandering Willie, which is encased in *Redgauntlet* – I have been careful, even while seeking to give my readers a taste of the macabre, to offer at the same time a rational explanation which does not offend common sense. That has seemed to me the only manner in which someone today can treat such matters, without making himself absurd by a display of credulity. It is quite different though when a man finds himself assailed in perplexity . . .

> Aye, but to die, and go we know not where,
> To lie in cold obstruction and to rot . . .

That fear of death, expressed so chillingly by Claudio, is natural enough. That is a very human fear, which, however well-founded a man's faith, must from time to time strike him. This new fear of mine is of a different order. It is not a fear of death, but rather a terror of being seized by something horrid and destructive, while still alive; of finding myself no longer the man I was, but possessed of another spirit, another incomprehensible being. For the truth is first, that I was eager that the scene which I saw on my earlier visit to the close should repeat itself; and true also that what I experienced on this occasion represented a progression to something worse, something still more vile. I acknowledge that and, doing so, know that I shall be driven to tempt fate by returning thither. But not tonight. It would not be serviceable to return tonight. Tonight's work, I am satisfied, is done.

We are not all of a piece. There is in man an inescapable and terrible duality, inherent in our nature. I have fought against this knowledge, against its recognition. I had thought to have escaped the black doom of Scotch Calvinism, with its brutal and arbitrary division of mankind into the Elect and the damned, which I have always found a repellent and presumptuous dogma. Yet, it comes to me now, when I woke this morning – or yesterday morning, as I see from the growing light it now is – I seized a glass from the table by my bed, and scrutinized my face – something I have never done in my life before on waking, and indeed I do not know how the glass came to be there – and for why? To see that I was the same man, wearing the same face, as had gone to bed.

If I told poor Anne that, she would look at me with terrified vague eyes, as the poor girl sometimes does. Seeing me daily, or near daily, when I was last at Abbotsford, I detected fear in her countenance, and I interpreted it as a fear that her father was not what he had been, but on the course to something worse. Her fear angered me. I felt my brows contract, and more than once it was all I could do to refrain from a sharp speech which the poor lass had done nothing to deserve. She was silent on the matter, but I do not believe it was my imagination that saw the fear start in her eyes.

I am proud of my children, and believe I love them as a father should. They are good bairns, all of them, and yet it has occurred to me as strange and worthy of remark that I often feel easier with those who are comparatively strangers, aye, and closer to them, than I do where my own bairns are concerned. I do not believe this sensation to be uncommon. A man feels his children to be part of himself, and yet they remain separate; they remain the other. They are flesh of a man's flesh, yet not his flesh. Their very closeness accentuates the difference between him and them. I do not know if women feel this way, and suspect they may not; but a man does – I do, and it pains and troubles me. Still I am sure it is natural, for it is also natural that a child in some degree should reject his or her father, if only to avoid domination.

Others have recognized this. Read through Shakespeare and you will scarce find one connection between parent and child which is devoid of resentment and misunderstanding. The very closeness of the relationship seems to insist on it.

> Merrily danced the Quaker's wife,
>   And merrily danced the Quaker;
> But the Quaker's lad went off to the wars,
>   A sad surprise for the Quaker.

Anne is a good lass, but if she now finds me a burden she would be glad to be free of, I canna blame her.

And, one has also to consider, when contemplating the bairns, by what obscure concatenation of circumstance they come to be as they are. They spring from my loins, but also, and more importantly, from their mother's womb; and had I married someone else, had I married Williamina, my children would have been quite different from what they are. The thought may be trite; nevertheless, it is odd to reflect that in these circumstances, none of them – not Walter or Charles, Sophia or Anne – would exist. So time and chance, in the words of the Preacher, govern all – even to the making of particular men and women.

How easy, dwelling on such a thought, it might be to believe in predestination – a perilous thought, for that doctrine can engender a most disagreeable arrogance, a certainty which nothing in common experience can justify, a self-righteousness that has been the curse of Scotland as the unco gude wallowed in their assurance that they were the favourites of the Almighty. I reject it, as I rejected the narrow – though in my father's case, benevolent – Calvinism in which I was bred. Yet there are moments, in the owl-light, when I feel upon me the controlling influence of an impersonal fate. In the mirk silence, prophecies sound; and if there is no destiny, then prophetic utterances are no more than childish folly:

> When Tweed and Pausyl meet at Merlin's grave,
> Scotland and England shall one monarch have . . .

Merlin's grave – that Merlin by the way who is not the Merlin of Arthur, but Merlin Sylvester, Merlin of the Wilds, Merlin of the Woods, residing at Drummelzier and roaming Tweeddale, eating grass like a second Nebuchadnezzar – is to be found in Drummelzier kirkyard, under an aged thorn tree. On the east side the burn Pausyl falls into the Tweed, and it so happened that on the day of the coronation of James VI of Scots as King of England, the Tweed was in spate, overflowing its banks to mingle with the Pausyl at the prophet's grave.

Was that chance or was the prophecy justified? Who can tell? We are to consider, in making a judgement, that in the intervening centuries the Tweed must frequently have flooded, and joined itself to the Pausyl at the prophet's grave, while Scotland and England remained separate and independent kingdoms.

How my experience this night sets my mind running on such matters, and makes the old ballads run in my head again:

> Up then crew the red red cock,
>   And up and crew the grey;
> The eldest to the youngest said,
>   'Tis time we were away.'

> 'The cock doth craw, the day doth daw,
>   The channering worm doth chide,
> Gin we be missed out o our place,
>   A sair pain we maun bide.

> Fare ye weel, my mother dear,
>   Fareweel to barn and byre,
> And fare ye weel, ye bonny lass,
>   That kindles my mother's fire . . .'

The day doth dawn, but the world is aye still, still as a Quaker meeting. I feel I have come through, and know an uncanny calmness for a man ruined and disgraced in the eyes of the world, and for one who has been exposed as I have been tonight. Still, as Corporal Nym has it, 'things must be as they may'.

Those years of my expeditions into Liddesdale and the other valleys in search of ballads did more, I now see, to form me than anything else I have attempted. They fed my imagination, filling a well on which I have drawn ever since, though I now fear that my credit there too is exhausted. And they formed me also as a social being, for on these jaunts (as we called them) I came to know men and women who share a common ancestry with me, but from whom in other circumstances my way of life would have been utterly divorced. There is nothing so good that does not have its dark side; and with the progress of civilization, we have lost, are daily losing, and will further lose, a sense of the wholeness of our society, an awareness of commonality which we used to have by nature. It cannot be otherwise. When the ballads were made nothing divided lord and hind in their apprehension of the world, or worlds, around them. Now that has vanished.

Now your scientific farmer, with his agricultural textbook in his hand and his head full of theories of crop rotation and selective stock breeding, with his daughters fine in silk and muslin, and his son arguing questions of Political Economy, is a different being, mentally, from the hands he hires.

Or a lawyer like Jeffrey, with his *Edinburgh Review* and his douce wee suburban estate at Corstorphine – his Sabine farm, as I have heard him call it, though he is less of a farmer, I suspect, than Horace himself could claim to be – with his careful elegant diction, and his society manners – what has he, or any like him, in common with either the heroes of the ballads or the shepherds of Liddesdale today?

He has been a frequent visitor at Abbotsford, where he is indeed always welcome, for I admire Jeffrey, have a warm affection for him, and would be a hypocrite were I to speak out against the refinement of manners and understanding with which he is associated. Yet I also recall one occasion when this gulf of which I speak, that yawns between the educated and the natural man, was made evident.

It happened that he was with me once when a great snowstorm came on. The winds blew and wreaths piled themselves against the dykesides. Jeffrey observed as we watched the snow clouds gather that the sheep were drawing out from the burnsides and making for the barer high ground of the hill where the drifts would not lie. 'Are not sheep the most foolish of all animals? Here is a great storm about to come upon us,' Jeffrey said, 'and instead of remaining where there is shelter, they are exposing themselves to the full fury of the blast. If I were a sheep, I should remain snug in the hollows'.

Whereupon, Tom Purdie, who had been leaning on a gate as he listened to the celebrated editor, removed his pipe from his mouth, gave Jeffrey a long appraising stare, and said:

'Sir, if ye *were* a sheep, ye'd hae mair sense.'

The truth is that every advance of civilization also at the same time, and inevitably, represents a loss, but it was my good fortune while compiling the *Minstrelsy* to be permitted to inhabit a world in which past and present were contemporaneous, in which indeed the distinction between them dissolved, leaving me entranced in a moment of eternity.

It was not surprising that Jeffrey found little to please him in my verses. He was especially severe on *Marmion*, a work which I made with the utmost delight, in the full confident exuberance of command, and in the happiness of those years at Ashiestiel. Some of the battle stanzas were composed as I galloped with my regiment of the Light Horse on Portobello sands, or wandered among the hills that divide Tweed from Yarrow. Awareness of my happiness, I believe, permeates the poem, grim though many of the incidents are. I viewed the work with a certain detachment, as is evident from a letter I wrote in the course of its composition to my friend Lady Louisa Stuart, who ever took a close and appreciative interest in my literary efforts. 'Marmion', I told her, 'is at this instant gasping upon Flodden Field, and there I have been obliged to leave him for these few days in the death pangs. I hope I shall find time enough this morning to knock him on the head with two or three thumping stanzas.' And so I did; and he was thumped merrily enough.

The poem, which I myself consider the most satisfying of my longer essays in verse, found favour with the public, but Jeffrey would have none of it. The Romance of Chivalry, he declared, was a blind alley, a false fashion which could not last. Well, I never thought of it lasting, but was glad enough to have the money it earned me, and to know – what is dear to an author's heart – that it had given pleasure to thousands with whom it was unlikely I should ever have any personal connection.

The next year – it would have been 1809, I suppose – I made a tour of the Highlands, for I had it in mind to produce a northern companion to the *Lay* and *Marmion*. I took some trouble with the details of this poem, which was to be called *The Lady of the Lake*, to the extent even of riding from Loch Vennachar to Stirling Castle to make certain that my hero could do the journey in three hours. I was rewarded by the favour of the public, and even of the critics. Over 20,000 copies were sold in a few months, and Jeffrey himself abstained from adverse comment. Its success was such as to induce me for a moment to conclude that at last I had fixed a nail in the proverbially inconstant wheel of Fortune, even though in sober solitude I knew that an author's vogue is like to be of brief duration, and that public taste is fickle: 'unstable as water, thou shalt not prevail'. I was fortunate to be able to take this balanced view, for assuredly authors are children of the moon, their reputation now waxing, now waning, their light now obscured by clouds, and only sometimes shining forth in what seems to them their proper splendour. I was fortunate also to have decided not to rely utterly on literature, though in this decision I can give credit to my good sense as well as my luck. I suppose I have written as much in my lifetime as any man in Scotland, perhaps in Britain, but I have always regarded literature as subordinate and auxiliary to the main purposes of life, and in conversation have preferred talk of men and events rather than of books and criticism; and I believe this has been to the advantage of my literary work, for I trust that, despite my antiquarian interests, my books do not reek of the study. It will be a sad day for literature if the time comes when novelists can conceive only of characters who would themselves find their chief pleasure in reading.

Thinking back over that period in my life has calmed me. The terrors of Hastie's Close have receded, and I can view my experience with a certain detachment. I suppose I was in a more nervous state of mind than I had understood, and so exposed myself to imaginings which presented themselves to me in exaggerated form. Yet there is a certain despondency in this new mood of calm, for whether these sensations came from without, or were produced by some projection of myself upon the outer world, the conclusion must be disquieting. Either I was assailed by demons, whose reality my intelligence rejects, or I admitted elements in myself which habitually lie too deep for thoughts to force themselves into my consciousness. There was evil there; and yet I do not believe I am a bad man, though in my present perplexities, 'the channering worm doth chide'.

10

Memories of Byron, 1814–24

I was surprised by my success as a poet, though I did not think it entirely undeserved. There was novelty and spirit in my verses, which pleased a public unaccustomed to such fare. One curious result was that they established a vogue for the picturesque scenery of my native land. This was especially true of *The Lady of the Lake*. Painters flocked to the Trossachs to transfer my verbal descriptions of landscape to canvas; and a host of travellers followed, not only ladies and gentlemen, but merchants and tradesmen taking their bit holiday. (It is to be remembered that the continuing war with Napoleon made foreign travel all but impossible; nevertheless the charms of Caledonia do not yield to those of Switzerland or even Italy, and it pleased me to think that by making verses for my own pleasure I had contrived also to stimulate the economy of my country.)

I knew that my vogue would not last, for the public, when it feeds greedily on an author, is usually soon satisfied; but I was unprepared for the swiftness of my fall from favour; it was some comfort, however, that my supplanter was a true eagle.

I confess that my first impression of Lord Byron had been unfavourable. As a very young man he published a volume of verses entitled *Hours of Idleness*. Their value was slight, though a tender critic might have reflected that they were the work of a mere youth. Yet something presumptuous in the publication irritated Jeffrey, and the little book was greeted with an icy blast from the *Edinburgh Review*. His young lordship responded with a sharp satire in the manner of Pope, though some way behind the master in felicity of expression. For some reason he chose to lay a cudgel upon my back, which at the time appeared unjust to me, even ungentlemanly. I summoned up my fortitude – no difficult task in the circumstances, for I found it funny enough to see a young whelp sprung from the nobility abusing me, of whose circumstances he was perfectly ignorant, for endeavouring to scratch out a living with my pen. 'God help the bear,' I said to a friend, 'if, having little else to eat he must not suck even his own paws. I could assure that noble imp of fame that it is not my fault that I was not born to a park and £5,000 a year, as it is not his lordship's merit, although it may be his great good fortune, that he was not born to live by his literary talents or success.'

This was certainly an unpromising beginning. Soon afterwards the young Byron went abroad – his travels taking him to the Levant, to Greece, Constantinople, and the ringing plains of wind-swept Troy; and indeed he all but dropped from my memory, and had any asked me, I should have been ready to wager that we should not find him again re-entering the poetic lists. I would, as the world knows, have been utterly wrong, and made to appear a fool, for he returned with two Cantos of a Romantic poem describing the travels of a noble but unhappy youth in that part of the world. *Childe Harold* took the town by storm, nay, not only the town, but the whole country. He followed it with a succession of eastern tales – somewhat, I confess or even boast, in my own manner – and, mellowed perhaps by fame, softened sufficiently towards me to send me the copy of one of these poems with an extravagantly flattering inscription, which modesty forbids me to repeat.

It was at this time that I brought out the *Lord of the Isles*, a poem at which I had wrought with rather more care than was my custom. One evening, a few days after publication, I invited James Ballantyne to call on me.

'Well, James,' I said. 'I have given you a week. What do folk say of the poem?'

James, usually so brisk, hesitated.

'Come,' I said, 'speak your mind. I am not a green girl to be laid low by adverse criticism. But I see from your look how the matter stands: in one word, disappointment. Byron has beat me, eh? So be it, so be it, but we canna hang our heads, James, we canna afford tae droop. Since one line has failed, we maun just tack our sails and try the ither yin,' and I held up a sheaf of the manuscript that was to be *Guy Mannering*.

James hummed and hawed a bit more, but did not deny my analysis, though he hastened to assure me that the novel would 'set a' to richts again. And when you're in London town, Scott, will you meet wi' Lord Byron?'

'I hope I may,' I said.

'Man, that'll be a rare encounter.'

'Oh, of course,' I said. 'I'll tell you though, James, what Byron should say when we accost each other:

Art thou the man whom men famed Grizzle call?

And I should germanely answer:

Art thou the still more famed Tom Thumb the small?'

But it was not, of course, with such compliments that we met.

Our first encounter was in the drawing-room of his publisher Mr Murray, in Albemarle Street. It was my first visit to the capital in six years, and I approached my meeting with Byron with interest rather than in anticipation of pleasure. I greatly admired the vigour and efflorescence of *Childe Harold*, while finding the hero somewhat given to self-pity (one cause perhaps of its vast success, for the public loves to be invited to share in a melancholy mood); but report had prepared me for a man of peculiar and affected habits, and of quick temper, and I had some doubts as to whether we were likely to suit each other in society. I was most agreeably and immediately disappointed in this respect, for I found the young man – some seventeen years my junior – to be in the highest degree courteous, and even kind, modest, and strangely gentle. He was full of wit and a gay humour that had to date found no place in his poetry, though it was, of course, subsequently to do so. We met frequently during my visit, talking almost daily for an hour or two in Murray's drawing-room. Our sentiments agreed pretty well, except on the matter of politics and religion, about which subjects I fancied he then had no very fixed opinions. I remember once, taking advantage of my seniority, remarking to him that if he lived a few years longer, he would in all probability alter his opinions.

'I suppose you are one of those who prophesy I shall turn Methodist,' he said, with a certain asperity.

I replied: 'You do me wrong, for I do not suppose that your conversion is like to be of so ordinary a kind. I would rather look to see you retreat upon the Catholic faith, and distinguish yourself by the austerity of your penances.'

The idea pleased him; he gave me that sudden ingenuous smile that lit up his countenance, removing all trace of the melancholy which he thought proper to assume in society; and conceded that I might well be in the right.

On politics we could not agree, for he affected a high strain of what is now called Liberalism. At the time I thought it arose principally from the pleasure it afforded him, as a vehicle for displaying his wit and satire against individuals in office, rather than from any firm adherence to the principles which he professed. I have since moderated that judgement, though I do not think he had any inclination to democracy, for he was certainly proud of his rank and ancient lineage. But his subsequent career, ending in the noble enterprise in Greece, attested to the sincerity of his sympathy with the oppressed, a sympathy which he also displayed in his maiden speech in the House of Lords, wherein he expressed his abhorrence of the industrial system which was depriving so many poor artisans of their accustomed employment, and driving them in desperation to acts of ineffectual violence. I could not approve the threat to the stability of the body politic which the rioters offered; yet I could admire the generosity of Byron's response. He was, I soon realized, a noble, generous, yet perturbed spirit, over-sensitive to the opinions of others, and at that time of youth, deficient in that robustness which allows a man to shake off criticism like a spaniel ridding itself of water after immersion in a river or pond.

He could scarcely be blamed. His countenance was a thing to wonder at, and so his beauty drew every eye upon him whenever he entered a room; his fame joined with his beauty to make him the cynosure of every eye, and exposed him to envy, jealousy, and even insult. Like me he was lame, in his case the result of a congenital disorder; or so I believe. I, not being blessed with beauty, thought little of my affliction; but Byron, thin-skinned and self-conscious, could not forget his, and had adopted a manner of walking which he believed to disguise his infirmity.

Withal, he was essentially manly, and we had the same view of the place of literature in a man's life. When he caught himself saying to me 'we authors' or 'we poets', he dissolved in giggles like a schoolboy. Tom Moore has told me of how once, in Venice with Byron, they stood overlooking the Grand Canal by night, and Tom launched into rapturous praise of the beauty of the scene. 'Hang it, Tom,' Byron said – as I trust I should have said myself – 'don't be so damned poetical.'

When he found the company unsympathetic, Byron could lapse into affectation. He never did so with me; I found him sincere; and I believe he was at his best with me. If so, it is a matter in which I take no little pride.

I was always conscious of his genius, though in conversation he would run on, lightly, even frivolously; but always ready to turn to grave matters about which he discoursed with feeling and good sense. He has written that he was 'born half a Scot and bred a whole one', and indeed his consciousness of his Gordon blood, and the pride he took in it, was a bond between us. In many ways he was an aristocratic Burns. There was the same tenderness, allied to the same contempt for cant. There was even a certain similarity of countenance, not surprising perhaps when one considers that they not only shared a genius of the same order, but that, though Burns is associated with Ayrshire and the south-west of Scotland, his family hailed from the Mearns, not so very far from the Gordon stronghold of the north-east. I have even played with the fancy that some Gordon laird may have got one of Burns's female ancestors with child, and that there might therefore have been a remote kinship linking the two poets. Certainly Byron's genius – I mean the nature of it and the forms of expression it took in its maturity – appears to me more characteristically Scotch than English. Even his sympathy for Greece 'rightly struggling to be free' may sound an echo ringing back to our own Wars of Independence.

When we parted, at the end of my London visit, we exchanged gifts, like the heroes of Homer – a comparison which, in justice to myself, I must state was made by Lord Byron rather than me, though the fancy did not displease me. I gave him a beautiful dagger mounted with gold, which had been the property of the redoubted Elfi Bey. But Byron outmatched me, for his gift was a large sepulchral vase of silver. It was full of dead men's bones, and had inscriptions on two sides. One ran thus: 'The bones contained in this urn were found in certain ancient sepulchres within the long walls of Athens' – raised to defend the city during the war with Sparta – 'in the month of February, 1811'. The other bore the lines of Juvenal: '*Expende – quot libras in duce summo invenies? Mors sola fatetur quantula sint hominum corpuscula*'. There was a letter with this vase, which I prized even more highly than the gift itself, on account of the kindness with which Byron expressed himself towards me. I left it naturally in the urn with the bones; but it is now missing. As the theft was not of a nature to be practised by a domestic – and in any case I have never employed a domestic whom I would have thought capable of such a theft – I have to suspect the inhospitality of some individual of higher station. Well, since I have chosen to make this public in a letter to Moore, which he has my permission to print in his *Life of Byron*, the said individual must enjoy his theft in secret, for I cannot think that he will choose now to boast of this literary curiosity.

Byron and I laughed a good deal about what the public might be supposed to think concerning the gloomy nature of our mutual gifts. Certainly they fitted the popular conception of Byron, and indeed he was given to moods of an almost morbid melancholy, in which his beautiful countenance darkened, so that one might suppose him one of Milton's rebel angels, now sunk in deep despair. When this happened, I either waited for the mood to pass, or diverted it by introducing some more easy and natural topic of conversation, whereupon the shadows would slip from him like mist rising from a landscape. He was also given, as I have hinted, to sudden starts of suspicion, when he would check himself, apparently considering whether there had not been a secret and perhaps offensive meaning in something casually said to him. Then, I preferred to let his mind, like a troubled spring, work itself clear, which, in my company, it invariably did in a short time.

I would rather say nothing of the misfortunes which drove him into exile, amidst a storm of calumny such as I believe few men have ever been compelled to endure. The failure of a marriage must always retain something mysterious to others, and also, I fancy, to the two people most intimately concerned. There is a certain impudence in speculating on such matters. I would refrain, but that so much has already been said and written that I believe that in justice it behoves me to give my own opinion.

Let me commence by stating what I take to be a general truth: that it is rare for the failure of a marriage to be altogether the responsibility of one party.

Lord and Lady Byron were ill-matched, and it is probable – though the union of opposites is often fruitful – that they should never have been joined together. I believe Lady Byron to be a good woman, and one possessed of a firm high-principled morality; but the evidence suggests that she is also a narrow and inflexible lady, whose passions are cold and steely while Byron's were hot and tempestuous. That he believed himself to love her I do not doubt; and indeed, through all the rage, indignation and incomprehension which he later expressed, I detect a continuing and, to him equally incomprehensible, attachment to her. Lady Byron was capable of a fierce and possessive jealousy, and Lord Byron incapable – in his glorious youth – of the great virtue of constancy. She was fiercely critical, and though I knew him to be given to self-criticism, often even to the point of self-laceration, he resented any suggestion of criticism from others. The habit of her mind was mathematical and rigid; his, poetic and exploratory. Had they come together when he had attained a greater maturity, and had Lady Byron been some years younger than his lordship, then I fancy they might have agreed well enough. But it was not so; they were yoked together as equal, yet unequal, partners, and discovered that they were also rivals. Lord Byron's temperament required a wife, or woman, who was sympathetic, tolerant, undemanding; he chose one in whom these qualities were altogether absent. Her jealousy of his close relationship with his half-sister, Mrs Leigh, in whom he had discovered these very attributes, was natural enough; it was equally natural that the storms of his married life should reanimate his love for his half-sister. Whether, as the world insists, there was anything criminal in that love, I do not know. It would not surprise me if there was such a connection, much as I might deplore it – for if it existed it must have occasioned sensations of guilt which all parties must have found distressing. If such a connection did indeed exist, it is sufficiently accounted for by the reflection that Byron and Mrs Leigh were not reared together, and that indeed, they were barely acquainted till Byron was adult – Mrs Leigh, I fancy, being some five years older than her half-brother.

Morality, of course, is to be supported, for without it the condition of society must be even sadder than it is; yet there is to me something intensely disagreeable in the judgement that passes harsh sentence on others for offences which the man who judges has never felt a temptation to indulge in (I think again of poor wretched Heber, and of how even a man of the highest principles and the most apparently steady virtue may be led astray by carnal desire; and when I do so, I hope I have attained a degree of sympathetic understanding which makes me readier to pity than to censure.)

I have – I may say in parenthetical passing – a particular, personal, and to me shameful, reason to express this hope, for I have myself been guilty of an act of moral censure and self-righteousness, which seemed to me proper at the time, but for which I now bitterly reproach myself. I have never written of this before, and I can do so now only in the certainty that this memoir is unlikely to see the light of day till long after I am in the grave; for I shall leave instructions to Lockhart that, while he may draw on it freely for the Life which he purposes to write, he must then place it under lock and key with instructions that it is not to be published in its entirety till all those mentioned in it have also taken that long journey into the dark.

My youngest brother Daniel was possessed of a rare degree of charm which however, as is often the way with those who have received this blessing or curse, contrived to lead him into a dissipated way of life. He was intelligent but not steadfast, and lacked the resolution which alone can enable a man of merry and agreeable temperament to reject the immediately attractive course of action in favour of a duller but virtuous one. Accordingly, he soon fell into evil ways. Believing that a change of scene was desirable, I secured him a post in the West Indies. While he was there, a rebellion of the negroes broke out. My brother disgraced himself by a failure of nerve which may have been no more than momentary, but which exposed him to contempt in the colony; and so he was returned home, his name – and mine – blackened. Back in Edinburgh, he lodged with my mother, who continued to treat him with that Christian charity which was natural to her, and who reproached me – it was almost the only, and certainly the hardest, reproach she ever offered me – for my failure to do the same. But like the God of the Hebrews I hardened my heart against poor Dan, refused to receive him, refused to name him as more than 'my relation', so denying him even the sacred name of brother and, in short, presented to him a front that was cold as ice and unforgiving as – well, Lady Byron's. Poor Dan in what I now understand to be the misery occasioned by broken hopes, shame, and the felt contempt of others, especially myself, sought refuge in the bottle and the unworthy companionship afforded by low taverns. He died, as a result of his dissipations, before he was thirty. While he was the prime agent of his own failure and decay, I cannot now acquit myself of the charge that my own adamantine rejection of him contributed to his unhappy end. To my present shame I refused to attend his funeral or to wear mourning for my brother. I have now learned to have more tolerance and compassion than I had then. Indeed – if I ever get through *Woodstock* and *Napoleon* – I have an idea for a character in a novel to be set in Perth at the close of the Middle Ages, who will display a like momentary cowardice, and, if I can bring it off, it may serve as some poor sort of expiation to the *manes* of poor Dan.

It is not only my memory of my brother which forbids me to join in the general censure directed at Byron both on account of his marital misfortunes, and of the nature of his life in Venice. That this was dissipated is beyond doubt; indeed in letters which were widely circulated Byron boasted of his amours, partly – I have no doubt – because it amused him to scandalize still further those who had already condemned him. It was as if he said, 'If they want a rake, I shall provide one.' But though I would never excuse a poet's life on the grounds that his manner of living was necessary for his poetry – a piece of special pleading which I think offensive – yet I am loth to judge Byron harshly even in his Venetian years. I am sensible that he was sorely wounded in mind and spirit; and I believe also he ever retained a certain quality of detachment which enabled him to view his debauchery with a candid eye. Then, if one is to seek justification in the work that resulted, why *Don Juan*, for all its profanity, occasional grossness, and the unpleasant, even offensive, nature of the personal attacks it contains – some of them directed against men for whom I have a high regard – might be held to justify even a treaty with the De'il. Where in English literature will you find such a medley? Such exuberance mingled with tenderness, such wit and high spirits, such shades of melancholy, such scene-painting, such an ability to move in half a sentence from frivolity to wise philosophy, such generosity, such keen contempt for cant?

As to the last phase of his life, that must be held to redeem anything and everything that had gone before. The cause was good, the enterprise noble, the commitment absolute. A young lady said to me once: 'I regret only that he died of fever rather than in battle, which would have been a more fitting and Romantic death for a poet.' Her feeling was natural enough – for a young lady of her stamp. In my own youth I might indeed have thought likewise. Now, Byron's acceptance of a role somewhere between that of a quartermaster and a diplomat appears to me evidence of his true greatness as a man. The odious Trelawny, who had modelled himself, it seems, on a Byronic hero, had no time, I am told, for the business that occupied Byron at Missolonghi. Indeed, he sneered at it, and took himself off to the mountains to join a band of fighters who were no better than brigands for all their professed patriotism. But Byron stayed in his quarters by that dismal lagoon while the rain fell, and scribbled letters about loans and supplies and accommodations. His acceptance of what he conceived as his duty – of the best way he could serve the cause in which he had engaged himself – a duty without glamour or excitement – his acceptance too of necessity and of the limitations of what was possible – all this establishes his true heroism to my complete satisfaction. In Greece Byron came to maturity, and, in doing so, realized, I believe, that the harder part of life consists in acceptance, leading to persistence, even if at times you seem to be dinging your head against a stone dyke. He got his teeth into the job and held fast as a terrier that has gotten a rat and will not surrender it. Affectation and Romanticism fell away from him, and he showed the rarest kind of courage – the dour cauld kind that hauds fast, and says 'no'.

When we were together, I ever thought myself, on account of the difference in our age, as being to some extent his mentor and even protector; and I have reason to believe from his conversation and writings that to some degree at least he himself saw me in that light too. Now, when I think of his labours in Greece, and then think on my present perplexities, on the temptation to despair which creeps upon me in the night watches, why then I feel that in some way our roles have been reversed; and that it is now Byron who speaks words of resolution and encouragement to me.

Had he survived the war in Greece, he would have surmounted a crisis in his life, and a new career of fame would have been opened to him, in which he would have obliterated the memory of such parts of his life as his friends would wish to see forgotten. But it was not to be; he leaves a memory, and a name, and, for me, a remembrance of warmth, and a sharp and indescribably painful sense of loss.

Light flickers on the reedy waste
　　Of Missolonghi's sad lagoon,
And dark, and sullen, clouds obscure
　　The weary, as if mortal, moon.

Frater, ave atque vale!
　　The Roman poet's echoing line
Speaks of the sword-keen grief that springs
　　In countless hearts, so sharp in mine.

Not only grief but also pride,
　　For Byron died in Freedom's cause,
At one with bold Miltiades,
　　With Wallace and the Great Montrose.

Lift high yon cup of Samian wine!
　　He died that Greece might yet be free,
As the mountains look on Marathon
　　While Marathon looks on the sea.

Frater, ave atque vale!
　　The wailing pipes take up the strain;
The echo sounds o'er Thessaly,
　　Again, again, again, again.

The laurels by the lake are stripped
  – while darkness cloaks the hills in night
To crown the hero-poet's brow
  – And Greeks themselves resume the fight.

Frater, ave atque vale!
  Rest, troubled Childe, the journey's done,
In honour rescued and restored,
  This battle lost, yet victory won.

I have known almost all the distinguished men of my time; yet taking everything into account, Byron excelled them all. As a poet Wordsworth achieves a sublimity which Byron could not attain; yet though I have a true affection for Wordsworth, as a man I must judge him inferior to Byron. Take poetry away from Byron and he would still have been remarkable; take it from Wordsworth, and what is left? Moreover, the vanity that is disagreeable – though I understand its source – in Wordsworth, was innocent in Byron. It ran deep no doubt; yet to me it appeared to belong to that part of him that remained boyish. There was an underlying humour in it. It was a physical vanity, too, for his profile was that of an angel, but there was ever an element of mischief in it;* it was part of a game he played.

His Grace of Wellington is, of course, a man whose sagacity far surpassed Byron's, and whose manners, bearing and dignity are all beyond reproach. I esteem him absolutely. Yet there is not in the Duke that divine fire which animated Byron. He is rooted in this earth.

* N.B. The last time I talked with Byron, he was merry and playful as a kitten. Now – *Sunt lacrimae rerum!*

Frater, ave atque vale!
How many tender memories mine,
Of laughter and companionship,
Of sense and nonsense, song and wine.

Light flickers on the reedy waste
Of Missolonghi's sad lagoon,
Love parts the misty clouds to show
The candid and translucent moon.

II

A Dream and an Argument, 1827

I have had the most horrid dream; I thought that I was dead.

It so happened that after a bite of supper of toasted cheese, which might account for it, and a dram of whisky, I sat in my easy-chair, meaning to rest for a half-hour or so before I resumed my task. I was weary after a day in the Court, where I still cannot escape the feeling that oppressed the man with the long nose, that everyone is looking at me, to estimate how I bear myself in my troubles. Fatigue then must have overcome me, for if I do not recall falling asleep, and could suppose that my vision was reality, that supposition is given a good dunt, by my certainty that I remember waking up.

Be that as it may, it seemed that there was a personage in my study with me, a most gentleman-like fellow, but not one that I could put a name to. He straightway excused his presence – and it did not seem that anyone had admitted him – by observing that I had set so many characters loose in the world from my study that I could scarce grumble at the occasional intruder.

Which was an odd thing to say, as it seemed to me, for an imaginary character can hardly be held to be equal to an uninvited guest. Nevertheless, I do not think I demurred.

It occurred to me that he was perhaps a lawyer sent by my creditors to conduct a new examination of my affairs; a thought that was disagreeable, since arrangements have been made and ought to be adhered to, as they certainly have been for my part.

'Not precisely,' he said. 'Call me an angel. All angels are lawyers in a manner of speaking, since we are sent to make a case, though' – he tittered in what even in my perplexity I thought an unangelic fashion – 'though the converse can scarcely be maintained.'

'What sort of angel?' I asked.

'Call me an examining or recording one. Or the devil's advocate. Or what you please. We are concerned here with you, Sir Walter, not with me.'

Then he accused me of dishonourable conduct.

'Dishonourable?' I said. 'In what way dishonourable?'

'Come, Sir Walter,' he said. 'Your love of secrecy – your concealment of your involvement – your financial involvement – in the Ballantyne printing business – do you call that honourable?'

'Why,' I replied, taking courage, for it seemed to me that if this was all the charge he had to bring against me, I had little to fear, 'I know of no principle that obliges a man to disclose his pecuniary affairs to the world. Moreover,' I added, 'James and John Ballantyne have been friends since my boyhood. If my engagement in their business was to my advantage, it also served them well, till this crash of bulls and bears on the London markets engulfed us all.'

He shook his head, but did not pursue the matter, as if it was no purpose of his to argue with me, but only to record my answers to his questions.

'Did not your denial of the authorship of your novels reveal an innate dishonesty?'

'Come, come,' I said, genially enough, I think, for I felt myself on *terra firma* here, 'it is a fundamental principle of Scots Law that no man is bound to incriminate himself. Besides the secrecy prevented me from taking myself too seriously, as authors are wont to do. We authors have the habit of rating authorship ower high, and are encouraged to do so by the praise of fellow-authors who offer it because they are anxious to elevate the profession, and hope for praise in their turn. Ca' me, ca' thee, as the saying goes.'

I felt that my answer displeased him, for he evinced signs of impatience.

'Come, Sir Walter, this is trivial stuff. Let us advance to the gravamen of the charge. You have presented – I speak with the voice of posterity here – a false picture of your native land. You are a traitor to Scotland, shame and dishonour lurk by your grave, sham bard of a sham nation . . .'

That touched me deeply.

'I have tried', I said, 'to make it possible for future generations to see Scotland whole, and I have tried to reconcile the divisions that still afflict us. Our history is one of conflict: between brother and brother' – and as I said that, I shuddered at the memory of my conduct towards poor Daniel, which, to my relief, he did not raise against me – 'clan against clan, Highland against Lowland. Covenanter against Cavalier, Presbyterian against Episcopalian, Jacobite against Whig, Whig against Tory. The opposed forces glower at each other across the wastes of history, and I would effect a reconciliation. I would have each see the virtue in the other's cause. I would have the victor learn that his victory is never complete, and should never be so, for his cause is aye changed by the battle, so that the world that comes into being is the heir of both parties in the quarrel. Now,' I said, warming to my theme, 'of these conflicts none was more enduring and cruel than that between Lowland and Highland. The Highlanders, whose language was once the tongue of the greater part of the country, were driven to the very extremity of history, and the catastrophe of Culloden saw their way of life utterly broken. By summoning up memories, however savage, by invocation of what was, I have sought to bind the past to the present and so, I hope, help to form a more intelligent and more sympathetic future.'

'Fine words,' said my inquisitor, for such I now saw him to be, 'fine words, Sir Walter, but the Highland chiefs you flatter are meanwhile clearing the glens of men and women to make way for sheep. Do you defend that, while you praise their ancestors?'

'I defend no inhumanity,' I said. 'Yet I observe that in every age, the forces of political economy, which arise from a general or particular perception of necessity, drive men, who in their personal relations may be kindly and benevolent, to perform acts which reek of inhumanity, but which their perpetrators contrive to justify on grounds of morality, as well as necessity. So you will find Christian gentlemen, who would be sair affrontit if you challenged their religious devotion or the honesty of their faith in Christ who taught us to love our neighbours as ourselves, Christian gentlemen, I say, in the southern states of the American Union, who hold slaves and buy and sell them as we do cattle. Why, Mr Jefferson himself, author of the noble sentiments expressed in the Declaration of Independence, owned black men as we own beasts.'

And then I spoke up for the wretched of the earth, the perpetual victims, the broken men and women, and for all those who suffer grievously in war. I spoke up for the defeated:

Dule and wae for the order sent our lads to the Border,
  The English, for ance, by guile wan the day:
The Flowers o the Forest, that foucht aye the foremost,
  The prime o our land, are cauld in the clay.

We'll hear nae mair lilting at the yowe-milking,
  Women and bairns are heartless and wae;
Sighing and moaning on ilka green loaning;
  The Flowers o the Forest are a' wede away.

'I defend no inhumanity,' I said again. 'Let the proud sad music of the "Liltin'" sound to the valleys and the hills and in men's hearts. If the day should come when we forget it, and abide only in the present and in hopes of the future, then, alas, my poor country, for all that makes Scotland Scotland will be no more. The brave days will be done, and we shall live in the ledger-books and no more in poetry and song. It is that awareness that I have worked to cultivate.'

As I spoke in this manner, the tears ran down my cheeks, for I was sorely moved, but my inquisitor threw back his head and laughed. I can hear that laughter yet, ringing down the corridors of a rational Hell, where indeed at that moment I believed myself to be imprisoned.

But I spoke up again, for my blood was high.

'To pay tribute to the defeated is not, as you appear to suggest, to be in love with defeat. I see what you are at. You would copy the hand that wrote on the wall at Belshazzar's Feast and delivered its terrible judgement. You have weighed me in the balance and found me wanting. Well, maybe so. In the end which of us is not found wanting? So, in a sense it maun be, for all of us. As Sir John says, "tush, man, mortal men, mortal men".

> Late at e'en, drinking the wine,
>   And ere they paid the lawin'.
> They set a combat them between,
>   To fight it in the dawin'

'Just so,' I said, 'just so it is for all of us. That combat is a contract in which we all engage, and at the close of day, victors and defeated alike, we maun pay the lawin'. But neither victory nor defeat is ever absolute, for something of the victor dies in his triumph, and something of the defeated and broken lives; and it is the duty of the poet to breathe life into dead bones, into what would otherwise be lost and sunk in the blackest tarn of History. It is in this way that he may enrich the experience of all men and women. The defiance and lamentation of the lost and broken ring down the waste of centuries, and if we are deaf to their cries we stop our ears to truth, pity, and poetry. The world rolls on, and in each revolution of the globe, in each turn of the cruel machine of History, much is crushed, destroyed, buried, and near obliterated. It is the task of the poet and novelist to rescue these broken things and re-animate them, and so save us from the tyranny of the present, from the rant of the conqueror, from the brutal dictatorship of success, which stifles thought and smoors the imagination. And, sir, let me tell you,' I said, 'it is by the exercise of the imagination that we live, and to keep the past alive is to hold open the gates of wonder . . .'

And then I woke. I had been thinking myself dead, suffering my inquisition in that rational Hell. I shivered as I sat in my chair, a Paisley shawl pulled around my shoulders to guard me against the draughts.

It is not strange to dream of death, and indeed there have been days and nights in the last months when I have been guilty of hoping that Death would not be over-long in summoning me. And if my dream, which is all it was, when awthing is said and done, tells me anything, it assures me that I shall be the same man in death as I hae been in life.

Which is consolation of a sort.

But it is strange all the same, that accusations of this nature should rise up against me from within my own being.

I mind once I was at the funeral of an old man so extravagant in his notions as to be properly thought by many to have left his wits at the world's end. One of the congregation – my cousin Maxpoffle as I remember – observed that the body was laid the wrong way in the grave.

'What do you mean?' said I.

'Weel,' he said, 'dae ye no see, Wattie? His feet are pointing the wrang airt.'

And so they were. Maxpoffle was all for having the appropriate adjustment made, but I told him to hold his hand, observing that a man that had been wrang in the heid all his life, could scarcely be expected to lie richt-heided in the grave.

But, on the evidence of my dream, I think I may; and that's consolation for ye, as Tom Purdie was wont to say.

What sad tricks the mind plays on a man! There is no surer mark of Shakespeare's genius, I have often thought, than the last act of *Macbeth*, and the manner in which he traces the vagaries of a disordered mind, brought like a stag to bay. But have I tried to be a good man? Yes, I truly believe so. If I were to subject myself, now I am awake, to a catechism, what charges would I bring? I think myself more often guilty of ill-feelings than ill-deeds. Are we to be judged on what we succeed in suppressing? When I pray, the line I speak with most urgency is: 'Lead us not into temptation, but deliver us from evil'.

In my youth temptation led me a merry dance, but the invitations that were extended to me were innocent enough, a matter of thoughtless dares, willingly accepted, and high spirits. So, for example, I scaled the Castle rock here in Edinburgh, a thing that would have caused acute anxiety to my dear mother, had she known of this foolish audacity. Then, later, in student days, it was a question of how far we could, or rather would – for we felt no incapacity – carry our cantrips. There was nothing, I believe, vicious in our merriment.

In my prime, worldly ambition drew me on; and again I felt it easy enough to acquit myself of any malignity in this respect. The desire to make a brave show, the wish to be well-thought of, these are innocent enough. Even the drive for riches may be excused, since in benefitting myself, I benefitted my family and dependents also. Some may accuse me of a greed for possessions, especially land, and, though I dislike the word 'greed' employed in this respect, I do not altogether deny the charge. Yet it is natural for a man to wish to be able to plant his foot on earth which he can call his own, and in building Abbotsford and extending my estates, I acted as the world expects a successful man to act. Moreover, again, though I confess that my acquisition of property, and its management, pleased me mightily, I worked at the same time for the good of others. There are many cottagers at Abbotsford who have sufficient reason to be grateful to me; as of course have my children.

As for my financial affairs and business dealings, I see nothing reprehensible in them. No doubt I was rash, but I never engaged myself more deeply than I had a rational expectation of being able to redeem. I had by my own industry opened up, as it appeared to me, a well-nigh inexhaustible seam of treasure; and indeed, though

I now have to crank up my imagination, where it once soared on the wings of the morning, the seam, as has been proved to me, is indeed not yet exhausted. But this is a matter too painful to dwell on now, though if I carry this work forward, I shall in time confront it face to face.

Age offers new temptations. In the present condition of my affairs, I hear sad seductive voices muttering of despair. 'Why put yourself to this trouble?' they insinuate, 'when there is no longer joy in labour, and all you sigh for is rest from toil?' It is a siren voice that summons me to easeful and inglorious repose. But this I can defy. Please God, I have aye done my duty; and ever shall.

There is another temptation that assails a man as the years pass, youth fades to a flickering memory, and the grave yawns. I do not refer to the desire for death, though that is a temptation close allied to despair, and one which every man, who feels his strength departing him, as the God Hercules deserted Antony, must feel on occasion. No, this temptation is more insidious, not hard to account for, difficult to combat. It was to this, I believe, that poor Heber succumbed. I feel it, though happily not in the precise form that attracted, and destroyed, him.

I have written in these notes of man's duality; but there is more to it than that. As we enter into manhood, the world spreads itself before us, offering what appears to be an infinite number of roads which we may choose to take. We go through life, and with each step that we take, the choice narrows. We fix our character by the decisions that we take. We determine what we are going to be, and each act of such determination requires us to reject other possibilities of what we might have been. We do this naturally and for the most part unthinkingly. Then comes a moment when we look back, when we are conscious of darkness waiting to engulf us, and we may feel a sharp stab of regret for all the possible routes, all the possible selves, which we left unexplored. This realization brings with it the whisper that it may not be too late to try out, or test, neglected parts of our nature. It arouses the Ulysses that lurks within all men who have striven to know themselves. Can it be supposed that he was content to remain at home in Ithaca?

I have known many men, too numerous to list, who, at some point in the middle of their journey, became weary of success, happiness, worldly ambition, domesticity, family life, and so committed acts which the world deems folly or worse, by which they destroyed themselves, or at the very least lowered themselves in the estimation of others: and I believe that in each such case, they were lured on by a spirit of dissatisfaction with their achievements, a feeling that they had imprisoned themselves in what they had made of their life, and by a wish that things could be different. That wish is a sweet cheat. When True Thomas lay on Huntlie Bank, and the Queen of fair Elfland summoned him, was he not yielding to a like temptation; or rather is the ballad not a poetic representation of what I have been attempting to describe?

> Oh see ye not yon narrow road,
>   So thick beset with thorns and briars?
> That is the path of righteousness,
>   Tho' after it but few inquires.
>
> And see ye not that braid braid road,
>   That lies across that lily leven?
> That is the path of wickedness,
>   Tho' some call it the road to heaven.

And see ye not that bonnie road
　That winds about the fernie brae?
That is the road to fair Elfland,
　Where thou and I this night maun gae.

It is the bonnie road that winds about the fernie brae that draws the disillusioned on, that attracts the man who feels that he has insufficiently explored, tested, or given opportunities to, his innermost nature. It lures on those who at moments wonder, with melancholy or anger, if they have denied a significant part of their own being.

When I feel myself drawn, ineluctably as it seems, to return to Hastie's Close, as if in search of some revelation which I both desire and fear, it is the bonnie road that winds about the fernie brae on which I have placed my foot.

I went there for a third time the other night. I went with self-reproach, even self-contempt, having told myself time and again that I would not; yet I went, and as I advanced towards the dank and sinister place, a lively expectation drove the self-reproach from me. I did not know what I hoped for, had no notion what I expected. Yet even that is not a true statement of my sentiments, for I knew I was opening myself to the opportunity to cease for the moment to be Walter Scott, Bart, of Abbotsford, a celebrated public figure, and become if only briefly quite another Walter Scott, a being who had hitherto been confined and denied; perhaps I hoped to become True Thomas. I do not know.

I turned off the Cowgate, my step unaccustomedly light, light as a bridegroom, it seems to me, on a long-awaited wedding day. A high wind sent clouds scudding over a thin moon, but it was still as the grave in the Close once I had rounded the corner and half-mounted the steps. Again: that silence as if the inhabitants of the surrounding houses had been stricken by some sleep-inducing fate. Again: that consciousness that in solitude I was not alone, though, as on my second visit, I saw no figures. Again: I pressed my back against the wall, receiving successive waves of heat and cold. And then a voice:

> And were you called to Elfland, cuddy,
>> Where the white lilies bloom,
> Or to that mirk, mirk land, cuddy,
>> The shades ayont the tomb.

'Who's there?' I called and my voice was hoarse. 'Answer me.'

> But look you now to the west, cuddy,
>> And see what I show you there;
> A land o sic sweet delight, cuddy,
>> Where the red rose scents the air.

> Come to a garden green, cuddy,
>> Where the red apple grows on the tree,
> And there I'll gie you your wage, cuddy,
>> A tongue that can never lee.

> And there in the garden green, cuddy,
>> Where the moonlicht fa's on the flowers,
> There in the garden green, cuddy,
>> We'll pass our pleasant hours . . .

The voice of an infinite sweetness died away, and I was like the lame boy who followed the Pied Piper and being slow found the door in the mountain barred against him; and I knew that the singer had been the slim girl, barefoot and with her head thrown back, as if laughing, though I had not seen her.

And then the voice, which likewise I knew to be that of the old woman who had sat smoking a pipe, interrupted my reverie:

'Aye, shirra,

> If ever thou gavest hosen and shoon
> Every nighte and alle,
> Sit thee down and put them on
> And Christe receive thy saule
>
> If hosen and shoon thou ne'er gavst nane,
> Every nighte and alle,
> The whinnes sail pricke thee to the bare bane
> – And Christe receive thy saule ...'

'Hosen and shoon he ne'er gave nane,' said another voice.

'Maybe so, maybe so,' said the first old woman, 'but he ance gave me snuff, and forbye for that he may pass the whinnes.'

'Snuff's nae hosen and shoon, hosen and shoon he ne'er gave nane – sae Christe receive his saule ...'

'Aye, biddy, but it was by the haund of my grandson that he gave me snuff, and forbye for that he may pass through the whinnes safe till Christe receive his saule ...'

Then the two dames cackled, and the fiddler from the shadows struck up a jaunty tune, mocking, sprightly and defiant.

I called out to the old women to stay and answer the questions that I wished to put to them, but the fiddle drowned my words, and then the music retreated and died away, leaving a note of sadness lingering in the air. I knew that a promise had been offered me, and then withheld; and that it was a promise which I was eager to accept, though well-advised to fear the consequences.

And the whins pricked me to the bare bone and even to the heart as I came away and turned for my lodging where I could look for no delight, not even for sweet repose, and then I looked back towards the close, and Dante's line formed itself in the misty air: '*Lasciate ogni speranza, voi ch' entrate*'. And yet it seemed that for a moment I had been offered hope – was it then a cheat, a sad delusion?

12

Waverley and Other Novels, 1805–28

These chapters of narrative are a sort of balm, for it is agreeable, but not, I think, reprehensible, to turn from the perplexities of the moment, and recall happier times. Moreover it occurs to me now that the public may derive some interest from some aspects of my personal history, and may be pleased to learn how I came to undertake the writing of novels. Indeed, it may be that it will prove seemly for excerpts from this otherwise gloomy and introspective work to be published separately; and in any case they provide material on which Lockhart may draw. Moreover, young Cadell, in his enthusiasm for the *magnum opus* – an enthusiasm which, however ill-founded it may prove to be, does something to cheer my wounded spirit – is eager that I should write a General Introduction to his edition; and these notes may serve to enable me to collect my thoughts, to determine what should be included, and what concealed.

Very well then: I was a story-teller from early youth. It was one of my chief pleasures, shared with an intimate friend of my boyhood (Mr John Irving, now a respected and distinguished Writer to the Signet, who may blush to find these childish follies brought to light). Indeed we were so addicted to the invention of narratives that we came to an agreement that each would prepare a story on alternate days, which he would tell to the other as we walked together. For this purpose we would frequent Arthur's Seat, the Salisbury Crags, or the Braid Hills, all of which gave us pleasing and Romantic views over our city, and which we deemed therefore to be well-suited to our present purpose. These locations had also the happy effect of separating us from our fellows, for we were conscious that the practice of recounting to each other tales of chivalry, Border warfare, or the supernatural in which the characters were engaged in 'dark dealings with the fiendish race', would naturally expose us to mockery, which, both being proud, we would have bitterly resented.

Then during my long illness in adolescence of which I have already written, I not only elaborated fantastic narratives to myself as I lay condemned to silence, but read with a voracity that astonishes me today. My mother procured for me romances and other tales of chivalry from the circulating library, originally established, I believe, by the celebrated poet Allan Ramsay (father of the Court Painter to George III, the delicacy of whose work renders elegant even that sturdy and homely Court). Moreover, at this time, I got my teeth into more substantial fare: memoirs, history, biography and what are called *belles-lettres*; and in this manner accumulated a store of knowledge, which I might even term 'treasure', on which I have drawn ever since.

The success of a few ballads and longer poems drew me out of the way of life in which I had first set my feet, and won me a certain literary reputation, which pleased me, though I could not think as highly of these works as some of the most generous enthusiasts for them contrived to do. Then, I know not how, the desire to attempt something new in prose fiction grew upon me. I was a great admirer of the novelists of the last century, especially of Henry Fielding, who strove to raise the prose romance to the level of the epic; and I conceived that I had in my native Scotland a subject which merited such treatment.

I was fortunate to have met in my youth a number of elderly gentlemen who had been 'out in the Forty-five' as the saying went, including one who in my childhood was my particular hero, for I saw him often, he being a client of my father. This was Alexander Stewart of Invernahyle, who had great glamour in my eyes, since he had not only fought at Sheriffmuir, and later served the Prince, but had also on one occasion crossed swords with the great bandit-chief, Rob Roy MacGregor himself. Once, greatly daring, I inquired of Mr Stewart whether he had ever been afraid in battle.

'Troth, Walter, my wee darling,' he replied, 'the first time I gaed into action, when I saw a' the redcoats rank afore us, and our people put up their bonnets to say a bit prayer, and then scrug them doon ower their een, and set forrard like bulls driving each ither on and beginning to fire their guns, and draw their broadswords, I would hae gien ony man a thousand merks to insure me I wadna rin awa.'

The manly honesty of this answer impressed me deeply, for even then I caught a glimpse of the complexity of the heroic nature, and I recall to this day the ironic laugh and the quick embrace with which he concluded this confession.

Then I had been much in the Highlands, when they were wilder and less visited than they are today, and the grandeur of the scenery and character of the inhabitants had made a profound – I may say indelible – impression on me. It seemed to me that the clash of an ancient civilization, still abiding by old traditions and ways of life, with the more civil and developed state of society south of the Highland line, offered a subject of significance which I was competent to treat. Though the philosophy of history had been a sealed book to me in my hot youth, yet I had gradually assembled much of what was striking and picturesque in historical narrative, and then in riper years attended more to the deduction of general principles. I was therefore in maturity furnished with a powerful host of examples, which I might use in illustration of them. I was, in short, like a gamester who keeps a good hand till he knows how to play it. Believing also that the Jacobite Risings, and especially the high, inspiring, and yet melancholy story of the '45, offered a fit subject for a Romance that might please and touch the public, it was a natural theme for me to settle on. I had been a fierce Jacobite, of course, from my youth: my great-grandfather having, as I have said, fought both in Dundee's campaign which ended with the hero's death in victory at Killiecrankie, and in the '15, naturally inclined me to that side; and I have never quite got rid of the impression which the gallantry of Prince Charlie made on my imagination, even though I am sensible – reason and reading having come to my assistance – that the Jacobite cause is more to be applauded in defeat than it could have been in victory. Even if the Prince, who had declared the Union with England dissolved, had been content to establish himself in Scotland and hold it as an independent kingdom against our southern neighbour – which indeed he never showed the slightest inclination of wishing to do – the results must have been unhappy. Indeed, dwelling on the wars with France, occasioned by the destructive principles of the Revolution and the inordinate greed, ambition, and callousness of Napoleon, I shrink – *horresco referens* – at what the consequences might have been of a revival of the Auld Alliance between my native land and France.

When all is said and done, I must be glad I did not live in the '45, for though as a lawyer I could not have pleaded Charles's right, and as a clergyman – had I been one – I could not have prayed for him, yet as a soldier I am sure, against the conviction of my better reason, I would have fought for him even to the bottom of the gallows.

The very confusion of my own sentiments, which, I was confident, mirrored that of so many of my fellow-countrymen, confirmed me in the idea that the romance of the '45 presented itself as the very subject for a novel, one which, I was convinced, no one could bring off more happily than I.

Accordingly, about the year 1805, I wrote, rapidly, as has ever been my wont, some six or seven chapters of a novel, which I then entitled 'Waverley – or 'tis Sixty Years Since'. I took as my hero a young English gentleman travelling in the Highlands and caught up in the drama of the Rising, choosing such a figure because I thought it useful to have affairs observed, and filtered to the public, through the medium of one who was not intimately engaged in the cause, and no firm partisan of either side. It seemed to me also that the choice of such a hero would enable me to view the, to him as to readers, unaccustomed nature of Highland society with a candid eye.

I showed these chapters to my friend William Erskine (subsequently Lord Kineddar) on whose taste and literary judgement I relied. His opinion was unfavourable, and so I laid the thing aside, being unwilling to hazard the reputation which I had won by *The Lay of the Last Minstrel* on so uncertain a cast, upon which so good and perspicacious a judge had frowned. In justice to my friend I should say that, though his decision was to be reversed by the favour the public eventually showed the novel, he is scarcely to be blamed, for the chapters he saw had not extended beyond the departure of the hero for Scotland, and consequently had not entered upon that part of the work which was finally found most interesting.

The work, though abandoned, did not leave me, and occasionally in the years that followed I thought of resuming it. But as it happened I could not lay my hands on the manuscript, and being unwilling, or too indolent, to try to renew it from memory, nothing was done. Meanwhile I did around 1808 undertake a task for Mr John Murray of Albemarle Street, which led me to consider again certain principles of prose fiction. He asked me to revise and arrange for posthumous publication certain writings of the distinguished artist and antiquary, Mr Joseph Strutt. These included an unfinished Romance, entitled *Queen-Hoo-Hall*. It was set in the time of Henry VI, and was remarkable for the scrupulous care which the author had taken to re-create the manners and language of that remote time. Since it was unfinished, I bestirred myself to supply a conclusion – admittedly hasty and artificial – but drawn from the notes Mr Strutt had left. The narrative displayed considerable power of imagination, but it did not please the public. Considering the reason for its failure, I judged that Mr Strutt had raised an obstacle to his success by his very erudition, by rendering his language too ancient, and by displaying his antiquarian knowledge in such a liberal manner as impeded the progress of the narrative, and laid him open to accusations of pedantry. I resolved therefore to try to avoid these faults if I should ever return to this sort of enterprise. In passing I may observe that an author cannot, with any degree of success, use language which dates much further back than the time of our grandparents.

Then one day while searching for some fishing tackle for the use of a guest at Abbotsford, I remembered that some had been put away in an old writing-desk consigned to a store-room or garret. I found the required tackle, and the manuscript of the first chapters of *Waverley* also. I read them, thought them tolerable, and my interest was rekindled. I set to, and wrote the tale rapidly, in a careless haphazard fashion, for I never took the time to form a scheme for the work, but rattled on as my imagination and zest led me. If some have discovered – or shall ever discover – a pattern in the book, I can claim no credit for it, but must assume that I was guided by some faculty of which I knew nothing, or that my hand, or rather my imagination, was in thrall to some force beyond my understanding.

I gave the manuscript to Mr James Ballantyne, who was enthusiastic. He passed it to Archibald Constable, already well launched on his remarkable career, which led me to dub him 'the Napoleon of the publishing and bookselling trade'. 'The very thing,' cried he, and promptly offered me an agreement whereby we should divide the profits of the enterprise equally between us, I stipulating only that James Ballantyne should be the printer.

The novel was, as the world knows, published anonymously. Now that I have confessed my authorship to the world, some may find this decision curious; others have declared it reprehensible. Yet it seemed sensible to me. Though I believed that I had lost my place at the top of the poetic tree, and would not regain it, I was yet certain that a speculative venture of this nature might do my reputation as a poet some damage, if, as I said to James, 'it doesna tak'. Then I was not certain that it was altogether decorous for the Clerk to the Court of Session to appear before the public in the guise of a mere romancer. I believe I wrote to my friend John Morritt of Rokeby in County Durham, 'Judges being monks, Clerks are a sort of lay brethren, from whom some solemnity of walk and conduct may be expected'. Moreover, I was conscious of the warning given me some time earlier by Constable's erstwhile partner, Mr Hunter, that I was in danger of flooding the market, and so falling out of favour with a weary, indeed saturated, public.

I must confess also that there was a considerable pleasure in anonymity. It spared me the attentions of many who might have wished either to flatter or upbraid me. It appealed also to a sense of mischief which some may find childish, as indeed my dear Charlotte, with affectionate raillery, professed to do.

'Scott,' she would say, 'you must toujours be ze lost heir of your own romances, or a little boy who dresses up to deceive his fellows.'

It may be also, I suppose, that there is something in the nature of a story-teller that inclines him to secrecy and deception. Novelists are after all liars. We seek to persuade our readers that an imaginary event has the force and significance of the real world; we aim to draw tears from them over the misfortunes of beings who have no corporal existence, and who are indeed no more than figments of the imagination. It is a strange trade, spending hours in the companionship of such beings, and I am fortunate that I have found it an agreeable one.

We went to considerable trouble to preserve my anonymity. I wrote the books in my own hand (except for a couple which I was compelled to dictate being at the time too weakened by illness to be able to hold a pen). James Ballantyne then had these manuscripts, or the copy as we say in the trade, transcribed by a reliable amanuensis, who was, like all those in the know, sworn to secrecy. Two sets of proofs were invariably cast off. I corrected one, and then James himself transcribed my emendments to the other set which was then returned to the printers. I believe we met with fair success, and it is a tribute to the integrity of mankind that none of the twenty or so people to whom the secret of my authorship was entrusted ever betrayed me.

I think it fair to say that few who knew me well had any doubt that I was the author of *Waverley*. They found there, and in subsequent novels, too many familiar scenes and characters, too many turns of phrase which they recognized as mine, in short a tone which to them was quite unmistakable. In Captain Medwin's not, I think, entirely reliable record of his conversations with Byron, he states that he asked whether Byron was certain that these novels were Sir Walter Scott's, and asserts that Byron replied, 'Scott as much as owned himself the Author of *Waverley* to me in Murray's shop. I was talking to him about that novel, and lamented that the author had not carried the story nearer to the time of the Revolution – Scott, entirely off his guard, replied, "Aye, I might have done so, but" – there he stopped. It was in vain to attempt to correct himself; he looked confused, and relieved his embarrassment by a precipitate retreat . . .' All I can say is that I have no recollection of such a conversation, and had it taken place, I am more like to have laughed than to have been embarrassed, for I certainly never hoped to deceive Lord Byron in this matter. Indeed, from the manner in which he spoke of the novels, I knew very well that he knew me to be the author, though, respecting my desire for anonymity, he was too well-bred to put the direct question.

Others were less so; and then I was compelled to follow one of three courses. Either I must have surrendered my secret – or equivocated – or issued a stout denial. The first two courses were unpalatable, for an admission to a person capable of such an impertinent question would have amounted to the announcement of my secret to the world, while equivocation would most like have had the same result. So I stood squarely by the principle of Scots Law: that no man is bound to incriminate himself; and since I was not on oath, I had no scruple in rebutting the charge, though it may amuse some to know that, acting on the same principle as allows a child to tell a lie to his fellows if he keeps his fingers crossed, I would generally add that, had I been the author, I would have felt quite entitled to defend my secret by refusing my own evidence.

I confess that, so many years after I entered on this course, it seems stranger to me than it did at the time; and if some choose to regard it as an example of moral infirmity, why then, I must bear the reproach.

Nor indeed did I stop at this point, for some three or four years after the publication of *Waverley* I brought yet another author on to the scene when I commenced to write what I chose to call the *Tales of My Landlord* putatively assembled by one Jedediah Cleishbotham, schoolmaster of the parish of Gandercleuch.

My motive this time was different, though there was a residual concern that 'the Author of *Waverley*' might appear more prolific than would be approved by either critics – who often hold that a modest rate of production is a truer mark of genius than fecundity – or the public itself. But, the real motive was otherwise. Though I esteemed Constable highly, and admired the energy of his business methods, I have never held that it is in an author's interest to be bound to a single publisher, who, in such a case, may all too easily come to think of the wretched author as his employee – something which, as one of the Black Hussars of Literature – I could never bring myself to tolerate.

I may say, here in passing, lest I find no other suitable occasion to do so, that I had an ulterior, and indeed altruistic, motive for resuming my work on *Waverley*. I had been greatly impressed, as well as delighted, by the Irish novels of Maria Edgeworth, whose presentation of the characters and nature of her native land was such as to persuade the English to look more kindly on them; indeed she may be said to have done more to completing the Union of the nations of the British Isles than any number of Acts of

Parliament could contrive to do; and I nursed the not ignoble hope that I might likewise present Scotland to those ignorant of the country, or prejudiced against its inhabitants, in such a manner as to promote a better and truer understanding between the nations. If I have indeed contrived to do so, then I trust I am not immodest in claiming that I have made some contribution to the happiness and future peace and prosperity of the United Kingdom.

Between the delivery and publication of this novel, I took a holiday, sailing round the Northern Isles of Scotland in the Lighthouse yacht, under the happy guidance of Mr Stevenson, the Surveyor of the Lights, a scholarly engineer whose contribution to the well-being of mankind, by his construction of lighthouses that save so many sailors from disaster, must be accounted far greater and more worthwhile than the achievements of a scribbler. The literary world may not agree, but the truth is that its inhabitants are too apt to measure value by some reference to literature, to suppose that nobody who lacks knowledge of it can be worth much. God help us! It would be a poor world if there was any truth in such opinion. I have read books enough, and been rarely happy in doing so, and I have met and conversed with the most cultivated minds of my time, but yet I have heard higher sentiments from the lips of poor uneducated men and women, heroically confronting difficulty and affliction, or speaking simply as to the circumstances of their family, friends or neighbours, than I have met with in secular literature. And, with what success, I cannot judge, I have in my own writings attempted to bring this out by allowing my humbler characters to speak with at least equal dignity, and often with a greater force of true and honest emotion, as my fine ladies and gentlemen.

This voyage introduced me to parts of Scotland which I had not previously visited, but my first port of call aroused mixed emotions.

The abbey of Arbroath is celebrated in the History of Scotland as having been the place where, during our Wars of Independence, the nobility, clergy, lairds, and burgesses of the realm came together to compose a noble Declaration addressed to the Pope, wherein they stated that it was 'for liberty alone that we fight and contend, which no honest man will surrender but with his life'. Yet, though I tried to keep my mind on this matter of high estate, I could not forget that it was with Williamina that I had first visited the noble ruined abbey; and the thought brought ready tears to my eyes.

I was delighted by the wild scenery of the Northern Isles which I was later to employ, to some effect, I trust, in *The Pirate*, and I was pleased to meet a well-attested witch, who made it her practice to sell favourable winds to sailors, but there, and in Sutherland, I was saddened also to see how the progress of civilization, and the demands it made, and the opportunities it offered, threatened to destroy old-established modes of life. I reflected that had I been an Orcadian laird, I would strive to maintain the crofting system, though I could not deny that it would be against my pecuniary interest, for it was clear that larger farms could be managed more efficiently and profitably.

In the outer Hebrides I followed with rapt interest the course of the Prince's wanderings after Culloden, and at Holy Iona, Columba's Isle, viewed the graves of the ancient Scottish kings, and thought how odd it was that the last to be buried there, Macbeth, should be more widely celebrated than all the others, thanks to a few weeks of labour on the part of an obscure English actor.

Then we crossed over into Ulster, where I was heartened by the evidence of the progress made by the descendants of my fellow-Scots established there by King James VI and I, when my holiday mood was broken by the sad news of the death of Harriet, Duchess of Buccleuch, at whose request I had written the *Lay*. I should have liked her to have the opportunity to read *Waverley*, which I flatter myself she would have enjoyed, but her inability to do so was naturally the least part of the grief her death caused me. Returned to Greenock, I sent a letter of condolence to the Duke, which I had composed on the crossing, but was surprised and deeply touched to find a letter from him, announcing her death, awaiting me. He desired, he said, to draw his friends closer around him: 'I shall love them more and more because I know that they loved her.'

I returned to Edinburgh to find that Constable had sold three thousand copies of *Waverley*, and was eager to come to terms of agreement concerning a third edition. If I could not say, like Byron, on the publication of *Childe Harold*, 'I awoke in the morning and found myself famous', it was only because I had already enjoyed as much fame as I wished, and because my name was not on the title-page.

It is not my intention to give a full account of my career as novelist, which would be tedious in the extreme, and would also smack of vanity and presumption. In any case, I shall have enough of that, if I do as Cadell asks and write an introductory preface to each of the novels in his *magnum opus* edition; but I feel a desire to say a few words about my practice as an author, and perhaps about the craft of fiction, for, though I write as it were by instinct, and have been condemned for carelessness, it is not to be supposed that from time to time I have not dwelled on this matter; and since the world in general has been pleased to grant approbation to my efforts, my thoughts on the subject may be of some interest to future generations.

In general I have written best when I have written fast, and those parts of a novel which have given me the most trouble and over which I have laboured longest have too often come feebly off. Some have reproached me – with reason – for carelessness of construction. In my defence I may say that I have repeatedly set out a scheme for my future work, dividing it into volumes and chapters, and have attempted to write according to a pattern which should lead inevitably to the conclusion or catastrophe. But there is some daemon who seats himself on the feather of my pen, and drives me on, often astray from my purpose. Characters, of whom I wist nothing when I commenced the tale, expand of their own accord, incidents multiply; the story lingers perhaps while I take my ease by a burnside and entertain my characters at an inn. In short my mansion, planned according to the best principles of a Classical architect, turns into a Gothic extravagance; and the thing may be completed even before I have attained the destination I originally proposed.

I scarcely regret this. Others may work more regularly, but I cannot, except when my imagination is slack and the ship rocks on the waves of a windless sea. But when I happen on a character like Bailie Nicol Jarvie, who, as I remember, was first intended to play but a very minor role in the story of Frank Osbaldistone and Rob Roy, why, my imagination brightens, and I am like a man mounted on a mettlesome steed, which he can scarce control, who decides that the better wisdom is to give the horse its head, cling on for dear life, and see where he arrives at. So I may be led many a mile from my road, and it is hard work to return thither with many a ditch or hedge to be louped. Yet if I resist this temptation, and work according to plan, my thoughts are dull, prosy, and flat. Then I write by effort and will, oppressed with a consciousness of flagging – which makes me flag all the more. I am like a dog turning the wheel of a spit. No, I maun go where the devil rides, even if I think myself bewitched the while.

I cannot reproach myself either for the speed of my productions or for the quantity. If I had written only *Waverley*, I might, I suppose, have secured myself a charming little reputation and be revered as a *petit maître*. The critics will ever have a tenderness for an author whose production is exiguous, who writes little, short, and seldom; and they will happily join to laud and boost him, for he renders their own task so much easier. But an author who bedevils them with a new work every six month can scarce expect to receive their constant indulgence. 'Here he comes again,' they cry, 'will the damned fellow never give over?' I understand their feelings, and can even sympathize; yet I have ever scorned to follow their recommended route. It is some consolation too to reflect that the best authors in all countries have been the most voluminous; and in general posterity plucks its favourites from those who have won the greatest success in their own day. A worthy book which fails to please the public is fortunate indeed if it is rescued from obscurity at a later date. Besides, I cannot think so ill of the taste of our own time as to suppose that posterity will utterly reject it.

Still, no man can tell the future, and reputation is a tender plant in which it is folly to trust. In this connection I am reminded of a learned advocate friend of mine who was charged with the defence of the notorious Jem McCoul, accused of having robbed the Bank of Glasgow of £20,000. The advocate-depute, appearing for the Crown, laid great emphasis on Jem's refusal to answer certain questions, which, he said, any man with a regard for his reputation would not hesitate to reply to. 'My client', said my friend, indicating Jem who was standing behind him, 'is so unfortunate as to have no regard for his reputation, and I should deal very uncandidly with the Court, should I say that he had any that was worth his attention.' I may not be precisely in the same case, but, where literature is concerned, I share Jem's happy state of indifference. My works have served me and my purposes well; I am grateful to those who have purchased the books, and happy if they have afforded them some amusement. But as to my future reputation, I must leave that to fortune. It would be gross to contemn the favour the public has shown me, and imitate the Irish judge, who discharged a prisoner with the words: 'You have been acquitted by a Limerick jury, and you leave this Court with no other stain upon your character and reputation'; yet I have never doubted that the favour of the public could be withdrawn as abruptly, and perhaps as deservedly, as it was granted. If the future is indifferent to me, so be it.

I have often been asked by kind friends which of my novels please me most. Now this is different from asking which I think the best, a matter that an author is rarely fitted to judge, for he may well give his approval to that which caused him most trouble, just as a fond mother may come to feel most warmly to the scapegrace among her sons – as indeed in the end I believe my own dear mother entertained the warmest, because most protective, love towards poor Dan, he seeming to require a greater expenditure of maternal affection. But the question which pleases me most is a fair one, and of another order.

I make a distinction between two categories among my novels. There are first the Scotch ones, especially those set in the late seventeenth and eighteenth century; and there are those set in more remote ages or in other countries. Now the distinction is this: that the former class, though supported by a ballast of solid reading, are nevertheless made on something of the same principles as the ballads. They concern a society which I knew intimately, and my reading is supported by observation and also by personal reminiscence. Moreover the conflicts portrayed in these novels are matters which touched me dearly and which are still in a sense or to some extent unresolved. I may say that these novels are, in a manner of speaking, conversations or sometimes arguments with myself.

The second class, however, are the result of bookwork. They may portray scenes of which I have at best a traveller's knowledge, and societies which I never encountered. The points at issue, though I would hope of some general application, are nevertheless matters long resolved by the passage of time, and such as cannot be supposed to touch me closely. The remoteness of the matter from the author gives the best of these novels a certain, perhaps curious, lightness; but in too many of them there are passages when I found it hard going and could only bring a chapter to a conclusion by the exercise of my will and the exhortation 'tis dogged as does it'.

In the first category I am inclined to put *The Heart of Midlothian* highest, but, though it is set in my native Edinburgh, though it has my favourite female character in Jeannie Deans, and though I fancy I never wrote a finer passage of sustained narrative than my account of the Porteous Affair (which on account of the discipline displayed is perhaps miscalled a riot), yet I do not place it among my favourites.

I have a tenderness for *Guy Mannering* because its setting recalls happy scenes of my early manhood. Moreover, I have done few things better than the character of Dandie Dinmont (and I am amused to learn that the type of scruffy and tenacious terriers which I gave him is now being called by his name). The heroine,

Julia Mannering, shares certain traits with my dear Charlotte, which also serves to make me think kindly of the book.

Let me say in passing that I have often been sair deeved, as we say in Scotland, by enthusiasts who profess to recognize friends and acquaintances in the characters who people my fiction. In truth the creation or depiction of character in a novel is a far more complicated and uncertain matter than those who seek out originals, with the zeal of a spaniel seeking game, can suppose. In the first place they neglect the obvious truth that a real person is invariably bigger, more complicated, and has been afforded far more experience, than any character in a novel can be. The person depicted in a novel consists of a few lines of description, a few snatches of dialogue, and a few actions which the author gives him or her to perform: what is that in comparison with a life that has been lived? Even when I have taken a true historical character, Claverhouse or Jamie the Saxt, about both of whom I am well informed, the personage in the novel is at best a sketch. I hit on a few aspects of the historical figure which I hope may convey an impression and, if I am lucky, even his essence; but it is no more the real man than one of Raeburn's admirable portraits can descend from the wall and mix himself a glass of toddy.

So what these enthusiasts call 'an original' is at best a starting-point offering material for a sketch.

Yet the matter is more complicated still, for three reasons. First, the author may take a trait from one person and another from another. He is like, too, to take the most of them from himself, and I confess I am as ready to charge myself with being the villain of any of my tales as to boast myself the hero. Second, the act of creating a character is for the most part unconscious, and I have known resemblances pointed out to me between the character in a novel and a real person of which I was perfectly unaware. Third, it has sometimes happened to me that in the course of a novel I have realized that he whom I thought a creation of my imagination was developing a resemblance to some friend or acquaintance, and on occasion, I have wrenched him in another airt.

Novels are made of what the author has known and what he has imagined, but the boundary between knowledge and imagination is a Debateable Land, nowhere more so than in this question of the relationship between fictional characters and the author's acquaintances.

There are passages in *Rob Roy* of which I think well, and I believe that that period in the history of the Jacobite cause is well and truly depicted; but I cannot acquit myself of passages of considerable tedium in that novel, while the villain Rashleigh is but a feeble creation, and the hero Frank Osbaldistone a dull stick even in comparison with some of my other heroes. Nor do I think as well of Diana Vernon as some kind critics have done.

No, the three Scotch novels of which I think most kindly may surprise some of my admirers, for they are not, I believe, those which have been best received.

The first is *The Antiquary*. The plot is sadly mishandled, and indeed I have a memory that I was well into the book before I had the faintest notion of my destination. Here, too, the villain is a mere piece of cardboard, though one who gave me a certain amusement in the writing, which, however, I doubt if many readers have shared. But the tone of his book pleases me. There is a holiday feel to much of it, and a humour that recalls good conversation. I derived much amusement too from poking fun at my own antiquarian interests, and I think the two lairds Oldbuck and Wardour genial creations. When I finished it, I wrote to my friend, the actor Daniel Terry, 'it wants the romance of *Waverley* and the adventure of *Guy Mannering*' – these being its two predecessors – 'and yet there is some salvation about it, for if a man will paint from nature, he will be likely to amuse those who are daily looking at it.'

I was a great admirer of the clever, elegant, and acute novels of Miss Austen, a young lady who died far too early, long before she had given all of which she was capable to the world. The precision of her writing delighted me, and also her ability to compose a truthful and significant narrative from the trivia of everyday life. I remarked once that I could do 'the Big Bow-wow strain' as well as any man, but that Miss Austen's ability to treat of the ebb and flow of everyday social life was unrivalled. In *The Antiquary*, however, as later in *St Ronan's Well*, I was bold enough to make at least an incursion into her territory, though in the former novel, I displayed a certain prudence by inserting a sub-plot in the big bow-wow manner.

There is another reason for my affection for this novel. It pays tribute, I believe, to the dignity, decency, and courage with which simple unlettered folk can meet disaster. I have written few scenes in which I take greater satisfaction than that in which the old fisherman Saunders Mucklebackit is found mending 'the auld black bitch of a boat' in which his son had been sailing when the winds rose, he was driven against the rocks, and drowned. Saunders's question, 'What would you have me do, unless I wanted to see four children starve because ane is drooned?' stands as a reproach to the self-indulgent grief in which more fortunate folk may wallow, and which they mistakenly believe evidence of their more refined sensibilities, when it testifies only to their easy circumstances.

I may say also that the manner in which I contrive to have an awareness of a supernatural world march alongside the ordinary conversation of social life still pleases me.

My second favourite among the Scotch novels may also surprise many, for it was widely condemned as exaggerated, melodramatic and overstrained. Yet I have a peculiar feeling for *The Bride of Lammermoor*. The story was drawn from a grisly legend which has attached itself to one of the great houses of our Scotch *noblesse de la robe*. There is no Scots lawyer who does not have a reverence for the great Viscount Stair, whose *Institutes of the Law of Scotland* have left succeeding generations in his debt. And yet repute has it that this polite and politic gentleman endured a family tragedy of well-nigh unspeakable horror, partly on account of the character of his Lady, who was better-born than her aspiring husband, and possessed of a pride as lofty as her lineage.

Lord Stair's rise in fortune, and his Lady's imperious and terrifying manner, were such that it was soon put about that she was a witch, in league with the Devil. She was freely compared to the Witch of Endor, before whom King Saul humbled himself, and it was even reported that she had been seen, in the guise of a cat, sitting on a cushion beside her husband while he acted as Lord High Commissioner of the General Assembly of the Church of Scotland. The improbability of this tale no doubt added to the zest with which it was related.

The Stairs had a daughter, Janet Dalrymple, a modest, comely girl, who fell in love with Allan, Lord Rutherford, and went so far as to form an engagement to him without her parents' knowledge. The young man was not acceptable to them either on account of his political principles – for he was a Cavalier opposed to the Revolution Settlement, while Lord Stair was a devout Presbyterian and Whig – or of his want of fortune. But the girl, with the obstinacy sometimes shown by tender natures, refused to give him up. Another suitor presented himself, or was found, and Lady Stair pushed his cause. In vain; Janet remained obdurate. Lord Rutherford also insisted on his rights, saying he would abandon his own claim only if Miss Janet herself requested him to do so. Lady Stair was therefore compelled to agree to an interview between the young lovers, which she intended should be their last, and which she sanctioned only on the acceptance of her demand that she should be present at it. Both she and Lord Rutherford argued their case with high passion, Lady Stair resting hers on the authority of the Scriptures and the Old Testament text (*Numbers XXX v 2–5*), which declared that a vow of engagement made by a daughter should not be binding unless her father had given the intended match his consent. Meanwhile the wretched girl, who had been subjected to weeks of bullying and moral pressure from her fierce mother, remained mute, pale, and motionless as a statue.

At last, when her mother commanded her to reject her lover, she tore from her neck the piece of broken gold which he had given her as a pledge of their engagement, and returned it to him. He flew into a passion, cursed both mother and daughter, and soon afterwards left Scotland, dying in France or Flanders a few years later.

Meanwhile Lady Stair hurried on preparations for her daughter's wedding to the groom she had chosen, a certain David Dunbar of Baldoon. The girl acquiesced, in a state of complete passivity, which must have aroused either the suspicion or the sympathy of a less determined woman than Lady Stair. On the wedding day she rode to the kirk behind her younger brother who afterwards recalled that her hand had been as cold and damp as marble.

The wedding was celebrated and the feast was followed by dancing. The bride and groom retired to the chamber, which had been set aside for them, and, according to custom, the groom's man pocketed the key, that no impertinent guests might break in on the first evening of conjugal felicity. But the festivities were interrupted by a series of terrible screams coming from the bridal chamber. The door was opened, and they found the bridegroom lying on the floor; he had been stabbed and was bleeding copiously. At first, in the dim light, there was no sign of the bride. Then they found her crouched in the corner of the chimney. She was dressed only in a shift, and that too was bloody. There was fixed on her face a smile of the utmost vacancy, and her head rocked from side to side. She uttered only one sentence: 'Tak up your bonny bridegroom.'

The lass never recovered and was dead and buried within the fortnight.

The young man was healed of his wounds, but refused to give any account of what had happened, and threatened anyone who inquired of him with a duel.

I had at one time considered making a long poem of this terrible and Romantic tale, and might have done so had I not turned to prose. I sharpened the conflict between the families of the doomed lovers, whom I called Ashton and Ravenswood, by making Sir William Ashton the new proprietor of the ancestral lands of Ravenswood, confiscated from the young lover's father as a result of his adherence to the exiled Stuart line. Then since I did not choose to attach to Lady Ashton the reputation actually enjoyed by Lady Stair for necromancy and acquaintance with the Black Arts, but was unwilling to deprive myself of an element of the supernatural, I invented a prophecy concerning the ill-fated house of Ravenswood ...

When the last Laird of Ravenswood to Ravenswood shall
   ride,
And woo a dead maiden to be his bride,
He shall stable his horse in the Kelpie's flow,
And his name shall be lost for evermore.

The device served well, I believe, to heighten the emotion, and it is
perhaps some evidence of my success that no fewer than four
different versions of *The Bride* have, I am informed, been staged in
the opera-houses of Italy.

    Another circumstance accounts for my own attachment to this
novel. It so happens that I composed it when I was in the throes of
a severe illness which lasted off and on for three years. I suffered
periods of intense abdominal pain, and was sometimes so weak
that I could scarce sit on a pony, on which indeed I was the very
image of Death on the pale horse, lanthorn-jawed, decayed in flesh,
stooping as if I meant to eat the pony's ears, and quite incapable of
going above a foot-pace. The pain could only be quelled by copious
draughts of laudanum, so that between the pain and the drugs my
mind was alternately disordered and befogged. I was quite unable
to sit at my desk and hold a pen, and a good part of the novel was
dictated to Willie Laidlaw. I was too ill even to correct the proofs
myself, and when the bound volumes were put in my hand by James
Ballantyne, I opened them with some trepidation for I found that
I could not recollect a single incident, character or conversation. It
may be imagined with what relief I discovered that the novel made
sense, and, what is more peculiar, has some claims to be thought
the best-ordered and best-crafted of my works. I know no clearer
evidence of the truth of my assertion that the essential work of
literary creation derives from some part of the mind to which we do

not have conscious access. 'There's a divinity that shapes our ends/ Rough-hew them how we will.'

I had recovered my health by Christmas 1819, but apart from that it was a bitter time, for a single week of cruel December weather took from me my dear mother, my uncle Dr Rutherford, and my aunt Christian Rutherford in whose language and conversation I had always delighted. Moreover, shaken by three years of illness and intense industry, I felt myself, though then still on the right side, as the saying goes, of fifty, to be already an old man. My mother had called me 'Wattie, my wee lamb,' to her dying days, and perhaps youth must vanish from us when the last of those who have fond memories of our childhood are taken from us. It was sadly affecting, as I sorted through her things, to discover the little preparations she had already made for presents – for the children, friends and dependents – which she had assorted for the New Year – for she was a great observer of the old fashions of her time, when the New Year was the season for gifts – and to think that the kind heart was already cold which delighted in all these acts of love and kindly affection.

I grow erratic in my course, and this chapter has already stretched out far beyond my original intention. But what of that?

> My mind is no like a Roman road,
> A clear straucht line on the map, see;
> But a gangrel path that winds its way
> Wherever the fancy taks me.

And I cannot pass on without the reflection that there is perhaps no love as pure, unselfish and steadfast as that of a good mother for her children. I have some sympathy with the Roman Catholic cult of the Virgin Mary which recognizes this, and in which the Virgin is generally presented as the Madonna or the Mother of God.

When I recovered from those years of illness, I found my energy diminished, and henceforward I was ever more tempted to look back, and to seek happiness in memory rather than expectation. It was in that mood that I wrote my own favourite among my novels: *Redgauntlet*. It begins as a pastoral. It has the two most engaging, I believe, of my youthful heroes – some would say the only two engaging ones – in Darsie Latimer and Alan Fairford. Some have detected elements of my dear friend Will Clerk in Darsie, and I would not deny their presence, saving only this qualification: that he is also in part a portrait of my own youthful Romantic and impractical self. There is much of me too in Alan, that side of my character which suffered me to submit to the drudgery of my father's law office (and Alan's worthy father Saunders Fairford is in part also an affectionate reminiscence of my own dear father). Then though it is a pleasant story of pleasant people (for the most part) and set in pleasant places, it is, I believe, suffused with an agreeable melancholy which derived from the autumn mood in which I wrote it. Indeed where young Darsie is concerned, the story may be held to present to the reader autumn's memories of spring.

It deals also with the last flicker of the Jacobite romance, and may be considered to form a triptych with *Rob Roy* and *Waverley*.

If I had written nothing else, I would not feel I had neglected such gifts as the Lord bestowed upon me, if I left behind *Redgauntlet*, as my sole literary memorial.

Of the novels made from book-work, I would select only two. *Ivanhoe* is also in a sense a tribute to my own youth, for it is in reality the elaboration of those tales of chivalry with which John Irving and I used to delight each other as we strode or wandered over Arthur's Seat. It was a new venture, which pleased the public greatly, and may indeed prove the most enduringly popular of my works. But for me it was in a sense a holiday task, for, though it is confessedly written out of books, the chivalric romances and old chronicles from which I made it were things I had so thoroughly absorbed in many years of delighted reading that they seemed to have become part of myself: so that in a sense *Ivanhoe*, like the best of the Scotch novels, may be said to have been as much remembered as invented.

The plot is full of improbabilities, but in this novel more than in any other I took as my guide that question: 'What is the plot for, save to bring in fine things?' Some readers have rebuked me for making Ivanhoe marry the admittedly insipid Rowena, rather than Rebecca, whom they have been kind enough to name the most spirited and delightful of my heroines. I have some sympathy. Yet I am enough of a historian to be aware that it was in the highest degree improbable that a noble knight should marry a Jewess; and I consoled myself with the reflection that while Rebecca was spirited and resourceful, poor Rowena was so insipid that if she did not get her man, the poor lass would be left with nothing. So there was a sort of justice to it.

I have been censured for historical inaccuracies, and admit myself guilty. *Ivanhoe* is not to be compared with a novel like *Old Mortality* which I took great pains to make historically accurate. It is Romance, and, if Shakespeare could give Bohemia a sea-coast, I did not see why I should not still have a Saxon landowner in the reign of Cœur de Lion.

No doubt as scholarship progresses, more inaccuracies will be discovered, and poor *Ivanhoe* be denounced as a tissue of fancies.

The time will come when scholars will undoubtedly know far more about the Middle Ages than I have been able to learn, for true historical scholarship has scarcely penetrated that period. Yet I may boast that I have done things which bring me into a closer kinship with medieval man than a scholar immured in a library may ever attain.

I have after all ridden in a cavalry troop. I have hunted the fox and the hare, flown a hawk, and speared a salmon. I have employed my own piper and chaplain, and lack only a jester or Fool, though Lockhart, whose tongue is sharper than mine, has been known to observe that certain of my guests at Abbotsford have played that role well enough. Indeed the mention of the dear place prompts me to add that if I have not built a Gothic castle, I have at least built a fine house with some Gothic decoration and appurtenances, and have therein an armoury that any Norman baron might envy.

My second favourite among the book-work novels is one which has found special favour on the Continent, *Quentin Durward*. I had long felt a peculiar interest in those periods of History which appear to serve as a bridge between two distinct epochs; and the fifteenth century afforded me an admirable example. It was a time when the principles of chivalry, more honoured admittedly in word than deed, were all but abandoned. These principles, however often flouted, had contrived to moderate the temper and selfishness of a largely unlettered age. Rude and cruel men were disposed by them to act, on occasion at least, more gently than their natures might have urged them to, but in the dark fifteenth century this softening influence was lost, and men acted with an egotism that seemed all too often to deny even the possibility of generosity and self-denial, principles on which the doctrines of chivalry had been founded, and qualities of which this may be said: that if the earth was to be utterly deprived of them, it would be difficult to conceive of the existence of virtue among the race of mankind.

No one more completely exemplified the mean and selfish spirit of this new age than Louis XI of France, a man whose history serves to make that instructive work of Machiavelli's, *The Prince*, all but redundant. Since Louis was also a man of great ability, possessed of a caustic wit, and at the same time as grossly superstitious as he was free of moral scruple, it seemed to me admirable to put him at the centre of my projected tale. I drew heavily on the incomparable memoirs of Philippe de Commines, but still sought a point of entry. I have ever found that it served well to allow the reader to see an historical character through the eyes of an imaginary one; and since it happened that Louis, in his terror as death approached – though his prayers to innumerable saints demanded apparently their intercession for the prolongation of his life rather than the salvation of his soul – was ready to place his earthly trust only in his bodyguard of Scottish Archers, whose loyalty to their untrustworthy master was in truth no greater than he deserved, I made what I may call the central intelligence of my novel a young Scottish gentleman who sought admission to that guard. Quentin Durward and his love-affair are little more than aids to keep the plot moving, but such strength as the novel has derives, I believe, from my decision to let the cruel and devious monarch be presented to the reader for the most part through the understanding of a young man from a ruder, but more robust and still more honest society.

But I think I have said enough about my literary productions, a subject which I have always preferred to avoid in conversation. I do not, however, regret this expatiation. Indeed it has eased my mind somewhat. I may say in conclusion that I have never been in the habit of reading over my novels again after they have appeared in book-form, except that, occasionally, when I have found myself stuck, as if in the mire, in the work under construction, I have read a few pages of one of my earlier books, to remind myself that there were always difficulties, and to persuade myself that I had in some manner or other circumvented them.

I may add, finally, that when engaged on a novel, I endeavoured, as far as possible, to shut the matter out of my mind from the moment I rose from my writing-desk till I woke the following morning, when I would allow myself half an hour or so to dwell on the story, a practice which meant that I came ready to the desk, while the long intermission, or cessation of mental activity on the book in question, allowed the story, I believe, to fructify in that part of the mind which is beyond the reach of conscious thought, but which appears to me to be the seat of the imaginative faculty.

13

Of Friends and Family, 1790–1828

At my age a man must expect to have more friends in the grave than walking the earth. Even so, though, like Macbeth, 'my way of life/Has fallen into the sere, the yellow life', I am not bereft of 'honour, love, obedience, troops of friends'; and if I were to catalogue the troops, the list would be long and do me some honour, I believe. It is consolation now that scarce a one has shown himself colder to me since I fell into difficulties, and my star waned.

I do not count those who were drawn to me chiefly on account of my celebrity, though some among them have been honest and engaging enough to have entered the ranks of those whom I am proud to name friend. I have been lionized more than sufficiently for the taste of any rational and honourable man; but if I am a lion still, I fear I am now but a ragged one.

> Oh speak not to me of a name great in story
> The days of our youth are the days of our glory.

If not glory – though there is glory in the boundless ambition and high spirits of youth – then at least it may be said that the friends of our youth ever retain the warmest place in the heart. Any man who attains either success or fame or wealth must wonder whether his friends love him for what he is or for the light which his celebrity shines on them. The friends of our youth stand forth as testimony that we can be loved for ourself alone; and I do not believe I have lost one of those intimates save through death. Will Clerk, Will Erskine, John Skene of Rubislaw, George Cranstoun and Thomas Thomson have been part of my life since I was a youth. We came together as equals, and equals we have remained in friendship, however 'great in story' any of us may have become. We shared our youthful hopes and ambitions with each other. We commiserated with each other, and offered sturdy comfort, when love affairs went agley. We rejoiced in each other's triumphs and lamented each other's failures. What can one say of a conversation, an endlessly agreeable social intercourse, that has lasted more than thirty years? Only this, I fancy, that it does some credit to us all, and that we should give thanks to the Almighty for his gift of friendship.

My friendship with James and John Ballantyne went still further back for it was first formed during the months I stayed at my uncle's place in Kelso. The world would say it was never a friendship of equals, with some reason, certainly, for both James and John were engaged in trade, and, though I was a secret partner in their printing and publishing business, I was also in a sense, I suppose, their employer; since they depended on me to provide them with the greater part of the materials for their business. Yet few have been as true friends to me as James and John, and in few men's company have I found an equal delight. James has ever been absolutely honest and straightforward with me; I have valued his advice; and if we are now sunk in the same quagmire, well, at least, we are aye thegither, and I have contrived to have James named manager of the printing-works, which are now held by the trustees; and since he is a man of infinite courage, I fancy he will come again.

Poor John is among the dead; a livelier, wittier, jollier fellow never lived. His only fault was his excessive optimism and his inability to understand his business. He was as lean as James is plump, and full of a nervous vivacity which never failed to lift the cares from my shoulders. You could not be with John and not be merry; and though his inattention to business might exasperate, with John it was a case of 'soonest met, soonest forgiven'. He found himself in the role of auctioneer, and it was an education to see him cajole a bidder into raising his offer. He was the soul of generosity, and when he died, left me £2,000 for the furnishing of the Library at Abbotsford, and it was not Johnnie's fault, though agreeably in character, that the dear man had in truth nothing but debts to leave behind him. But even in extremity his vivacity never deserted him, and he spent some time elaborating the best style of the bookshelves which I should install. As for his generosity, I mind a day at his auction-room when his eye was caught by a poor student – of Divinity, I believe – a subject in which Johnnie took but little interest. 'You look ill,' he said to the young man. 'That I am, in body and in mind.' 'Come,' said John, 'I think I ken the sort of draft that wad dae ye gude' – and he slipped him a draft for £10, 'particularly my dear,' he added, with a wink, 'if ta'en on an empty stomach.'

A few days after he was making his plans for the Library at Abbotsford, I stood in the Canongate Kirkyard, and watched them smooth the turfs over Johnnie's grave. It was a cold grey slatey day, but as we turned away, the sun broke through the clouds over Calton Hill. I remember sighing, and saying to Lockhart who had accompanied me to pay my last respects to my poor Johnnie: 'I fear there will be less sunshine for me from this day on.' My fear was justified.

I have already spoken something of James Hogg; but the subject of this extraordinary man is well-nigh inexhaustible: such a combination of sense and nonsense, rudeness and sensitivity, pride and servility, good humour and vile temper, courage and poltroonery, grace and boorishness, was surely seldom united in one being; like Dryden's Zimri, he seemed to be 'not one, but all mankind's epitome'. He infuriated me often; and yet, like Johnnie, has always demanded, and received, forgiveness. I have bailed him out of the innumerable scrapes into which his rash thoughtlessness has led him. Once, I remarked that a vile sixpenny planet shone on him when he was born, that seemed to condemn everything he attempted to be broken by his own folly. And yet Hogg has a rare genius, which on occasion I have myself unkindly insulted. I once suggested that he should put aside thoughts of supporting himself by a literary career, and concentrate on his farming (though his brother Robert, who is my head shepherd at Abbotsford, has a gey poor opinion of brother Jamie's capacity as agriculturist or pastoralist; 'Jamie is clean gyte,' he says, 'he doesna ken yin end of a tup frae the tither, or you wad think he didna, gin ye were tae judge him by his inability to tell a gude beast frae a bad yin.') James was for a time as if mortally offended by my advice, which, of course, he misunderstood. I never intended that he should abstain from poetry – and indeed if he would not die if poetry was taken from him, he would certainly feel sadly diminished – but rather that he should treat poetry and literature as I did, as an activity for leisure moments, and, for the sake of his family and the excellent Mrs Hogg, should bend his efforts to supporting them by the farms which, thanks to the intervention of the Duchess of Buccleuch, he had been leased on very favourable terms. But Jamie was only intermittently a farmer; oddly enough at moments that sometimes did damage to his other ambitions. So for instance, when I obtained him a seat for the Coronation of His Majesty, thinking that he could write a favourable account of the occasion, and perhaps do himself some good with the ministry and even obtain a pension for his efforts, he replied that It was verra kind o ye, Scott, but the thing canna be done.' Unfortunately – and he dwelled some time on the grievous misfortune it was – they had fixed the Coronation for the same day as St Boswells Fair, and, since he had only just taken over the farm of Mountbenger, which was not yet stocked, folks would think him out of his wits if he went gallivanting off to London instead of completing the stocking of his farm. And nothing I could say could move him, though it was not many months later that he was deeving me with the demand, 'Can ye no dae something for me, Scott, wi the ministry? Ye ken I'm as gude a Tory as ye are yoursel.'

In recent years Jamie has achieved a considerable celebrity as a result of the Conversations, the 'Noctes Ambrosianae', which have been appearing in *Blackwood's Magazine*. Lockhart had a hand in the early 'Nodes', but since he departed to London to edit the *Quarterly*, they have mostly been the work of John Wilson who appears in the guise of Christopher North. I never cared for Lockhart's connection with Wilson, who is, though a man of talent and energy, something of what the French call a *'faux bonhomme'*. We do not have an expression in our language that exactly corresponds, though, as Byron remarked in another such case, we do not lack the thing. The 'Nodes' purport to be – and to some extent probably are – the records of actual conversations, and there is no doubt that one side of Hogg is well-caught in the character of The Shepherd. But it is only one side of him, and not the better one.

Jamie himself, while flattered by the celebrity he has attained in this manner, has too much sense not to be pained by the portrayal. 'I am neither a drunkard nor an idiot nor a monster of nature,' he wrote to me. Poor Hogg is indeed none of these things, though, in our native manner, given to drink copiously when the occasion offers. I do not think Wilson has done him service, but I doubt whether he has the resolution to withdraw from that set. I have almost always found Hogg agreeable in the Borders, but his manner, even his character, deteriorates when he crosses Middleton Moor, and Hogg in Edinburgh has frequently irritated me. Yet with all his faults, I love the man, and look forward to seeing him again at Abbotsford when I repair there.

It was through William Laidlaw, then farming Blackhouse in Yarrow, that I first met Hogg, who had – briefly, I suppose – been his father's shepherd. Laidlaw was invaluable to me in my ballad-hunting years, and later, when he had run into difficulties on his own account, and I had bought Abbotsford, I invited him to join me as my factor; and have never regretted it. We do not agree on politics, for Willie is inclined to be a Whig, but his good nature, his industry, his resourcefulness, and his perpetual good cheer, all make me love him. Take a difficulty or problem to him, and his reply 'What for no?' is like sunshine after rain.

I have always held by the good old Scots tradition that a man's servants should also be his friends, even though I have never perhaps gone as far as the Aberdeenshire laird, who, having fallen out with an old servant, nerved himself to tell the man that they must part, only to receive the reply: 'Aye, aye, laird, and far are ye ga'in?'*

---

* In the Aberdeenshire dialect, known locally as the Doric, the sound 'wh' is pronounced 'f'. So 'where', which is 'whaur' in the Borders, becomes 'far' in the north-east.

Nothing, however, is so offensive to me as to observe the manner in which certain folk who think highly of their consequence treat their dependants, as if they were machines without human feelings or the right to conversation. So Peter Mathieson, my coachman, whom the bairns call 'Pepe', Robert Hogg, John Nicholson, my footman who came to me as a boy and whom I have taken care to see is now a well-educated young man, my piper John of Skye (who doubles as a hedger and ditcher when his piping skills are not required), and my butler Dalglish, are all men whom I regard as properly part of my household, and, I may even say, my family.

Tom Purdie, on account of his admirable independence of mind, has a special place, and has indeed had such since I rescued him from the dock of the Sheriff Court. Tom does not treat me exactly as an equal, but he conceals his deference so well that I have known visitors who thought he treated me as an inferior. I recall one occasion when we had a disagreement concerning the thinning of a young plantation. A certain coolness prevailed. Then, on our return from an expedition, Tom asked me if he could have a bit word. Whereupon he told me that he had thought the matter over, and, on consideration, decided 'he wad juist tak my advice this time'.

Tom has all the old Scotch prejudices. Once he took an English friend of mine to try for a fish near Melrose Bridge. On the way to the river he regaled him with the history of the grand fish he had caught himself. By and by my friend, who was an experienced and skilful angler, hooked a vigorous fish, and after playing him nicely, landed him. 'That's a fine fish, Tom,' says he. 'Oh aye,' says Tom, 'a nice eneuch wee grilse.' 'A grilse? Why, it must be equal in weight to the heaviest fish you were telling me you had taken in this pool.' 'Weel, I wadna say that,' says Tom; so to settle the matter the fish was weighed, to my friend's great satisfaction. 'Weel,' says Tom, letting the salmon fall to the ground, 'ye are a muckle fush efter a' – aye, and a muckle fule to let yoursel be kilt by an Englander.'

I cannot end this account of my domestic friends without mention of four-footed ones. I have never lived without dogs, and could not happily do so. I like to have a couple with me in the study while I am working, and will break off from time to time to promise them a run when I get to the end of a chapter. My noble cat Hinse of Hinsfeldt is also accustomed to sit on the top of the steps I use to reach the upper shelves of my bookcases, and gives the impression, in the best feline manner, of exercising a sternly critical supervision over all that happens around him. As for the dogs it is invidious to select favourites, for a man should have an equal affection for all his children, among whom – I may say – I really think I include them. Yet human nature being by instinct partial, it is hard for a parent to avoid favouring certain of the bairns above the other, though the wise parent will attempt concealment of his inclination. So, since the poor dogs canna read, I may say that of the many I have had around me – for I do not care to think of *owning* them – there are two that stand fondest in my memory.

The first was Camp, a sort of bull-terrier, of uncommon fidelity and sagacity. In his youth he would always accompany me on my rambles in the hills around Ashiestiel, and delighted in showing me the easier route. When on a rock above me, he would lean down and give me a lick to either cheek or hand, as if to encourage me. A sad accident to his back half-crippled him and he could no longer be my companion on these expeditions. It became the custom for someone then to tell him when I was seen returning home, and he would make his way – somewhat painfully, I fear – either to the hill or the ford, never, to my knowledge, mistaking the direction I was taking. When he died and we buried him in the garden behind our house in Castle Street, the whole family stood around the grave, and there was not a dry eye among us.

Then there was Maida, a noble deerhound, given to me by MacDonald of Glengarry, who of all the Highland chiefs with whom I am acquainted most surely maintains the old habits of patriarchal responsibility towards his clansmen, being more concerned with their well-being than his ain balance at his bankers. Maida was worthy of such a donor, a dog of the greatest dignity, good sense, and kindness. When we set off for a walk with the other dogs, Maida was accustomed to trot gravely a few steps before me, indifferent for the most part to the gambolling and sportive sallies of his fellows; but I always suspected that he would relax his dignity when I was not present, and then romp and engage in mock battle with his companions with sufficient zest. Maida was so often made the subject of the painter's art that, latterly, wearied – as I am – of such attention and prolonged sittings, the mere production of a sketch-book was sufficient to cause him to take his leave.

The chief drawing-room dog was my dear Charlotte's spaniel Fynette, a graceful, engaging, and often naughty, bitch, of a type bred originally in France till the advent of the Revolution caused the Duc de Noailles to send his kennel for safe-keeping to his friend, the Duke of Newcastle at his seat of Clumber Park, whence Lord Montagu obtained Fynette, as a suitable gift for Lady Scott, remarking that the spaniel was from an *émigré* family also.

We have always had greyhounds or lurchers and a scattering of terriers of the Dandie type, who in honour of the original of Charlieshope are habitually called by the contents of the cruet-stand: Pepper, Salt, Spice, Nutmeg, Mustard. To this catalogue I might also add a small pig which conceived a violent affection for me, and tried to attach himself to my person whenever possible, and to join the troop of dogs on our expeditions. That did not often serve, but at least I determined that he should be spared the usual fate of the porcine race, and so he grew old in the swinish indolence which is, I suppose, what nature intended for the breed, till man intervened and converted them to bacon, hams, and chops.

(I might add that I early formed a repugnance for eating any beast with which I had been personally acquainted; and this feeling has grown stronger with the passage of time. Indeed, around the age of fifty, though I had been in my youth the most enthusiastic sportsman, which I do not regret, I developed a distaste for killing any living thing, and was happy to desist from such activity. This was a purely personal decision which I would not impose on any other, or choose to interfere with their sport.)

In the last twenty years I have known most of the great men and women of the day. Naturally I stand in a special relationship to the great family of Buccleuch, and Dukes Henry, Charles, and Walter, together with their Duchesses, have been my constant, faithful, and ever generous friends. It is with the pleasure that comes from familial pride that I am happy to add that I know of no great noblemen who have shown themselves better, and kinder, landlords and masters than the chiefs of my own house. Their care for their tenantry and servants, and the paternal responsibility they have exercised throughout the countryside, have been alike exemplary.

My southern acquaintance has been too extensive to list, and I may say only that I count myself fortunate to have been granted such opportunity to acquire some understanding of the habits and manners of our sister kingdom. There have been particular friends like Mr Morritt and poor Heber, who share my antiquarian interests, and there have been brother-poets – if I may so flatter myself – like Wordsworth and Southey from whose companionship and friendship I have had both pleasure and, in an intellectual sense, profit.

Friendship is a balm that softens and sweetens the asperities of our progress to the grave. Yet its chain, however bright, does not stand the attrition of constant close contact. I agree with the old lady who said that three days was just the right length of a visit.

It is otherwise with family. You choose your friends but your family is the gift of God and your own work. For one reason or another my relations with my brothers slackened as we passed into manhood, separated from each other by distance and a diversity of interest. Of Lady Scott and of my mother I have already written in this memoir; and there is nothing I can now add, beyond repeating my sense of my own good fortune in being born of one and finding the other. I have been equally fortunate as a father.

My elder son and heir Walter is not a clever lad, but he is a good one, which is more important. He has now laid aside youthful follies, and is making a brave career for himself in his regiment of Hussars. The tranquillity of his company has always delighted and soothed me, and if in his early days as a lieutenant in Dublin I occasionally had to speak to him harshly, it was only my duty to ensure that he did his. He is a notable sportsman, and will, I am certain, make a good and benevolent laird of Abbotsford when I am dead. He has made a happy marriage to a sweet girl possessed of a good fortune, the niece of my friend Adam Fergusson's wife. It is true that the girl's mother is a sour Presbyterian blister, and a snob, though her husband made his fortune by pickling herrings in Dundee; I was much amused when one reported to me that she had declared herself not altogether satisfied with the match, and had only let it go forward because the young couple were so attached to each other. Otherwise, says she, her dear Jane might hae looked higher: 'It is only a baronetcy, ye ken, and quite a late creation.' Miss Austen or Miss Edgeworth, I fancy, might have made much of Walter's mama-in-law.

My daughters are good girls. Sophia, my eldest child, has a nature of uncommon sweetness, and she has given me grandchildren who are my delight as I feel age grip me. Her tenderness has made her into a most accomplished coddler of the bairns; well, better that than harshness. More children suffer from a deficiency of love than from an excess; aye, and suffer more harm too from coldness than from warmth.

Anne has a satirical touch which I have tried – in vain – to check. I call her Beatrice sometimes after Shakespeare's heroine of the ready wit. She is perhaps of a somewhat nervous disposition, and inclined to be strict with me. But she has shown fortitude in the calamities that have fallen upon us, though she was surprised, even indignant, one day to come upon me and Will Clerk laughing in the study a few days after the great Crash. 'Why, papa,' says she, 'you would not think to hear you, that you have lost a fortune and Mr Clerk a sister . . .' Well, for my part I should hope not: *agere et pati Romanum est*. Still, I fear it is a dull life for the child tied to this ragged lion who must consume the hours, that might be given to pleasant conversation, in unremitting toil.

I fear my youngest child Charles is one of the lilies of the field rather than a toiler. Intelligent, charming, amusing, brought up in the plenitude of my fortune, he has lacked the spur that drove me on in my youth. Once he even suggested, during his residence at Brasenose College, Oxford, that he might become a parson. 'My dear,' I said, 'if you really feel disposed for the chimney-corner of life, and like to have quails drop upon you ready-roasted, be a parson in the name of God! I have nothing to say against it, for there must be parsons, but it is against my principles and feelings to recommend it. I consider that taking Holy Orders is a sneaking and disreputable line unless its adoption is dictated by a strong feeling of Principle, such as you, my dear, have never evinced.' The boy took the hint, and I have been able, by appealing to the benevolence of His Majesty, to secure him the promise of a place in the Foreign Office, where I daresay he will do very well, since I believe that his charm, intelligence, and good manners will secure him a degree of success in that department which his indolence, lack of strong convictions of any sort, and dilettantism, will do nothing to impede.

I cannot leave the subject of my family without animadverting to my son-in-law Lockhart. I do so with a certain hesitation, for he is to have charge of my papers, and there is something disagreeable always for both parties in praising a man to his face. Perhaps it is more seemly to begin with his faults. Lockhart has a withdrawn, proud, and even secretive manner which disguises his natural goodness from the world. He is over-given to the exercise of a sarcastic wit, and like many people who are acutely sensitive where their own feelings are concerned, is often either ignorant or careless of the pain which his sharp tongue can inflict on others. Moreover, I never knew a man of such virtue, sense, and genuine kindness, who had such a capacity for making enemies for himself. Nor is he always wise in his acquaintance; I have already mentioned my distrust of his close friend Wilson. He recently introduced an extraordinary young pup to Abbotsford, a bejewelled and ringletted Jewish Dandy, by name Benjamin D'Israeli. When I heard that a Mr D'Israeli was to visit us, I was happily expecting the pup's father, Mr Isaac D'Israeli, whose *Curiosities of Literature* is an erudite work that has offered me both instruction and delight. My first impression of the young Ben was that he was an intolerable coxcomb and popinjay. Moreover he came with a hare-brained scheme to make Lockhart editor of a Daily Paper which he was bent on launching. I deplored this for more than one reason, since it seemed to me impossible that association with such an enterprise could bring Lockhart either honour or profit. To do justice to the pup, I amended my first impression – something I have rarely had occasion to do, since I have usually found that when I had no great liking for a person at the beginning, it has pleased heaven to decrease it on further acquaintance. But this young man – though foppish and exaggerated in every notion – displayed signs of intelligence, if not of taste, and of a curiously sympathetic under-standing. I was touched too by the manner in which, in conversation with him, my stiff Lockhart softened and revealed his true, delicate, and judicious self. So there is more perhaps to young Ben than appears at first sight; but, as Tom Purdie observed, 'Whit a sicht thon is, Shirra'.

Since Lockhart and Sophia removed to London, I miss them deeply, and find great delight in the summer months they pass at Chiefswood on the Abbotsford estate. He is the only member of my family circle who has ever penetrated my secret world, which I generally guard like a fierce watch-dog, and from which I have been accustomed to draw. Only to Lockhart, I think, could I ever have offered the confession that I could never have brought myself to abandon literature for ten times my income.

I had thought to calm myself to dwelling on friends and families. But the happy memories thus aroused have a melancholy tinge, and have brought on a sort of fluttering of the heart. I know it is nothing organic and is entirely nervous, but the effects are dispiriting. Is it the body brings it on the mind, or vice versa? I cannot tell; but it is a stiff price to pay for the rewards imagination brings me at other times. It is strange too that thinking on my friends in this manner now makes me conscious of my utter solitude. Our way through life runs on two parallel courses; the one social, the other solitary; and society pleases us as it rescues us for the present hour from our awareness that in the essential matters of life, we have no companion.

I could not write of Charlotte here, for last night I dreamed that she lay in the bed beside me. I stretched out my waking hand to touch her, and encountered ... nothing. I rose, shakily, and crossed the room and drew the curtains; but it was still ink-black without. I thought for a moment of repairing to the study, to smoke a cheroot and steady myself with a dram; but I did not do so, for I feared the consequences for the morn. To such a sad state has my way of life sunk! So I retired again, and lay wakeful and restless for what seemed an age, though I daresay it was not above half an hour. Then I slept but fitfully, my mind being disturbed by new and more horrid dreams. In one I saw my dear Will Erskine, who had a horror of sport and an almost feminine delicacy, stretched across a cartwheel, the shirt torn from his back, as if he were about to be flayed; poor Will, who has been in the grave these five years. What mean such images? Whence do they come? I might as well ask, like Macbeth, 'canst thou not minister to a mind diseased?' For if my mind should go – as in the night-wastes I sometimes fear will be my fate – what then of my plans for our salvation, what then of my determination to work my passage, what then of the consolations of love, friendship or philosophy? All will be swept away like stooks from a flooded field when Tweed is in spate ...

Then I drifted back to uneasy sleep, and woke with those lines that are pounding me in my ears:

> And were you called to Elfland, cuddy,
>   Where the white lilies bloom?
> Or to that mirk, mirk land, cuddy,
>   The shades ayont the tomb?

14

Financial Affairs (written *c.* 1828)

I owe it to myself to give some account of my financial affairs and of the catastrophe which engulfed me. If I find this difficult, it is not only on account of the proper pride which makes me reluctant to divulge my business and my folly to the world, but also because I do not understand them very well myself. I have, since my youth, when my father trained me to do so, been punctilious in the keeping of my personal cash-book, and scarce a day has gone by that I have not entered there my incomings and outgoings. But the larger affairs of business have baffled and bored me, and have therefore, to my shame and present confusion, been neglected. In self-exculpation I can say only this: that I have ever been confident of my ability to earn the money which was advanced to me and which I spent on the building of my house and the enlargement of my estate; all went swimmingly for many years, and might have continued to do so but for the flurry of panicking bulls and bears on the London stock-market, and the sudden nervous crisis experienced by the banks.

Horace advises us, on the model of Homer, to plunge into a narrative, *in medias res*. That has rarely been my method, and indeed I know some have complained of my lengthy introduction of a story. So I think I had better abide by my practice, and begin at the beginning.

When I determined against supporting myself by my earnings at the Bar and took on my sheriffship, then my clerkship to the Court of Session, becoming in this way a mere salaried official, with no prospect of increasing my earnings in the main business of my life, I naturally had to look to what I could get by my pen as the main means of establishing myself in that way of life to which I aspired. It was my ambition to become a landed proprietor, both because the prospect pleased me, and because I wished to have property to hand on to my children. I make no apology for this ambition, which is one shared by the common run of mankind, and which I was fortunate enough to be in a position to gratify.

Then it seemed to me good to have my works printed by my old friend James Ballantyne, but, his business requiring capital if he was to handle the full load of my work, it was again natural enough that I should invest the legacy I had inherited from my Uncle Robert by buying a third share in James's printing firm. There was nothing disreputable in this, but nevertheless, believing that it was no part of the world's business to know of my pecuniary affairs, I preferred to keep it secret. In retrospect this may have been an error, for it introduced a certain note of unreality into my affairs. The business became a sort of bank from which I could draw, while at the same time its expansion required me, from time to time, either to invest more in it, or to grant a loan against future profits to it. But it served both James and myself well for many years, and I do not believe any of my publishers, especially not Constable, my principal one, had any true cause for complaint.

Constable, I may say, was a great man, in his way, with a genius for his business which excelled any other person in his line in Britain. The Emperor, as he liked to be called – or his Czarish Majesty, as I dubbed him – was a being of inordinate ambition, penetrating vision, and an unusual fertility of invention. It is fair to say that my admiration for him persisted till the very end, but to add that it also exceeded my affection.

Never thinking it a good thing for an author to be bound to a single publisher, and around 1808 or 9 being displeased with the truculence and ill-manners of Constable's then partner, Alexander Hunter, I was easily tempted to spread my interest wider. And so, with James and his brother John, I established a rival publishing firm, John Ballantyne & Co, in which I invested the greater part of my literary earnings which were not otherwise committed. The success of *The Lady of the Lake* seemed at first to justify the venture, but subsequent publications, though of literary worth, failed to find public favour, and the house was left with a good deal of stock which had not succeeded in finding a market. (I particularly regret the failure of a History of the Culdee Church, which was a work of true scholarship and historical importance that deserved a happier fate than to be piled, mouldering, in the basement of John's shop in Hanover Street.)

Within a few months I was aware of the rashness of this venture, and in the winter of 1810 even contemplated a change of direction. There was some talk that Lord Melville, the former Minister for Scotland and the father of my old school-friend, Henry Dundas, might go to India as Governor-General, and in my financial perplexities, I was ready, if he would take me with him, to pitch the Court of Session and the booksellers to the Devil and try my fortune in another climate. Many a Scot had made his fortune in India since Lord Melville first assumed the power of patronage there some quarter of a century earlier, but, even while I was considering the matter, His Lordship died, and so I stuck to the last I knew. This was all the easier because my affairs suddenly improved. From the 1st

January 1812, I would at last receive the full stipend for my clerkship, a portion of which had been diverted to the previous incumbent. With my sheriff's remuneration, and my wife's income, I could count on some £2,000 a year, and I was confident that, even if there were no profits to be had from the publishing and printing businesses, I could still earn at least another thousand by my pen.

It so happened that the lease of Ashiestiel was almost up, and my attempts to purchase house and estate were in vain. I therefore began to cast around for a suitable lodging, and happened on a little farm on the banks of the Tweed, a mile or so down river from the point where it is joined by the Ettrick water. It was then the property of Dr Douglas, the minister at Galashiels, and I secured it for £4,000, which I obtained by borrowing half from my elder brother John and half from the Ballantyne firm – on the security, I may say, of a poem, of which I had not yet written a line.

My joy at being at last a proprietor in my beloved Borders may well be imagined, and my original intentions for the property were modest, for I could not then foresee that the Author of *Waverley* would soon open to me a store-house of wealth of undreamed-of proportions. The original purchase did not extend over more than 110 acres, and the farmhouse, or rather cottage, was inadequate even for our simple needs. I therefore promptly had masons in, and the re-modelling of the cottage commenced.

But no sooner did I seem settled than new dangers reared up before me. The year 1813 saw much financial uncertainty throughout the country. Bills were called in, credit restricted and bankruptcies soared. The Ballantyne firms were in no condition to float on such a turbulent sea. Looking into the matter, I believed that the printing business was basically sound enough, but that the publishing firm could not be sustained. Yet I could not permit it to go bankrupt, for that would have revealed my connection to the world, and I should all too probably have been compelled to part with my share of the copyrights to my own works.

There was nothing for it but to make my peace with Constable and seek his help. This was granted, but on his own terms. He took over some of the stock and bought a quarter share in the copyright to my poem *Rokeby*, which together reduced liabilities by some £2,000. Then he conducted a careful examination of the two businesses and concluded that they might just be solvent, since assets and liabilities were almost equal to each other. The difficulty was that certain of the assets could not be realized, and, he judged, some £4,000 was urgently required. With great kindness and generosity, the Duke of Buccleuch offered to guarantee a bank overdraft to that figure, and the crisis was averted. It had been, as the Duke of Wellington was to say of Waterloo two years later, 'a damn'd close-run thing'; but we had come through, and with trading conditions improving, there was no need to draw in my horns.

Retrenchment soon appeared unnecessary because of the great and unforeseen success of *Waverley* and the novels which followed. There was, it is true, a hiccup some three years later, but it seemed to me of little account. James had fallen in love and proposed to a certain Miss Hogarth, whose brother, as head of the family, was prudently reluctant to sanction marriage to a man whose financial situation appeared to him to be unsound. Accordingly, James for the time being retired from the partnership and became the salaried manager of the printing works, while I took over sole proprietorship of that business. The publishing firm ceased business the following year, when its debt – amounting if I remember to some £10,000 – was transferred to James Ballantyne & Co, as the printing firm continued to be named.

Meanwhile the success of the novels meant that I found no difficulty in raising money for my building operations at Abbotsford, and for the purchase of some of the small farms and holdings around, by means of which I was able to enlarge the estate to more than a thousand acres. Indeed, in a few years, with the purchase of the land around Cauldshiels Loch and the estate of Tofthills, renamed Huntly Burn, my land extended from Abbotsford to Darnick, and I was the proud proprietor of all the territory named in the ballad of Thomas the Rhymer.

I was aware, of course, that my foundation of credit was insecure, for we had formed the habit of drawing bills on Constable, in anticipation of literary profits, which we backed by granting him bills drawn on the printing business. In justice to myself, I should say that Constable, though an entrepreneur of near-genius, was no more timid or prudent in his business methods than I was myself, and no more reluctant to take credit wherever he found it available. Meanwhile I told myself that it was but reasonable that I should run into a certain degree of debt while I was engaged in establishing my estate; that it was no great matter if my expenditure in one year considerably exceeded my income, since I was not only certain of being able to redeem any short-coming from future literary earnings, and was in any case acquiring capital in the form of land – to say nothing of the copyrights, or the share in them which I retained. It was true that I was always in arrears, but then I was accustomed to live in such fashion, and assured myself that, if need be, I could aye get my feet clear by a modest economy and a considerable expenditure of creative effort.

A few years later – in 1821, I think – I was happy to be able to re-admit James as a partner in the printing business, which had been making reasonable profits over the last few years thanks to its monopoly of printing my own novels. There was still a substantial floating debt – indeed I believe it was larger than it had ever been – somewhere between £20,000 and £30,000. This had come about partly because of the renewal of old bills, and the interest due on them, and partly, I confess, because I had been drawing fairly freely against the security of the firm in order to finance my building at Abbotsford and the extension of the estate. But I reflected that I was making at least £10,000 a year from my novels and had earned £80,000 by my pen in the last ten years, and I knew that when Abbotsford was completed, and in a fit state to be settled on my son (as it was on the occasion of his marriage), my expenditure would fall to a decent level, and there was no reason to suppose that it would not then be far exceeded by my annual literary earnings.

Yet on the re-constitution of our partnership, James and I agreed, with many a prudent nod and wink, that we would neither of us draw more than £500 a year from the business and that profit above that should go to the reduction of the firm's debt.

What I did not realize, and for this I believe I should reprove myself, is that my financial position depended ultimately on the prosperity of Constable's business, for so much paper had been exchanged between the two firms, that if Constable were to fail, then heigh-ho, down goes Ballantyne, and Sir Walter with it.

But Constable and his new partner, young Cadell, were flying high. He seemed to me not only the Napoleon, but also the Maecenas, of the book-trade. He paid me, I recollect, £1,000 for my poem *Halidon Hill*, which was the work of two wet mornings when the weather confined me to the house. His letters from London, where he often found himself – since naturally the main market was there – breathed confidence, optimism and high spirits. He was a man to whom any difficulty seemed an opportunity rather than a deterrent. Meanwhile, recovered from my three years of illness, I felt my own power as great as ever. The future was set fair.

We passed the next few years on easy seas, with only the occasional tremor. Constable's confidence was infectious, even if in 1823 he had requested that the Ballantyne firm's debt to him, which he declared to stand at £20,000, should be reduced by more than half. But, by 1825 Abbotsford had been completed, and young Walter was married and set up for life. My expenses were, as I had anticipated, diminishing, and my mind was serene.

Constable visited us at Abbotsford that spring. He was in a state of high enthusiasm which might be better termed excitement. The business of printing and book-selling, he told James and me, was only in its infancy – I indicated a decanter of whisky and suggested we take a drappie to wet the baby's heid. He proposed, he said, to bring out a new *Miscellany*, in cloth rather than boards, to be sold at a cheap price in monthly numbers, costing perhaps half-a-crown.

'If I live another half-dozen years,' said he, firing up, 'I'll make it as impossible that there should not be a good library in every decent house in Britain as that the shepherd's ingle-neuk should want the saut-poke! Aye, and what's mair? Why should the ingle-neuk itself want a shelf for the novels?'

'As I have said, Constable,' I replied, 'you are the grand Napoleon of the realms of Print.'

'I'll bespeak that line for my tombstone, Sir Walter. But stay – Napoleon. What would you say to a life of Napoleon by the Author of *Waverley*?'

'Done,' said I, before we had even discussed the terms on which the thing should indeed be done; and I set to work almost straightaway on the research, the sort of book-learning in which I have aye taken pleasure, sending to Paris for among other things a hundred volumes of the *Moniteur*, Nap's official gazette.

I spent that summer and autumn digging at Napoleon and toyed with a new novel which was to be *Woodstock*. In November came evil tidings from London, for the Stock Exchange had suffered one of those periodic outbreaks of speculation that seem as inescapable as the plague used to be. By the autumn the peak was past, and the consequences beginning to be felt. The bankers, aware of their earlier rashness, were now restricting credit, and calling in debts as a shepherd folds his sheep.

Lockhart, who had been in London, in connection with his prospective editorship of the *Quarterly*, wrote to me concerning rumours that Constable's London agents, Hurst and Robinson, were in Queer Street; it was said they had lost £100,000 in a speculation involving hops. Knowing how deeply Constable was committed to them, the tale caused me some misgivings; but I comforted myself with the assurance that the Great Man would certainly let me know at the earliest opportunity if there was any substantial cause for concern. Then Lockhart returned north, and in a few days received a letter from a London lawyer declaring that Constable's London bankers had closed his account.

I could not believe it; but I could not sleep either, and so ordered my carriage to be harnessed and drove through the night to Constable's estate at Polton. He was suffering from gout, but was quick to assure me that the rumour was false. Nevertheless he admitted that there were difficulties, but 'none that cannot be surmounted, Sir Walter', though he added that it might be necessary to raise some money to support his London agents, 'for I do not conceal from you that their ruin would involve me, and therefore you, through the Ballantyne business and in other respects also, in considerable embarrassment.' We agreed to raise £5,000 for this purpose.

Things got worse in London, and in mid-December a great private bank closed its doors, the first of several, I believe. On the 14th, at Constable's instigation, I committed myself to raising a £10,000 mortgage on Abbotsford – as I was entitled to do under the terms of Walter's marriage settlement – and to make the money available to Constable that he might shore up Hurst and Robinson, for I now realized that he stood in much the same relation to them as Ballantyne's did to him.

On the 18th came word that Hurst and Robinson were down. I felt as if a strong cold hand had seized me by the throat. But that night Cadell arrived to tell me this rumour too was false. The house still stood, and that evening in a fit of verse-making I scribbled lines to the old tune, 'Bonnie Dundee'.

Christmas was a cheerless time, and I forced myself to my desk to obliterate the cold sinkings of the heart which threatened to unman me. The mortgage was executed and the money went to Constable.

In mid-January, the 16th, I returned to Edinburgh in bitter weather and a black frost. 'Came through cold roads to as cold news,' I noted in my journal, for I learned that Hurst and Robinson had dishonoured a bill of Constable's, and the world had cracked. Since Hurst and Robinson could not meet their liabilities, their creditors turned on Constable who had backed their bills; his turned on Ballantyne's; and so good-night.

It was hard to establish who owed what to whom, so intricate had been the relations between the three firms; but the upshot was that Hurst and Robinson were in debt for £300,000, Constable for £256,000, and Ballantyne's, which meant Sir Walter, for £130,000. Most of our debt was held by the banks, though a few bills were now in the possession of private traders and speculators.

It was a bitter moment when I had to confess to Lady Scott and Miss Anne that I was a ruined man; and I cannot blame poor Charlotte that her charity failed her. She was already declining in health and now chided me for putting an unthinking trust in others.

Well, it is the trust others have put in me which has caused me most distress. There is a Spanish proverb: 'Who wishes not to sleep late in the morning, let him borrow the pillow of a debtor.'

I early resolved two things: first, that I should refuse all the offers of help which came flooding in on me. Among them there was one which touched me deeply: old Mr Pole, who taught Sophia and Anne to play the harp, offered me some £500, probably all he had in the world, saying that since he had got it as a result of my patronage, it was mine to make what use I cared of. I had the resolution to decline, but not to keep the tears from starting to my eyes. Walter's Jane offered to sell her holdings in the funds, and Sir William Forbes, a banker himself and the man who supplanted me in Williamina's affections – but a good and loyal friend all my life for all that – expressly proffered whatever aid he could give. A newspaper even proposed that a subscription should be raised for my benefit – a fine thing that would have been – here is a popular author whom the public has already supplied with countless thousands of pounds, now seeking their charity because he had not the wit to keep a gude haud o' his siller. No, these suggestions and offers did credit to the generous hearts of those who made them, but I would have none of it. To enter into fresh debt owed to my friends, in order to clear myself of debts which were the result of my own folly, that must be repugnant to any man of honour.

And so, since honour and industry were all that were left to me, I would have no man's help.

I resolved that I would not, if it could be avoided, take the easy refuge of bankruptcy, but to accept the government of trustees and clear the debt in full. 'My own right hand shall do it,' I said. Like King James at Flodden I 'saw the wreck my rashness wrought', and determined to drive myself even to death to repair the matter.

As for Constable, I pity him, and yet cannot acquit him of blame, or for his luring me into taking that mortgage on Abbotsford, raising a sum of money which the estate can ill afford and which was then drowned in his shipwreck. My feelings towards his Czarish Majesty were mixed, for as I said to Skene, 'he aye paid well and promptly, even generously, but, devil take him, it was all spectral money. He sowed my field with one hand and as liberally sowed tares with the other.'

Yet now that my first anger and resentment have abated, let me pay tribute to him. While I live I shall regret the downfall of his house, for there never was a publisher who did better by his authors. No doubt: he went too far while money was plentiful, but if you reflect how so many booksellers grudge every penny the mere author extracts from their grasping hand, well, Constable shines out in the full glory of the midsummer sun.

When I first visited my dear Abbotsford after the disaster, and after I had taken my resolution of how to combat it, dear Willie Laidlaw asked me how I was.

'I feel like the Eildon Hills, Willie – quite firm, but a little cloudy.'

'And what for no?' he replied.

'Well,' I said, 'I maun harness myself to my yoke. I can count myself fortunate that I have seen all that society and the world have to offer, and I find myself in agreement with the preacher that all is vanity, and much, vexation of spirit.'

'Aye, aye,' says Willie, 'and you speak a true word there.'

15

Scotland, England and the Royal Visit of 1822

It so happened that the period of greatest uncertainty and wretchedness concerning my own financial affairs coincided with one of my rare entries into the public controversies of our own day. In general I care little for politics from one year's end to another. I would not go so far as Dr Johnson who observed that he 'would not give half a guinea to live under one form of government rather than another. It is of no moment to the happiness of an individual' – and indeed I believe that the good Doctor might have changed his opinion had he lived to see the horrors of the Revolution in France. Nevertheless, most of the time I have been content to let things take their course without my interference, and certainly in this country changes of government have made little difference to the happiness of individuals – though it may be another matter if the present agitation for Reform is permitted to shake the fabric of the State.

Yet when something happens to stir me, then I will strike with the best and the fiercest; and I have often thought it has been my good fortune to have lived in quiet times, for in a more turbulent age I doubt if I should have 'scaped hanging.

Now the financial crisis, that pulled this ragged lion down, alarmed the Government, which, eager to seek a remedy for the disease, and too impatient to examine the cause, resolved on a measure which would have limited the Bank of England to the issue of notes of a value of £5 and upwards, and have taken the privilege of issuing bank-notes from the private banks altogether; and it was proposed that this measure should apply to Scotland also.

I at once saw that it would be in every way harmful, for the shortage of coin in Scotland was such that the passing and acceptance of bank-notes had become the ordinary and common mode of doing business; and the withdrawal from the Scottish banks of the right to issue their own notes would have had the dire effect of bringing the trade and manufactory of the country to a standstill. I therefore resolved to strike, and did so with some vigour, in three letters published in successive issues of James Ballantyne's *Weekly Journal*, and attributed to one Malachi Malagrowther, the letters subsequently being published by Blackwood in pamphlet form.

The letters made a considerable stir. My authorship was recognized, and by stirring up a hornet's nest – for I am glad to say that there was much in the matter of my epistles which the Whigs also detested – I showed that I was still to be reckoned with. I was not to be an object of Pity – 'poor Sir Walter that has had sae sair a fall'.

My intervention infuriated some of my friends in the ministry who felt, no doubt, as if a dog which they had supposed faithful had turned and nipped their ankles. Well, I had never hired myself to any man or party, and was not going to begin to do so in the twilight of my life. What's mair, as Tom Purdie would have said, what's mair, hinny, it amused me that I should be turning patriot and giving direction as to the management of the financial affairs of the kingdom, on the very day I signed the Deed of Trust on behalf of my creditors, and was thus proclaiming myself incapable of managing my own. Aye, it was rare work for a near-bankrupt scribbler.

I carried the argument far beyond the point narrowly at issue, and surveyed the course of Scottish affairs since the Union, and the manner in which they had been conducted. Indeed, I rested a major part of my argument on the Treaty of Union itself, and in particular on that article which guarantees that no alteration be made to laws which concern private rights 'excepting for the evident utility of the Subjects within Scotland'. No evidence of such utility had been offered; and therefore the proposed measure clearly contravened the Treaty, and ought to be abandoned.

That Union itself was a shabby business. I have no doubt of that, or that, if I had been living then, I would have struggled against its making with all the force and eloquence that I could muster. There is a part of me that has never been reconciled to it, that sighs for the auld independent kingdom, when we made our ain laws, and went our ain way, whatever the consequences. And it grieves me when I see folk tinkering with the inherited institutions that yet survive. If Jeffrey, Cockburn and their Whig friends are given their head they will whittle away whatever is distinctively Scotch until we become mere Northern Englishmen, awkward, crotchety, and girny, it may be, but without the individuality that even now distinguishes us.

There were certain areas, I am aware, even in the sacred field of Scots Law, where the Treaty of Union effected marked improvement much to be desired. Before the Union, the question whether a right of appeal to the Scots Parliament from the decrees of the Court of Session existed had been hotly disputed. In 1674, for example, a number of members of the Faculty of Advocates were suspended by the Court for daring to presume the right of such appeal; and at a time when the judges were more distinguished for legal knowledge than for either impartiality or integrity, the denial of the right to appeal to a Higher Court made acts of partisan injustice more probable, and indeed more common. The Treaty, however, by securing the right of appeal to the House of Lords, ended that state of things and so contributed to the impartial and independent character which, much contrary to the practice of their predecessors, the Judges of the Court of Session have since displayed. But, of course, an act of the Scots Parliament itself could have served as well.

The subsequent success of the Union, which I do not deny, had depended on the willingness of the Government in London to permit Scotland, under the guardianship of our own institutions, to win her silent way to wealth and consequence. The growth and magnificence of the great city of Glasgow affords evidence of the value and utility of Union. 'Nane', as I had my own dear Bailie Nicol Jarvie say, 'were keener against it than the Glasgow folk, wi' their rabblings and their risings, and their mobs, as they ca' them nowadays. But it's an ill wind that blaws naebody gude – Let ilka ane roose the ford as they find it – I say, Let Glasgow flourish! which is judiciously and elegantly putten round the town's arms, by way of Byword – Now, since St Mungo catched herrings in the Clyde, what was ever like to gar us flourish like the sugar and tobacco trade? Will onybody tell me that, and grumble at the Treaty that opened us a way west-awa-yonder?'

The Bailie is unanswerable. Common sense and reason are his supports. And there is another matter which should not be forgotten and which has reconciled countless Scots to the Union. Even if the old parchment of the Treaty should become obsolete, the peace that now exists between the two proud neighbouring nations, often so cruelly at war with one another, cries down blessings on the Union that has enabled the Borderers 'to hang their broadswords on the wall and study war no more'. I am as fixed in my love for Scotland as any man, and as good a patriot – *fier comme un Écossais* – but I had rather Scotland should dwindle into becoming a mere Northumberland than that we should remedy the loss of our national consequence by even threatening a rupture which should break that bonnie peace. Yet there is no harm in wishing that we may have or retain just sufficient of a sour temper, just so much national spirit, and just so much resolution, as will enable us to stand up for our rights, and our institutions, conducting our defiance of any encroachment on them with every feeling of respect and amity towards our sister nation, my dear England.

And I believe that the late war with France – brutal and cruel necessity – has done much to inculcate a sense of British patriotism, in the cultivation of which Scotsmen have not been remiss. For was it not a Scot – James Thomson from Ednam, near Kelso – who gave us that fine song 'Rule, Britannia!', and were not some of the finest patriotic verses made in the French Wars the work of another, my friend Thomas Campbell?

Yet I would resist any levelling process. I deplore anything which would sink us in uniformity. Indeed I am certain that it is to the advantage of the Union and the Kingdom – aye and to the advantage of England too – that the culture of its constituent nations should remain proudly distinct. I have been lionized in London as much as any man – and more, probably, than is altogether good for any man. I accepted this, not only as a species of tribute to anything worthwhile which I may have achieved – but if it had been that alone, I trust I would soon have wearied of it – but also, and more importantly, as a recognition of the distinct character of my native land. The Union will be the weaker if Scotland grows less Scotch, just as it would be if, by some at present unforeseeable turn of events, England became less English. I would add, however, that its preservation will depend on the tact and fine sensibility displayed by our southern neighbours, who are so greatly favoured by nature, and who must therefore always be the richer and preponderant partner. If, however, the day should come when they forget that the Union is a partnership, then either we must sink into resentful subjection or cut ourselves loose, with all the attendant risks. But if that day comes, let the break be made in an amicable and generous spirit on both sides.

It was with such thoughts in mind that I responded with alacrity to the suggestion a few years ago that His Majesty should pay a visit to his northern kingdom. No reigning monarch had set foot in Scotland since Charles II, having been crowned at Scone, set forth on that bold campaign that ended so disastrously at Worcester – unless, of course, as a loyal Jacobite, you insist that James VIII was truly king when he made his belated and feeble contribution to the '15 Rising.

I knew already that His Majesty was sensitive to Scottish sentiment. He had responded with enthusiasm to a suggestion I put to him while he was still Regent that the ancient Regalia of Scotland should be disinterred from the lumber of the Crown Room in Edinburgh Castle where they had so long lain unregarded, and I was proud to be named as one of the Commissioners of Inquiry charged with undertaking the task. Many believed that the Regalia had in fact been taken south at the time of the Union, or shortly afterwards, though the Treaty stipulated that they should never leave Scottish soil. On the 4th of February 1818, a dusty iron chest was prised open by a sergeant of the Castle Guard, and there, in perfect order, as if they had been sleeping under enchantment in a fairy tale, were the Crown and Sceptre fashioned in the reign of James V, and the noble and magnificent Sword of State which Pope Julius II had sent to James IV, and the great silver mace once ceremonially borne by the Lord Treasurer of Scotland. It was a moment of deep emotion such as I cannot render into words; and Sophia, who had accompanied me to the ceremony, was close to fainting. Not all my fellow Commissioners felt the sacramental gravity of the moment; one – who for the honour of his family I shall not name – displayed an improper levity and went so far as to propose placing the Crown on the head of one of the young ladies present, remarking that it would become her rarely. He was about to lay hands on the mark of royalty, but I stopped him with a sharp cry: 'My God, No'; and, to give him his due, he displayed contrition, confusion, and was uncharacteristically silent thereafter.

His Majesty had already given another sign of his profound understanding of our national sentiment, for he had commissioned the famous sculptor Canova to raise a magnificent monument to the exiled and unfortunate Stuart kings in St Peter's in Rome; and though I have not seen it I believe that the inscription bears not only their names but their royal titles, and records that it was raised by the order of the Prince Regent. In this connection, I might mention also the humanity of his father, the late King George III, who granted a pension to the last scion of the doleful House of Stuart, Henry, Cardinal-Duke of York, by that time the titular Henry I & IX, when his bishopric and benefices were torn from him by the ruffianly French, and he was thrust into poverty in his old age.

There was an immediate political reason which rendered a royal visit to Scotland desirable, for the economic distresses which were in part the consequence of the slackening of trade brought about by the ending of the war, and in part the result of the profound changes then taking place in methods of manufactory, which were aggravated by the callous denial of responsibility for the welfare of their workers displayed by a number of employers, had re-kindled a dangerously Radical mood in the country-side and towns, which I indeed attempted to combat by putting our volunteer force, the Buccleuch Foresters, on the alert.

My ambitions, however, transcended this narrow purpose. I saw that a successful royal visit might be the means of reconciling a greater number of my fellow-countrymen to the Union with England, and that it might also serve to heal the still bleeding wounds left by the memories of the suppression of the Jacobites, and to promote a better understanding between Highland and Lowland. In short, it appeared to me that to promote such a visit was to give practical expression to the arguments which I had deployed in my novels. Only one prince of the House of Hanover had ever visited Scotland, and his example had been unhappy, for he was the notorious Duke of Cumberland whose ruthless cruelty after Culloden had left his name stinking in Scotch nostrils, even though the University of St Andrews honoured him by inviting him to become its Chancellor, and though the Town Councils of Edinburgh, Glasgow and Aberdeen had all given dinners in his honour.

The project was not without a degree of risk. His Majesty, though a man of intelligence and sensibility, had been unpopular during his Regency, and this unpopularity had been increased rather than diminished by his attempt to divorce his wife, Caroline of Brunswick. Though I am no friend to divorce, holding that a man should stick to the vows he made, however hard he might find it to do so, I had some sympathy for His Majesty, for my own single encounter with the Queen had not given me a favourable opinion of her: for on that occasion, in London in 1806 or 7, she had most indecorously attempted to flirt with me. I was not therefore surprised to hear of her subsequent gross immorality.

The London mob, always sentimental and at the same time eager to express its democratic prejudices, took up the Queen's cause vociferously; while her counsel, Henry Brougham, a man of great intellectual gifts that were equalled only by his moral infirmities, defended her with brilliant and unscrupulous art that would have been better displayed in a more worthy cause. The divorce was abandoned, and the Queen was the heroine of the London mob.

His Majesty was wounded, sensitive to his unpopularity, and reluctant to display himself before his subjects. It required a certain tact to convey the assurance that in Edinburgh he would be received with all the respect due to his rank, and that his visit might, if properly handled, revive an enthusiasm for monarchy that had lain too long dormant.

Still there was hesitation. His Majesty was in poor health, suffering from gout and the dropsy. Then Lady Conynghame, on whom he relied deeply for comfort, was urging him to make a tour of the Continent, where, she assured him, his presence would do much to restrain the dangerous drift towards Liberalism which was alienating so many nations from their legitimate monarchs, and where, furthermore, his health would benefit from the gentler climate.

Nor were all his Ministers in favour of a visit to Scotland. Poor Lord Londonderry, whose mind was already disturbed, and who would bring his own life so cruelly to an end, even as His Majesty set sail in the *Royal George*, the visit having at last been determined on, gave him conflicting advice – now one thing one day, and the opposite the day after – an inconsistency that all too faithfully reflected the vagaries of his own poor agitated intelligence. In short, one week the king would come, and the next he would not.

I had persuaded myself that he would not come this year, and was looking forward to some easy weeks at Abbotsford, and then to a trip into the Highlands as the guest of Glengarry, when the Lord Provost of Edinburgh, Mr William Arbuthnott, called on me in Castle Street one morning and informed me that the visit would certainly take place. Furthermore, he said, there was not long to make all the arrangements, he did not know where to begin, and relied on me utterly to determine what form the matter should take.

The Lord Provost was, he said, acutely conscious that there was no traditional way of welcoming a monarch to his northern capital which could be taken as a model for the projected visit. This was of course true, and I did not think it right to disturb him further by mentioning what was uppermost in my mind: the weeks that the Prince had spent in Holyroodhouse in the autumn of 1745, though I was certain that His Majesty would be mindful of that time himself. Therefore I merely promised that I would think on the matter, and the next day discussed it with my old friend William Adam, the Lord Commissioner of the Scottish Jury Court. He reminded me of the Commission of Inquiry set up to discover the Honours of Scotland, and proposed that a similar body be formed now. This made good sense and we quickly co-opted David Stewart of Garth, as the principal authority on the history, culture, customs, arms and dress of the Highlanders, my old friend James Skene of Rubislaw and my distant cousin Sir Alexander Keith of Ravelston, whose membership of the Committee was the most appropriate since he was now the Scottish head of the great family that had supplied the hereditary Earls Marischal of Scotland, and which had suffered grievously for its loyalty to the Stuarts.

When we met, I mentioned that in a private conversation with His Majesty some years previously, I had remarked to him that, the Old Cause now being dead, there could be no doubt that he himself was the true heir of the old traditional Scottish kings as the direct descendant of Mary of Scotland and her son James VI & I, and that he had been much struck by the notion. Accordingly I had no doubt that he would play the true part of a King of Scots with all the grace and dignity of which I knew him to be capable on any public occasion. I added that his enthusiasm had been such that I was sure he would fit himself out in a manner becoming a King of Scots.

'Do you mean that you think he will wear the kilt?' asked Stewart.

'I am certain of it.'

The motto of the visit, I suggested, should be *Righ Albainn gu brath*, that is *Long Life to the King of Scotland*, for it was only by elevating the status of Scotland and by reaffirming our national dignity that the Union of the two kingdoms could be made complete.

Since I was aware that the public ceremonies would have something of the aspect of a pageant, I did not scruple to turn to my theatrical friends for advice. The first was Daniel Terry, whom I also requested to return to me as quickly as possible one of my dearest possessions, the sword which had belonged to the great Marquis of Montrose, which Terry had taken to London to restore and provide with a suitable scabbard, and which I had promised to Sir Alexander Keith for this great occasion. In Edinburgh, I relied on the imaginative skill of Mr William Murray, the manager of Edinburgh's Theatre Royal at the East End of Princes Street. I was especially pleased to do so, because Mr Murray was the grandson of Murray of Broughton of whom I had that dark childhood memory which I have already related; and I believed that by employing him in this manner, I would not only do something to enable him to retrieve the family honour which his grandfather had so besmirched, but that it would also signify the binding of the wounds of Scotland's bleeding history, and so effect the reconciliation of the different strains in the land which I saw as the happiest consequence of the visit.

I decided early on four major events which would express the nation's sense of itself. At the centre of them all would be the King, as the heir of Robert the Bruce and all the Stuarts, even down to the unhappy Prince Charles Edward himself. First, the Honours of Scotland should be conveyed with due ceremony from the Castle to Holyroodhouse, to await the King. Second, the royal landing at Leith, where Queen Mary had set foot on Scottish soil after her long years in France, should be followed by a ceremonial procession to Holyroodhouse, with all the pomp, and dignity, that could be mustered. Third, at some appropriate moment during the visit, the King himself should return the Honours to the Castle, where he would show himself to the crowd from the battlements. Fourth, there should be a great gathering of the Clans under their loyal chiefs, which should demonstrate to all that Gaelic Scotland also acquiesced in the restored monarchy. I kept these points central, and all else was subsidiary to them.

Our plans were soon interrupted by an impertinent letter from a certain Mr Thomas Nash, who held the post of Controller of Accounts in the Lord Chamberlain's Office. No doubt with the best intentions, but with a sad lack of understanding, Mr Nash challenged the authority of the Committee. He reminded us of what had been done when the King had visited Ireland the previous year, and suggested that this should be regarded as the model or precedent for what was to be done in Edinburgh. I answered him roundly. Ireland, I said, was not a historic kingdom, but a lordship of the English Crown. I therefore wished to hear no more about that country, or indeed about England or English practices either. 'When His Majesty comes amongst us,' I wrote, 'he comes to his ancient kingdom of Scotland, and must be received according to ancient usages. If you persist in bringing in English customs, we turn about, one and all, and leave you. You take the responsibility for the success or failure of the visit entirely upon yourself; and this was sufficient, for he shrank, prudently, from such an onerous responsibility.

I knew better than anyone, of course, that many ancient usages had been quite forgotten, and that it would be necessary to employ a degree of imagination to devise acceptable substitutes. One of my happiest strokes, I believe, was to make suitable use of the Royal Company of Archers, and to present them as the ancient bodyguard of the Scottish kings. I knew they were no such thing, that the Company had been formed in the late seventeenth century, long after there was no monarch resident in Scotland, that, though it had been granted a Royal Charter by Queen Anne, it was essentially a sporting and social club; it had come close to being disbanded on account of the Jacobite sympathies many of its members had displayed at the time of the '15; but it was clear that the King must have a bodyguard, and there was no company better fitted to supply him with one. Furthermore, I was at this time brooding on the idea for a novel which the next year came to fruition as *Quentin Durward*; and it seemed to me that if the Kings of France were defended by a Guard of Scottish Archers, the Kings of Scotland should be equipped in no inferior manner. Accordingly, with the help of

Mr Murray, a suitable uniform was devised, and the Archers were fitted out in suits of Lincoln Green slashed with white satin, a flat bonnet sporting eagle's feathers, a hunting-knife at the belt, a long bow, and a quiver of clothyard arrows. They made a brave show, and were so pleased with the garb that I believe they immediately afterwards took an oath to retain it for ever.

It is not my intention here to give a full account of this remarkable visit, for the details can be found easily elsewhere, and, of course, it was daily recorded in the Press, in general fairly, though the recently established Edinburgh newspaper, *The Scotsman*, consistently displayed a querulous, canting, levelling, Whiggish spirit, though even it could not ultimately deny the extraordinary success of the venture, far beyond what even the most optimistic of its promoters had hoped for.

For my part, I was exhausted almost before it was underway. I was afflicted, too, by a rash, the product, my doctor advised, of nervous irritation, which lowered my vitality and rendered it unseemly for me to wear the kilt. (I was amused, by the by, to get a letter from young Walter, currently in Berlin, who told me how the ladies had been shocked when he declared his intention of appearing at a ball in the garb of old Gaul, and had urged him at least to cover his thighs with 'those flesh-coloured things that are worn upon the stage'. With a fine show of spirit the boy appealed to the King of Prussia who told him that the women were a parcel of silly bitches and that he should wear his kilt as he pleased.)

I had occasion, too, for private sorrow which marred the King's arrival, for on the very day when the *Royal George* dropped anchor off Leith, my dear friend Will Erskine, only lately raised to the bench as Lord Kinedder, breathed his last. Already grieving for the recent death of his wife, his end was hastened, I believe, by a vile calumny put about: to wit, that he was the lover of an apothecary's wife. A man of a firmer temperament might have laughed off such nonsense, but Erskine, over-sensitive and fine-spirited, was dismayed and felt himself to be degraded. His health rapidly failed him, and his noble life ebbed away. He was buried at Queensferry by the estate in which he took such pleasure, and I believe I have rarely felt more wretched than when I stood in that grey kirkyard in the thin rain coming off the Forth. I would fain have skirted Edinburgh and made for the refuge, nay the sanctuary, of Abhotsford, but instead I had to bestir myself and make merry.

During the visit, the King's graciousness conquered all with whom he came in contact, and delighted the people who thronged the streets whenever he made a public appearance. There were also pleasant intimate dinners for those whom he chose to invite to attend him more closely. He lodged, of course, in the Buccleuch Palace of Dalkeith, since Holyroodhouse was not considered to be in fit state to receive him, though some £4,000 – I believe – was spent on refurbishing those apartments which were to be used for the Levees and Receptions which His Majesty gave there – I daresay I should have been more impressed by this figure had I not been well acquaint with the bills from masons, joiners, plasterers and decorators at Abbotsford. But I recall with especial pleasure a dinner there when the young Duke Walter, then a boy of fifteen, I think, sat on his right hand, and His Majesty showed his delight in the Scots fiddle music played by the famous Nathaniel Gow and his musicians. He would send the young Duke from the table to request particular pieces from the players – in the choice of which he impressed all by his knowledge and taste. When the young Duke grew somewhat weary of his role as messenger, His Majesty clapped him affectionately on the shoulder, and said, 'As the youngest member of the company, my dear, you must make yourself useful. When you reach my age, or that of your kinsman Sir Walter, then you may in your turn exercise authority over the young'; and he pressed a glass of champagne on him, waving away some proffered brandy with the words 'far too strong for one of His Grace's tender years to drink'.

I believe His Majesty can rarely have been happier than on the day when he carried the Honours of Scotland from Holyroodhouse back up to their historic lodging in the Castle. The enthusiasm of the crowd – so unlike the hostility to which he was accustomed in London – exhilarated him. The day was wet and misty, but, despite his bodily infirmities, he made his way to the Castle battlements where he stood, waving his bonnet, and acknowledging the cheers of the crowd for a full quarter of an hour. When he emerged on to the battlements he turned to Sir Alexander Keith and said 'Good God! What a fine sight! I had no conception there was such a scene in the world; and to find it in my own dominions; and the people are as extraordinary and beautiful as the scene.' They urged him to come in out of the rain. 'Rain?' said he, speaking as if the soul of his ancestors did indeed at that moment inhabit his body. 'Rain? I feel no rain. Never mind the weather. I must cheer my people.'

There is one other memory, tranquil, moving, and melancholy, that rises above my souvenirs of the gaiety and exuberance of the festivities. Before he took his leave of us, he went alone to Queen Mary's apartments in Holyroodhouse. Before he left London he had insisted that these apartments should not be touched in the course of whatever repairs and re-decoration were made. He arrived without ceremony, dressed like a country gentleman coming to town, and spent almost an hour there, sometimes – I was told – standing without moving for five minutes at a time, while he imbibed the atmosphere of the Queen's chamber, whence the unfortunate Rizzio had been dragged to his brutal murder, crying out to the Queen who was powerless to help him, and whom the ferocious and drunken earls threatened to 'cut into collops' herself, if she attempted any resistance. Then His Majesty would run his hand over the bed in which his ancestress had slept, and let it rest on the bed-post to which Rizzio had clung. He spoke little, but he felt much. 'Rarely,' he said to me later, 'no never, Walter, have I felt the past surge so powerfully against me, or been so keenly conscious of the influence of my heredity and my Stuart blood.'

When the captains and the King had departed, and I was able to return to Abbotsford and rest, criticism muted during the three weeks of the visit was naturally more loudly heard. I was reproached for what some called the 'Celtification' of Scotland. It was argued that I had imposed a false image of my native land. Lowlanders, who had feared and loathed the Highland clans for generations, it was said, had been encouraged by me to accept them as the personification of Scotland. There were many who were not slow to point out that during the '15 and even more during the '45 Lowland Scotland – and especially the cities of Edinburgh and Glasgow – had been loyal to King George and had repudiated those whom they called the Pretenders.

I knew this as well as anybody, better indeed than most. But I also knew that, just as I had myself Whig and Jacobite strains in my own family and my own heredity, in this I seemed to myself the very image of Scotland. For centuries we had been a nation riven by deep divisions, and yet capable at vital moments of coming together as one. We were almost the first people in Europe to acquire a strong sense of national feeling, and I was aware of how this had been diluted, and of how many among us were prepared to settle, even if at times resentfully, for the status of North Britons. Well, I was proud to be British, but could never consent to style myself a North Briton. I believed that to be oblivious of our history was to mortgage our future.

Now whatever distinction there might be between the North of England and the Lowlands of Scotland, it was, except in terms of our national history, a fine one. To restore a full sense of national consciousness in Scotland it was necessary that Highlands and Lowlands should come together, and that the old animosities should be stilled. Then inasmuch as nothing marked Scots out as distinct so clearly as the Highland tradition, it was evident that the most efficacious way of forming a renewed sense of national identity was to make use of that, and to persuade all Scots that we shared in those traditions, which indeed in a sense we did, for in the early Middle Ages, before Malcolm Canmore married the Saxon princess Margaret, Gaelic was the tongue spoken over almost the whole of Scotland.

I trust I do not claim too much if I say that in managing the King's visit I was attempting to give visible expression to the impulse which drove me to write *Waverley*, *Rob Roy* and *Redgauntlet*.

I may add two footnotes. During the visit I spoke to Sir Robert Peel, the Home Secretary, and a man I already knew and highly esteemed – as did Byron who had been his schoolfellow at Harrow – about the great cannon Mons Meg which had been removed from Edinburgh Castle after the '45, and which now languished in the Tower of London. I suggested the time was ripe for its return, and Sir Robert, with his quick sympathetic understanding, undertook to arrange it.

I also took the liberty of suggesting to His Majesty that the act of reconciliation between the Houses of Hanover and Stuart, which he embodied in his own person, would be made complete if he would now lift the attainder which still afflicted Jacobite families, and, if it was alas impossible to restore forfeited estates, since this could not be done without injustice to their present proprietors who had purchased them in good faith, it would at least be possible, and seemly, to restore the titles of which those loyal to the Stuarts had been deprived. His Majesty responded to the suggestion with that quick and tactful enthusiasm which he had displayed, to the delight of all, throughout his time in his northern capital; and the thing was done.

There is only one regret: that the King's indifferent health made it impossible to repeat his visit to Scotland and perhaps travel more widely throughout the country where I have no doubt that he would everywhere have been greeted with the same loyal acclamations that so delighted him in Edinburgh. Certainly, when the royal yacht slipped down the Forth, there were many hearts which spoke the refrain: 'Will ye no come back again?'

16

Of Death and Dreams, 1829

I had thought to have done with this ragged memoir, for it is long since I wrote in it, having, in some fashion, employed it to write me into a better frame of mind, so that my legitimate work proceeded apace, and to my fair satisfaction. Besides which, that served what I fear is now its primary purpose well enough, and has considerably reduced my debt to my publishers. There have been moments when I feared that I was attempting more than my health could bear. Well, if so, 'at least we'll die with harness on our back'.

Constable died more than a year back. I had no cause to regret him, and yet I did, our connection having been so close, and we having shared triumphs and disasters. If he wronged me in the end, it may be that I wronged him in my turn; and that, bound together, we were agents of our mutual destruction. It is strange; no man understood better the art of publishing and selling books than Constable, and, without an affectation of modesty, I can say that no man in our time has better understood the art of making them than myself – and yet. Well, you have to climb high to suffer a great fall. There was something of the tragic hero in him, for he was felled as much by his own character as by circumstance. His pride and vanity were inordinate, and, till near the very last moment, he could not believe that he could be broken. For my part, I had had doubts, fears which I kept secret that the thing was too good to last. I was in one way more fortunate than he; for when the crash came, I had my mental and imaginative resources to fall back on; I could aye work, which is the only medicine I know for heartache, but he, cast down in his pomp of pride, bankrupt, was as enfeebled as Napoleon on St Helena.

Casting back over what I wrote concerning the King's visit to Edinburgh, I see I all but omitted everything concerning poor Londonderry, whom, I fancy, posterity may recognize more easily as Viscount Castlereagh. I never knew him well, as I did his rival Canning, and on the few occasions I met him found him awkward and shy in conversation. But his achievements in the guidance of our foreign policy were notable, and the thought of his end gars me shiver. It seems that he approached His Majesty a few days or weeks earlier in a state of mental perturbation. Indeed he burst into the Monarch's study unheralded, seized him by the arm and exclaimed 'Have you heard the terrible news? I am a fugitive from justice, accused of the same crime as the Bishop of Clogher. I've ordered my saddle-horses, and intend to make for Portsmouth and take ship to some remote quarter of the world ...' He remained with the King some half-an-hour refusing all comfort, but – which is the more remarkable – occasionally breaking off from his mad recital of his fears to talk rationally about his forthcoming mission to Vienna. At last they got him away, back to his own house, where they summoned the Duke of Wellington, to whom Castlereagh poured out the same story. The Duke told him it was a delusion; then, thinking that blunt methods might shock the wretched man into sense, told him he could not be in his right mind. He was put to bed and bled, which eased his agitation somewhat, and they took his pistols, knives, and razors into safe keeping. But a few days later he got hold of a pen-knife and cut his carotid artery.

His Majesty received the news during his voyage to Scotland, and since he had come to revere and rely on poor Londonderry, I believe his distress was considerable. From a hint he subsequently dropped to me – though only a hint, for one cannot expect kings to make confession to their subjects – I believe he blamed himself for not having taken firmer methods to secure Castlereagh's safety. But when a man is of a mind to be rid of this life – whether he is out of his mind or not – it is hard to thwart him. Desperate suicides will aye find a desperate way.

It is inconceivable that there could have been substance in Castlereagh's fears. The wretched Bishop of Clogher –son of an Irish peer, I think – had been taken in the act of sodomy with a private in the Grenadier Guards in a London public-house. No one who knew Castlereagh's proud self-control could suppose him guilty of such a crime. And yet the thing preyed on his mind. It was on such an act that his disordered fancy fastened. Strange, strange it seemed to me – then.

Now – when I have learned to know better the wayward motions of my own mind, when that energy which formerly surged forth and led me into the realms of imaginative creation seems turned in on itself, when I work with difficulty and dream dreams that disturb me, I have a better understanding of poor Castlereagh's terrors. For it seems likely to me now that they were the expression of that duality of which I have written; that in his disordered terror he gave vent to that Double whose existence he had denied, suppressed, drowned in a flood of activity, and which now revenged itself on him in his weakness. For in my weakness, between waking and sleeping, I have been afflicted by like fancies and images – though taking a different form from his, equally horrible and alarming.

I kept away from Hastie's Close for several months after my third visit, though often tempted to return there in a questing spirit, yet always resisting, for fear of what I should learn, for fear too of being dragged, not then unwillingly, into some degradation. I told myself that the temptation was unworthy of me; and turned back to labour. Yet the thought was ever with me, like a nagging tooth, not so painful that extraction is necessary, yet always a lurking and unwelcome presence.

Eventually I succumbed, about some three weeks ago, I cannot remember. I made my way there eager-reluctant; yet as I drew near, and expectation quickened, my self-reproach was stilled.

I do not know, of course, what I sought, for each of my visits had been inconclusive, like a book which has been printed without its final chapters.

The night was thick and gloomy, and the haar hid the rooftops. I leaned as formerly against the wall of the close, my chest tight, and my senses – so often dull nowadays – alert as a young man's. But nothing happened. The magic – whatever it might be – was absent. I remained there for an hour by the striking of the Tron clock, and then limped away, sorely cheated of I knew not what. In the morning I felt strangely heavy, dull of eye and of brain, and had to drive myself to my desk where, as I recall, I made little progress.

This mood of lassitude remained with me. In company I attempted to disguise it, but I believe it was remarked on. My memory too began to show signs of rapid deterioration, which grieved me, for should it fail, then the last vestiges of my power will have been stripped from me. Often in the late afternoon, at the dying of the winter light, I would find myself sitting, blank of mind and of eye, in my chair, as if in the grip of a paralysis, bereft of will, inspiration, everything.

For a fortnight, when sleep at last came upon me, I was awakened in the middle of a dream which grew more horrible nightly. Yet there was nothing, it seemed, to it. In my dream I found myself in a Gothic mansion, or rather castle, perched on a high rock, with the sound of water flowing below. The castle seemed empty of humanity, and the only evidence of other life was provided by fluttering bats, and the croaking of ravens on the battlements aloft. I was in a dimly lit room, and having felt my way around the walls which were covered with some soft but damp hangings, I came on a heavy door which I opened and which allowed me to advance into a long passage. In this lobby, as in the room, though there was no other presence, I was sensible of invisible watchers, and I believed, though I could not hear them, that they commented scornfully on my movements. I advanced along the passage, and opened a door at the end, and found myself in another room, identical, it seemed, to the first. At this point a sentence was spoken in a language I did not understand, and which I knew I had never heard before. Then, as the words died away in whisper, I woke up, sweating. That was all, except that each night I believed that I had started in the room where I had finished the previous night, and was therefore advancing towards something which could only be terrible.

I could speak to no one of this dream, which seemed like a reversion to childhood, though I had no recollection of nightmares then; I found that I was afraid to retire to bed.

It was that fear which drove me last night to go back to the Cowgate and Hastie's Close. Nothing I encountered there could be more horrible than the terror that awaited me in bed, for that had increased with every step along that dark corridor.

Again, for a time it seemed that the magic had departed. I knew a hollowness of feeling. Then, as if a stage curtain had been drawn, a thin light flooded the close and the music struck up. At the top of the steps the girl appeared, and held out her hand, but not to me. A figure emerged from the shadows, a boy with long hair, a torn shirt and breeches that ended in rags about his knees. He was barefoot, and his hair and cheek were streaked with what I knew to be blood. They held my gaze, and at first I could not recognize him. And then I saw that he was Green-breeks, and called out to him, asking whether he did not know me. He looked as he had in the days of our 'bickers', indeed as if the sword-blow which had felled him then had proved mortal. He danced with the girl, a measure that began in grave fashion and grew faster and faster and more lively as the music quickened.

The fiddler, whom I could not see, broke off, and then resumed in a slow languorous tune, that was sweet and sad at the same time. The graceful movements of the boy and the girl held my gaze. I stretched out my hand to touch them, but they slipped away. This happened three times, and I knew that they were either incorporeal or that it was not intended that I should lay hand on them. And yet I wanted to, so much.

> The golden lad and silver lass,
>   The auld wife dour as lead;
> The fiddler wi his merry dance,
>   That summons up the dead.
>
> The mune ahint the dusky clouds,
>   Denies the world its light;
> The western hills roll far away,
>   Like years, into the night.

Now, Walter, tak dead Michael's hand,
  That cleft the hills in three,
Now, Walter, tak dead Michael's hand,
  For you twae maun agree.

Thin-flanked from nether regions, he
  Has come to speak with you,
And gin you list not to his words,
  This night now shalt thou rue.

Sae, poet, tak dead Michael's hand,
  And feel the bones of death;
Sae, poet, touch dead Michael's lips,
  And taste his icy breath.

The golden lad kens silver lass,
  And auld wife dour as lead;
The fiddler leads a merry dance,
  That aye delights the dead.

Oh, he has touched dead Michael's lips,
  That drank the bitter wine,
And round and round the sacred tree,
  The baith o them maun twine.

The baith of them maun twine, my dear,
  The dance maun hae its way;
The dancer yields his will, and he
  The music maun obey.

Down in the glen where fairies are dancing,
  Down in the hollow where all is entrancing.
There in the milk-white field that is moonlit,
  Rest for the weary, and freedom from all guilt.

Cease from battle,
Let war's rattle,
Fade away,
Fade away.

Come to the land where the asphodel blows,
Where its sweet musky scent is preferred to the rose;
The dancers, the dance, and the music are one,
And the race that is prized is the race never run.

Where golden lad and silver lass,
  And auld wife light as lead,
Follow the fiddler in his dance,
  That quickens up the dead ...

And as I listened a great desire came over me, and I advanced up the steps, my legs lighter at every stride I took. I attained the top, and stretched out my hand and laid it on Green-breeks's blood-encrusted hair, and he did not flinch, but smiled at me, a smile of an infinite sweetness and regret. I let my hand drop, and the mists closed round him and the girl, and the music died away; and I looked down, and in my left hand, I was still holding something which I found to be a rickle of bones as if once it had been a hand. I raised my eyes, and I said, 'In the name of God, no,' and the bones crumbled to dust, and when I laid my hand to my lips the dust stained them and tasted dry and sour.

I limped home through the empty streets, a prey to conflicting emotions, for sometimes it seemed that I had won a great victory and survived a trial, and at others that I had been deprived of what I most deeply desired, though I could not put a name to that. I put my left hand to my lips again, and the smell of death was still upon it. I could not believe that I had really held the skeletal hand of Michael Scott, astrologer, philosopher, and tutor to the Emperor Frederick II, known as *stupor mundi*, the wonder of the world – Scott around whose name so many legends have attached themselves in his native Borderland, whom Dante, calling him 'thin-flanked', had consigned to the eighth circle of the Inferno, and of whom I myself had written in the *Lay*; but then I could not believe either than I had not done so. And I did not know whether I had been threatened with something fearful, or whether a promise of delight had been extended to me.

I found Anne in our lodgings, in a dressing-gown.

'Where have you been, Papa? I heard you go out, and then not return, and I grew anxious.'

'Walking, my dear. I could not sleep, and thought I might tire my body to rest my mind.'

'But you look so pale and agitated.'

'It is nothing, my dear. I am ready for rest now.'

'And strange, as if . . .'

'As if what?'

'As if you had struggled with devils.'

'Come,' I said, 'that is fanciful. A Romantic, Mrs Radcliffeish notion, purely Gothic. There are no devils, I sometimes think, save in our own mind. It is all right, child. Come, let's away to bed.'

17

Of George IV and Prince Charles Edward

News came last week of the King's death. My correspondent reports that his last words were: 'So this is death! Oh God! They have deceived me.' *Se non è vero, è ben trovato*, as the Italian proverb has it. Death, the great leveller, destroying consequence, and all earthly pretension, must aye make mock of monarchy. The radical papers have been scurrilous in their notices of his obituary, none more so than that detestable rag *The Times*. But the Tory Press has scarcely used him more kindly. Yet I believe that, self-indulgent and alternately obstinate and vacillating as he was, he tried to do his duty. No man can say more for himself than that. And he could play the part of the monarch to perfection, for he had natural grace and charm of manner; and perhaps playing the part is as much as is now required of kings.

I knew him – but only socially – for near a quarter of a century. He was always kind and courteous, even admiring, towards me; and thoughtful too. He offered to make me Poet Laureate, an honour I declined because I had no wish to be seen as a sort of retained hack, and also because I think the position a futile one. Then, when I retired from the Clerkship of the Court of Session, he conveyed to me the desire that I should become a member of his Privy Council. I declined that honour, too, for I did not think it became me, especially in my sadly altered circumstances; the invitation was honour enough, I said.

Of his intelligence I cannot judge, for it is impossible to estimate the intelligence of one who has the power to dictate the terms of conversation, and who may leave off a topic when he pleases, and deny his interlocutor the right to return to it. In society a Prince must be like the conductor of an orchestra. Yet, with this reservation, he had a refinement of taste and sensibility of intelligence not commonly found in Princes. He was a great patron of painters and architects, and I believe has done more to beautify London than any previous monarch. His restoration of Windsor Castle is also said to be beyond praise. Of the Pavilion at Brighton I am not qualified to speak, except to say that he talked of it in terms which recalled my own feeling for Abbotsford.

I was naturally gratified that he found something to admire in my work, though I consider that his admiration for Miss Austen's novels offers better evidence of his discriminatory ability. When Byron talked with him, he reported that 'he spoke of Homer and of yourself with equal fervour, and, to do him justice, appeared equally well acquainted with the writings of both'.

He had no doubt that I was the author of the Waverley novels, though he was too well-bred to inquire directly of me. Once, when I dined with him – an intimate little supper in Carlton House – he offered a toast to 'the Author of *Waverley*'. I drank happily and retorted that 'I shall be delighted to convey Your Royal Highness's compliments to the gentleman in question if ever I should be so fortunate as to meet with him'. He enjoyed that sort of jest, and had indeed a ready wit and a warm, sometimes broad, humour. He excelled, and delighted, in conversation, having talents of mimicry that, had he been born in another walk of life, could have made his fortune on the stage; he had a fund of anecdote which he recounted very well and with considerable art. There was indeed something – and splendidly – theatrical about him, in both his private and public life, for he was always extremely conscious of the impression he made; and therefore his largely undeserved, but extreme, unpopularity in London grieved him more than it would have done a more robust and less sensitive man. This was a great tragedy, for, had he managed his private life more decorously, he had talents which could have ensured great popularity, which would have been to the benefit of his kingdoms by promoting stability. As to his private life, it is not for me to judge. I shall say only this: we who are fortunate enough to be able to marry where we choose, and do so in the certainty of there being at least affection between husband and wife, should not rush to condemn Princes who are compelled to make marriages which are not of their choosing. I believe also that, for all their private virtues, both George III and Queen Charlotte were unsympathetic, even harsh, parents.

George IV had a great reverence for courage, and military achievement. He had Lawrence paint him portraits of his great Captains and Admirals, which he hung in his favourite drawing-room at Windsor. His deference to the Duke of Wellington was wonderful to see – even though in relaxed mood he would 'take off the Duke to perfection. He was a Whig in his youth, partly as an expression of revolt from his father – it is wonderful how the heads of the House of Hanover hate their elder sons, in every generation - partly because he fell victim to the charm, which was formidable, of Charles James Fox. Then his other great friend was Sheridan, a man who made his way in the world supported by no consequence but his genius. Though my politics were clean opposed to those of Fox and Sheridan, I would be a fool if I did not recognize their great qualities. If it is true that a man's quality may be judged by his choice of friends – and I think it is – then George IV emerges better from such a test than most men, certainly most kings; for kings tend to prefer their inferiors, while as Prince and King, George sought out those who were his intellectual, and moral, superiors or equals.

When he became Regent, with Fox dead and Sheridan in decline, he deserted the Whigs, for which they never forgave him. Indeed his support for the Tory ministry and his determination to prosecute the war against Napoleon *à l'outrance* was the chief cause of the Whig bile which to a great extent accounted for his unpopularity. Thinking they had been deceived by him, they did not scruple to deceive the world concerning him. In old age his Toryism grew more settled, for he feared the levelling tendency of the age, even as I do. The Whigs, by the bye, never lost their initial tenderness for Boney. At Holland House I once heard Lady Holland refer to him as 'that poor dear man'. Since I was her guest, I kept silent, but with some difficulty.

His virtues inspired affection, even tepid affection, rather than loyalty, and his vices an easy contempt. Though he had dignity and presence, no one ever feared him. He was denied any opportunity to display martial courage, which I think he would have had, though I am certain that his direction of any army would have been as incompetent as his brother York's proved to be. His claim to have led a cavalry charge at Waterloo – and I am told, latterly, at Salamanca also – suggests that he felt this denial severely. But he lived when the heroic age of Princes was no more. He was a metropolitan creature.

He could not inspire devotion as Prince Charles Edward did. In exile he might never have roused himself from self-indulgence, and it is impossible to imagine him leading an adventure like the '45. Whatever may be said against the Prince, the audacity of his enterprise admirably satisfies the test laid down by the great Marquis in the lines:

> He either fears his fate too much,
>   Or his deserts are small,
> That dares not put it to the touch,
>   To win or lose it all.

The Prince was a hero to me in my youth, and I still cannot disengage myself from the Romance of his cause. It is true that those who were closest to him thought least well of him, discerning the faults of character – rashness, obstinacy, unwillingness to take good advice, secrecy, selfishness, and a tendency to despair – that were to combine to make his later life such a wretched mockery of the other qualities he displayed in his great year. There is some justice in the view expressed by one Jacobite chief, that they might have set the Prince's father back on his throne, if the Prince himself had retired to bed and left the management of the campaign in the hands of Lord George Murray. Even more hostile was the verdict of Lord Elcho, who on the melancholy field of Culloden cursed the Prince for 'a damn'd cowardly Italian' – which I think unjust.

The earlier judgement may be questioned, too, for it is doubtful if Lord George, in the absence of any support from the English Jacobites and of the promised landing of French troops, would have advanced as far as Derby; while it remains one of the great imponderables of history, to speculate on what would have happened had the Prince's will prevailed, and, instead of turning back at Derby, his army had pressed on to London. Reason and good sense counselled withdrawal; but since reason and good sense counselled that the adventure should never have been embarked on, and yet since they had got so far, with unbroken success, they might have been wiser to continue to disregard these warning and doubting voices, and try one more throw of the dice.

Certainly there was panic in the capital. George II had packed his bags and was prepared to scuttle off to Hanover. No strong feeling of loyalty bound men to the ruling dynasty, and the great Parliamentary lords would, I fancy, have been as quick to accommodate themselves to a change of regime as their great-grandfathers had been in 1688. The Tory squires, who were dinner-table Jacobites, would have welcomed the Prince, initially at least.

But there's the rub. Considering the characters of James VIII & III and of the Prince himself, they might have found it even harder to keep their throne than to win it, for there is nothing that suggests that either had the sense or political skill to play the part of a modern monarch. George IV might resist his ministers, as he long did over the issue of Catholic Emancipation where he was in the wrong, but he knew he had to give way in the end. Even his father, as obstinate a man as could be found – except for the Stuarts in male line of descent – eventually acquiesced in the independence of the rebel American colonists. But the Prince would persist in a course even when it had been demonstrated that it must be against his interest, simply because he had determined on it, and others were bold enough to advise against it. Of all his ill-fated family, he most resembled his grandfather James VII & II, who lost the secure throne he inherited from his brother, because he would have his way, and so ignored the warnings which well-wishers offered.

Charles II, after his experience of exile, held to only one fixed point: that he would not go on his travels again. The family have been sad wanderers since his brother ignored the implications of Charles's determination. In exile, James relapsed into a morbid religious superstition, and his disappointed grandson took to the bottle.

For that he deserves sympathy rather than blame. He was a man whose whole life was concentrated on one object, who had ventured everything on a bold throw; and having lost the game, cared not what else he lost. So he sought oblivion as release from pain and disappointment, and the crapulous old man in Rome's Palazzo Muti was a far cry from the gallant hero who raised the standard at Glenfinnan, and who answered Lochiel's advice that he should go home, with the bold words, 'I have come home'. Then, having been defeated by the despotism of fact, he retreated into the imaginary world which liquor can create. As he lay dying, a piper played 'Lochaber No More' in the courtyard below the window of his chamber. His natural daughter Charlotte once found him in tears during a conversation with a visitor, on whom she turned sharply with the words 'You have been talking to him about his Highlanders...'

Here I am, in my sixtieth year, a man who has seen much, and achieved enough to have won the respect of his fellows, but when I think of the great adventure of the Rising, I become a lad of fourteen or fifteen again. Jeffrey once said to me, 'Depend upon it, Sir Walter, we would all have stood by King George and the legitimate government had we been alive then. The true hero of those years was the Lord President,' – Duncan Forbes of Culloden – 'who first tried to deter men from joining the Prince, and then, after his defeat, to mitigate the severity with which the rebels were treated.'

'I do not accept the word "rebels",' I said. 'A man can rebel only against a government which he accepts as legitimate.'

'As all the chiefs had done,' Jeffrey said. 'At any rate they had all sworn oaths of allegiance. Come, Sir Walter, your attachment to the Jacobite cause is unworthy of your own good sense.'

'Maybe so,' I replied, 'but I should think the waur of myself if I reneged now.'

And so I would. At a time when calculation and rationality were commencing to dominate men's minds, the Prince threw down the challenge of the irrational. That is where the poetry lies, for the poet must ever bring an alternative vision to the character of mind which deals only in profit and loss. I have a profound admiration for Dr Adam Smith, and yet a world that was formed only on his principles would be a dry and barren place, where all emotions are tepid, but greed.

Fifteen years after Culloden, and as many before Dr Smith's *Wealth of Nations*, James Macpherson gave 'Ossian' to the world. It was a largely fraudulent production, for while it seems probable that Macpherson drew some of his materials from Gaelic poetry which he received orally, his contention that he had translated an authentic manuscript cannot be sustained, since he defied every attempt to make him produce the original. The case against him cannot be refuted. Yet in some mysterious fashion, Macpherson gave the world what it was longing for; and our national vanity may be flattered by the fact that a remote and almost barbarous corner of Scotland produced a bard who gave a new tone to poetry throughout Europe; a bard who captivated poets and conquerors alike. Napoleon never travelled without Cesarotti's Italian version of 'Ossian' and it solaced him on his way to St Helena. The imperial apartments in the Tuileries were decorated with huge murals depicting 'Ossianic' scenes, which included the bard himself welcoming the ghosts of Napoleon's soldiers. Now it seems to me that 'Ossian' is the poetic equivalent of Jacobitism and the '45.

This is why I have insisted on its importance for Scotland. We live in a mercantile age, which is rapidly becoming an industrial one. The progress of our manufactories is wonderful, and must add – has already added – to the comfort of individual life and the wealth of the nation, but if this is all we subscribe to then we shall be diminished.

I have seen the walls of Balclutha, but they were desolate. The fox looked out from the windows, the rank grass of the wall waved round her head. Raise the song of mourning, O bards, over the land of strangers. They have but fallen before us, for one day we must fall. Why dost thou build the hall, son of the winged days? Thou lookest from thy towers today; yet a few years, and the blast of the desert comes; it howls in thy empty court, and whistles round thy half-worn shield. Let the blast of the desert come! we shall be renowned in our day . . .

That Romantic and melancholy music moved all Europe. If the day comes when it no longer does so, if the day comes when we forget the Prince and the tragedy of Culloden, if we consign Flodden, and further back the Wars of Independence, to a sort of dry as dust History, of no significance, then our own courts will be empty, desolate as the walls of Balclutha.

18

Waterloo and Paris, 1815
(written 1830)

They have taken to keeping things, which they think disturbing, from me, but they cannot conceal what I would wish, at certain moments, to hide from myself: that I am deteriorating fast. My memory is not what it was, and I have had at least one apoplectic fit. Work, which used to be play to me, has now become drudgery. I grind out my new novel, *Count Robert of Paris*, doggedly, but with no joy in the enterprise. Indeed, almost my sole satisfaction is to think of the inroads I have made on my debts. Let me live to struggle but two or three years more, and then, all will be well, honour redeemed, and I may dwindle to the grave.

Meanwhile this summer's new revolution in France has aroused old fears, though at the moment it would seem as if the former Duc d'Orleans, who has assumed the title of King of the French (not France!), has matters in hand and under control. Yet I cannot help thinking that only a few months after the First Revolution broke out in 1789, something of the same sort might have been said. The truth is that when Demos has been stirred from slumber, he is a rare brute to pacify, a thought that alas cannot be got into a Whig head, the absence of which accounts for the manner in which our own Whigs are agitating the very fabric of the State to achieve their own ends. Well, you require the resolution of the old Earl of Angus to bell-the-cat that is democracy.

The old Bourbon king, Charles X, whom I knew during his previous exile when he was called the Comte d'Artois, has been foolish, but I believe the French would have been wise to thole his foolishness. Once start tinkering with Constitutions, and you have opened up a game which the De'il himself delights to play. Our Government, I am glad to say, has invited him to take up again his old quarters in Holyroodhouse – a bitter home-coming for him, I fear. To my distress this proposal was greeted with hostility in Edinburgh, a mood engendered, I believe, by an ungenerous article in Jeffrey's *Edinburgh Review*. I thought it my duty to respond briskly, and appeal to the better feeling of those who had so long been my fellow-citizens. I therefore despatched a letter to James Ballantyne's newspaper, writing as one who had recently left his native city, never to return as a permanent resident; and I recalled that 'the Frenchman Melinet, in mentioning the refuge afforded by Edinburgh to Henry VI of England, in his distress, records it as the most hospitable town in Europe. It is a testimony', I said, 'to be proud of, and sincerely do I hope there is little danger of forfeiting it upon the present occasion.'

I believe my words had some effect; at any rate His Majesty thanked me for my intervention on his behalf.

I could not but reflect, considering his woeful position, on how I had seen him, proudly restored to France, with his brother Louis XVIII, in 1815, and, doing so, recall the expedition I made with Alexander Pringle of Whytbank, Robert Bruce – both fellow members of the Faculty of Advocates – and my young kinsman John Scott of Gala, to the Field of Waterloo, and then Paris, less than two months after the great victory had been won. Happy days, when I had health and vigour and a desire, an insatiable curiosity, to see everything that was to be seen.

Waterloo made an ineffaceable impression on me. I delighted in plotting the arrangement of the battle, and in collecting souvenirs from the terrible field. Yet even while my heart throbbed with pride as I contemplated the courage and glory of my countrymen, even while I enthusiastically garnered every anecdote and memory that came my way of the great battle, I felt my old boyish enthusiasm for war seep away; and though I have from time to time rekindled it while describing military prowess in my novels, the sight of that field compelled me to feel the misery and brutality of war, far outmatching its splendour. What a business it is that a poor lad from Ettrick or Yarrow should bayonet a peasant boy from Gascony all because a Napoleon must needs be a great man! War is glorious only when seen at a distance; the reality is blood, terror, the screams of the dying, confusion, waste. Of course there is magnificence too, for nothing so surely tests the quality of a man. But now, in tremulous age, I cannot but ask myself whether such tests are necessary. Is war, or the desire for war, an ineradicable part of man's nature?

The moral questions it raises cannot be easily answered. There are moments in a nation's life when there seems to be no alternative. 'Wha would be a traitor knave, Wha sae base as live a slave?' And yet, I find myself wondering whether my Quaker ancestor may not have had the wisdom of it. But if so, are good men to submit to evil? I have observed that a sombre look crosses the Duke of Wellington's face when he talks of battle.

It was strange to breakfast at an inn on the outskirts of the Forest of Soignes, where the Duke himself had slept the stormy night before the battle. It was near there that his gallant quartermaster, Colonel Sir William de Lancey, recently married to the daughter of an Edinburgh acquaintance of mine, fell, struck by a cannon-ball; then to see the tree, beside which Wellington surveyed some stages of the struggle, also scorched by cannon. The battlefield itself still gave horrid evidence of the fight. I was shown a sort of precipitous gravel-pit into which our heavy dragoons had forced a great number of Napoleon's cuirassiers who lay there, a still living and struggling mass of men and horses, piled together in common destruction. The shattered state of the neighbouring farmhouses also offered vivid testimony to the desolation caused by war, and around the little chateau of Hougoumont, the stench of putrefying corpses showed us that the burial of the slain had been but imperfectly and hastily performed.

Yet parts of the ground were already being ploughed by the Flemish peasants – living proof of how the work of the world continues beyond the mischief that men do – and I consoled myself for the evidence of cruel waste by the reflection that the corn which must soon wave there would remove from the face of nature the melancholy traces of war, and so tranquillity would be restored, and even the dead might lie easy in quiet earth. When Byron visited the battlefield the following year, this transformation had been completed, and he acknowledged it in one of the most beautiful of his verses, which I cannot deny myself the pleasure of recalling:

> There have been tears and breaking hearts for thee,
> And mine were nothing had I such to give;
> But when I stood beneath the fresh green tree,
> Which living waves where thou didst cease to live,
> And saw around me the wide field revive
> With fruits and fertile promise, and the Spring

Come forth her work of gladness to contrive,
With all her reckless birds up on the wing,
I turned from all she brought to those she could not bring ...

As my survey of the battlefield continued, I found myself victim to a confused admixture of emotions, such as, I believe, the contemplation of war and the field of strife must provoke in anyone who lays claim to intelligence and sensibility. On the one hand I was lost in admiration of man's courage and ability to endure. On the other I longed for the day when the prophecy of Isaiah shall be fulfilled, and 'nation shall not lift sword against nation, neither shall they learn war any more.'

'O house of Jacob, come ye, and let us walk in the light of the Lord.'

That evening, returned to Brussels, our hostess, Mrs Gordon, presented me with a manuscript collection of French songs found on the battlefield. It still bore traces of blood and clay, and I could not but reflect that it had probably been the possession of a young French officer who – the nature of the songs persuaded me – young and gay and caring little for the merits of the quarrel on which he was engaged, perhaps considered the war which was to determine the fate of Europe as but an agreeable, natural, and animating exchange for the pleasures of Paris, which he should find as a result all the sweeter on his return. But that was not to be, and I was saddened by the contrast between the light and airy quality of the songs, the hours of mirth and ease which they promised, with the circumstances in which the booklet was discovered, trampled in the blood of the writer, and then cast aside by those who had come to despoil and strip him on the field where he lay. I fancied that he was a flower of a French forest, one of the brave, who 'foucht aye the foremost', and who now, like the sons of Ettrick and Yarrow, 'lay cauld in the clay'.

Of all the remains of Waterloo which came into my possession, I count none more precious than this, or more moving in the involuntary associations it must arouse.

We progressed to Paris following the route of the victorious armies, amid scenes of wretchedness and devastation, for, while our British troops behaved with discipline, dignity and humanity, the Prussians took a terrible revenge for the hardships which Napoleon had inflicted on their country. Meanwhile disbanded French regiments were roaming the countryside, dirty, despairing, and resembling *banditti* rather than soldiers. If war's rattle and the groans of the dying were now behind us, all that we saw bore witness to its awful consequences. Outside an inn, one day, I saw a middle-aged Frenchman, in a tattered uniform, sitting on a bench, flanked by a British grenadier with a glass of brandy and water, and a German soldier smoking a pipe. They none of them spoke, and the Frenchman looked from one to the other in a manner which indicated his incredulity or incomprehension of how he came to be there with such companions.

We could not enter Valenciennes, which was still held by a French garrison whose commander refused to surrender: an empty gesture of defiance, though a spirited one, which however laid the town's inhabitants open to the threat of a Prussian bombardment. So we proceeded to Chantilly, through miles of magnificent forest, but the great palace of the Prince de Conde had been destroyed by the Parisian mob in the early stages of the Revolution; only the stables remained, which were of a magnificence that gave some idea of what the palace must have been. The stables in their turn were now given over to the Prussians who were engaged in wrecking them as if in calculated insult. I could not but reflect on what the emotions of the great Conde, whose grandson had built these stables, but who had himself led so many invading armies into Germany, would have been if he had been told that these Prussian vandals were marching unopposed on Paris, holding in their disposal the fate of the House of Bourbon and the Crown of France.

As so often on this journey, Johnson's great lines echoed in my head:

> Yet Reason frowns on War's unequal Game,
> Where wasted nations raise a single Name,
> And mortgag'd States their Grandsires Wreaths regret
> From Age to Age in everlasting Debt;
> Wreaths which at last the dear-bought Right convey
> To rust on medals, or on Stones decay.

Or, as Shirley put it:

> The Glories of our Blood and State
> Are Shadows, not substantial Things;
> There is no Armour against Fate,
> Death lays his icy Hand on Kings.

I could not, while surveying the ruins of Chantilly, but think of Napoleon himself, so recently returned in triumph to the Tuileries, now consigned to a little rock in the remote Atlantic; the most ambitious and audacious of men, now reduced to vain imaginings, profound and unassuageable regret, but whether – ever – for the misery he has brought on men, who can tell? I only pray, now, that in the six years he was compelled to pass, wasting away, on St Helena, he at least vouchsafed repentance to the Almighty, even though he could never bring himself to express that in conversation with those around him. To them he sighed of his lost glory, his defeated ambitions; spoke of pity for his own condition, never for those he had ruined, and whose lives he had treated as if they were his own insensible possessions. Of his genius, his transcendent qualities, I have no doubt; but what is one to make of genius which expresses itself in utter indifference to the sufferings it imposes on mankind? Yet, if I encountered a Napoleon, two hundred years back in time, would I not have been so dazzled by the glamour of his achievements, extraordinary as they were, as to be blind to the cost? Is there, I wonder now, any difference between what the Emperor demanded of the French and what Prince Charles Edward called for from his Highlanders; and did not the Prince bring ruin on them as Napoleon did on all Europe?

And have I been guilty, by means of my writings, of encouraging men to see the glory of war, and to forget its price?

That is a thought I find painful to entertain.

I trust that the price has always been implicit in what I have written. At any rate I believe I have never concealed the manner in which commitment to a cause, leading as it so often does to fanaticism, is used by men to justify the most barbarous cruelties, and indifference to the tender and natural impulses of humanity. And how much worse it is when men are driven by a conviction of their own utter righteousness, as the most extreme and loathsome of the Covenanters were. How closely nobility and virtue may be joined with a repellent harshness! I have often observed that men rarely act so vilely as when they are buoyed up by the conviction that the Lord, or destiny – which is perhaps another name for the same idea – is guiding them. In like manner, *Liberty* has so often been made the pretext for crushing its own best and most ingenuous supporters, that I am always prepared to expect the most tyrannical proceedings from those who boast themselves democrats – aye, and the most cruel persecutions from those who claim liberty for their own tender conscience. The vilest deeds are often performed by those who profess the most noble purposes, and it is one of the most wretched features of our existence that it is so much easier to inflict pain than to create pleasure; moreover, the infliction of pain, if presented as a duty executed in deference to some high ideal, easily becomes a pleasure in itself. The witch-finders enjoyed hunting their wretched victims – and so did the Spanish inquisitors; and their consciousness of their own virtue gave an irresistible zest to the enterprise, like the touch of vinegar a salad requires.

When we arrived in Paris we lodged at the Hotel de Bourbon by the Tuileries. We found the city one great garrison of foreign troops, where challenges were issued by soldiers on guard duty in a dozen languages at least. The sight of our British troops caused me to reflect that not since 1436 when the armies of Henry VI withdrew from Paris had an English drum been heard in the city.

We were fortunate to have the good services of the distinguished traveller and archaeologist, M. Jean-Baptiste le Chevalier, who, I was pleased to discover, retained many happy memories of the long visit he had made to Edinburgh as a travelling tutor in the years before the war, when he had been on friendly terms with Professor Dugald Stewart and Professor Andrew Dalzell, both of whom had been so unfortunate as to be required to instruct me. Under his amiable guidance we surveyed the magnificent galleries of the Louvre, where Napoleon had collected artistic spoils from all

Europe. These works of art were now as was proper to be restored to their rightful owners, but I was grateful to the defeated Emperor for having made it possible for me to see such a remarkable collection. Nothing impressed me more than a Romantic masterpiece by the great Neapolitan painter Salvator Rosa; it was entitled *The Witch of Endor*, and its sulphurous gloom was magnificently picturesque.

The mood in the French capital was uneasy. One could not but be aware of the resentful shame of a proud nation, so long accustomed to glory, now crushed beneath the heel of its enemies. The conviction that the Bourbon king was being restored by allied arms against the wishes of his subjects was too pervasive to be ignored, and boded ill for the restored dynasty. Meanwhile, many who had suffered in the Royalist cause expressed their indignation at the retention of those whom they considered traitors, such as M. de Talleyrand and even more conspicuously the police chief and former Terrorist, Fouche, whom Napoleon had created Duke of Otranto. His presence in the ministry must offend sensitive nostrils; yet it was justified, if only because none knew better where the bodies were hidden. I did not believe however that he would long hold his post, once the King was firmly back on the throne; and this indeed proved to be the case.

I was honoured to be presented to the Duke of Wellington. The Duchess of Buccleuch had kindly furnished me with a letter of introduction, but since I spent much time in Paris in the company of one of his bravest officers, General Sir John Malcolm, the letter was scarcely necessary, though this did not diminish my gratitude to the Duchess. Of Wellington, concerning whom I have already written in this memoir, it is here sufficient to say that he was as remarkable as I expected, and that his outstanding quality was his complete self-possession. He seemed to me to offer an excellent illustration of the truth that men of genius are not only fit but much fitter for the business of the world than those less gifted, providing always that they will give their talents fair play by curbing them with application. I was never in the company of a man with such a noticing eye and such sound judgement. He treated me with a kindness and consideration which I regard as the highest distinction ever conferred on me.

At a dinner of Lord Cathcart's I was also introduced to the Czar Alexander. It so happened that I was wearing the blue-and-red uniform of the Selkirkshire Lieutenancy, and, seeing my lameness, the Czar's first question, delivered in a very elegant French, was in what action I had been wounded. I replied that my lameness was the result of a natural infirmity.

'Oh,' said he, 'I thought Lord Cathcart mentioned that you have served.'

Seeing that the Earl looked somewhat embarrassed, I felt I could not deny the matter.

'Yes, indeed, Your Majesty,' I said, 'I have served, in a manner of speaking, but only in the yeomanry cavalry, which is a home force, resembling the Prussian Landswehr.'

'Under what commander?' he asked, this no doubt being the stock response of royalty to such an admission.

'Under M. le Chevalier Rae,' I said, wondering if my old friend would recognize himself under such a designation.

'Were you ever engaged in action?' was the next question, strengthening my suspicion that conversation with royalty generally must consist of question-and-answer sessions.

'In some slight actions. Sire,' I said, keeping a straight face with the more difficulty when I saw Lord Cathcart ready to break into a fit of Homeric laughter. 'Such as the Battle of the Cross-Causeway and a skirmish at Moredun-Mill.'

Fortunately, before his Imperial Highness could probe further, and perhaps demand of me which enemy forces had been engaged there – an honest answer to which would have surprised him, I fear, and lowered me still further in his estimation – he was apprised that another was waiting to be introduced, and I was dismissed.

It would be absurd on such a brief acquaintance to pretend to have acquired any sense of the Czar's complicated and difficult character, which was to give rise to wild speculation on the occasion of his sudden death some ten years later; but watching him through the evening, I had the sense of a man of fine sensibility unhappy in the role he was compelled to play. I was aware of course that, like our own James IV, he was reputed to be racked with guilt for the supine (at best) part that he had played in acquiescing in the assassination of his father, the Czar Paul; and I had the impression of a haunted spirit. My knowledge, too, of how he had been first dazzled, then – as it were – seduced, and finally revolted by Napoleon added to the interest with which I observed him.

A few nights later I dined with Lord Castlereagh and the Duke's aide-de-camp Colonel Stanhope. The talk turned on the Czar – 'the imperial dandy', as Stanhope called him. I remarked on the impression I had taken away, and said that he looked like a man who had not only seen a ghost, but lived with one.

'I should not be surprised,' Castlereagh replied. 'The Czar is possessed of a most delicate sensibility. Besides, we all know that such things exist. I must tell you, Mr Scott, that I have encountered a wandering spectre, in a house in County Limerick where I was stationed as a young officer.'

The account he gave of his supernatural experience was not in itself remarkable, for I have heard countless such stories from the old men and women of Selkirkshire, but it was remarkable coming from a man celebrated for his good sense, and sometimes censured for his lack of imagination. Yet I had no doubt that he placed an absolute trust in the authenticity of his experience.

My surprise redoubled when Colonel Stanhope, with an apologetic cough, confessed that he too had seen a ghost, which investigation proved could not have been a natural occurrence.

Like Castlereagh, Colonel Stanhope died some years later by his own hand. They were both men of sound sense and credibility; I tremble when any friend relates visionary experiences of this kind, and even more so at the thought that I have undergone such myself in recent years.

Curiously, the morning after this supper-party, when their confessions were fresh in my mind, M. le Chevalier asked me if I had ever heard that Napoleon was said to be haunted by a familiar spirit described only as 'l'Homme Rouge'. 'It is reported that it appeared to him at Vilna,' M. le Chevalier said, 'to warn him against the projected invasion of Russia, and also, they say, before Waterloo. For my part, I am sceptical, not, you understand, mon cher Scott, that I assert that there are no such beings, but that I question the way in which they are so often said to appear to men of power to warn them against a particular course of action. I believe it is certain that they are reported only subsequent to the disaster which they are said to have predicted.' This is undoubtedly true, and I made use of this idea in *The Bride of Lammermoor*; yet I felt it uncanny that, in writing *Waverley* only the previous year, I had supplied Fergus MacIvor with such a spirit, the 'grey spectre' which appeared to him on the eve of the battle which was to lead to his capture and execution at Carlisle. But it is one thing to do that in fiction for a Gaelic chief, another to believe it of a man like Napoleon.

It was evident even in my month in Paris so soon after his defeat that he was already receding into legend and myth, a process which has since gone very much further with the poems of Beranger and the memoirs of his time in St Helena. But even then I recall a conversation after the execution of General la Badoyère for treason. One lady talked of this as *un horreur*, an atrocity unparalleled in the annals of France.

'Did Bonaparte never order such executions?' I asked.

'The Emperor? Never,' was the emphatic reply.

'But what of the shooting of the Duc d'Enghien at Vincennes, Madam?'

'*Ah! Parlez-moi d'Adam et d'Eve.*'

So soon can iniquity be swept aside when partisan feelings are aroused.

Every step we took in Paris seemed alive with historical association. We visited the site of the old Temple, where the unfortunate Louis XVI and his Queen were imprisoned in the months before their execution. Our guide there gave further evidence of Napoleon's superstition, for he asserted that the Emperor had ordered the Temple's destruction on account of a presentiment that he himself might one day share the fate of the unfortunate Louis, a presentiment which, if he indeed felt it, he forestalled effectively enough by having the building pulled down.

Napoleon certainly in conversation generally affected to despise superstition, and was quick to mock it in others. Yet he had undoubtedly a share of it in his own bosom, and he had strange and visionary ideas concerning his own destiny. Well, I can scarcely reprove him, for while I would deny any such conviction myself, I have been aware more often than I would care to confess in conversation that, when I write with my greatest fluency, I feel myself to be in the possession of some being other than myself, over which I can exercise but little control.

Before leaving Paris we visited Malmaison, where the Empress Josephine had lived after her divorce, and died soon after Napoleon's first abdication, and the Emperor's own favourite residence of St-Cloud; its gardens so enchanted me that when, a few years later, I required a garden scene in *Kenilworth*, I drew partly on my memories of this afternoon passed there, and partly on the poetry of Tasso and Ariosto, which had delighted me since my youth.

It saddens me now to think of these days in Paris, though I have not found the actual re-creation of them painful. But the contrast between then and now is as stark as the two portraits which Hamlet compelled his mother to gaze upon, and does not bear consideration.

On our way through London, I had my last meeting with Byron, though I had no reason then to suppose we should not speak again. Young Gala was intoxicated by his beauty, though he deplored to me the bitterness which he discerned in his talk. It was true that though he listened with close attention to my account of our experiences, and took great interest in all which I had to relate of Waterloo, he did not pretend to anything but disappointment at the restoration of the Bourbons, and could not share my unmixed pleasure in a feat of British arms which had led to such a conclusion. Yet the tenderness with which he spoke of his cousin, Major Howard, who had fallen there, spoke of his true nature; even more beautifully expressed in the lines of mourning for Howard in the third canto of *Childe Harold*.

Once, certainly, what might have been thought bitterness broke out. I recounted the story of a gallant officer who had been shot in the head while conveying a message to the Duke, and of how he had staggered on, completed his duty, and then fallen. Byron knew the young man – perhaps – I cannot now recall – they had been schoolfellows. 'Ha!' he exclaimed. 'I daresay he would do as well as most people without his head – it was never of much use to him.' This rather shocked young Gala, but seemed to me an expression of Byron's refreshing freedom from cant. It also pleased me as calling to mind the remark of the old woman concerning the unfortunate Duke of Hamilton, executed by order of Cromwell after he had led the Engagers to defeat in Charles I's cause at Preston: 'Folks said his heid wasna a very gude ane, but for a' that, it was a sair loss to him, puir gentleman.'

'And I suppose, in truth that could be said of any of us,' Byron smiled. 'I know there have been occasions when I would willingly have stopped the working of my head, even if I had left it on my shoulders; but I suppose I would have regretted even that.'

'Well,' I said, 'regrets, fears and wishes are often fair mixed. Did you ever hear the story of the auld wife at Carlisle in the Prince's year? When the Jacobites descended on the town, the word went round that they were no better than savage barbarians – as bad as the Cossacks, we might say now – and that the town would be given over to looting and rapine. So the auld wife locked herself safe in her chamber. But time passed and nothing happened. So, at last, she pops her head out of the window and cries out, "Pray, tell me, when is the ravishing to begin?"'

'And vowing she would ne'er consent, consented,' Byron laughed.

So the afternoon ran on, with Byron again, as I had seen him before, merry as a kitten.

When we took our leave, I said that I hoped that I might see him at Abbotsford before long, though I warned him that the accommodation was not of the finest, for it was still a building-site.

'I hope I may,' he said. 'Nothing could give me greater pleasure than to be your guest in your ain keep. But . . . temple-haunting martlets, as I daresay you have, who can tell? I have a presentiment . . . no, that is foolishness. I may however go abroad again before long. England confines me finer than a coffin, and my affairs are in such disorder – "sic a sotter" as my old nurse used to say – that I really do not know.'

'Try the air of Scotland, my Lord,' Gala said. 'It's caller air, and we'd be blithe to see you in the Borders.'

'You cannot think', he said, 'how often I dream of Deeside where I spent my youth. I was born half a Scot and bred a whole one. One last thing, before we part . . . I am about to become a father. If the child is a boy, will you stand godfather, and consent that I name him Walter?'

'Nothing could give me more pleasure.'

He embraced me impulsively, in a manner French, Italian or Greek, rather than Scots – and certainly not in the chilly English fashion which depressed his spirits.

My last memory of him is of a smile that lit up that beautiful countenance, and yet left his eye melancholy.

He never paid that visit to Abbotsford. I wish he had. If he had returned from Greece . . . but that, like so much now, doesn't bear thinking on.

19

Abbotsford: Its Building and Significance, 1830

Horace asked only for 'a little piece of land, with a garden, near the house a spring of living water, and a small wood besides'. When Maecenas granted him his farm in the Sabine Hills, he asked 'no more, Mercury, but this: make it mine for ever'.

Nothing runs deeper in our nature than the desire for a bit land of our ain, and Horace could not have loved his Sabine farm more, or more truly, than I have loved Abbotsford.

Some have censured me, I know, for what they call my lust for land, and others have thought the zeal with which I added to the little hundred acres, that was all that came with the farm-cottage I bought by the banks of the Tweed, a sign of craziness. They did not understand. I had no lust for possessions as such, and had I never made my fortune could have been content with a but-and-ben and a small piece of ground. But having opened for myself, as I found, a seemingly inexhaustible treasure-house, I could not deny myself the opportunity to make dreams reality.

When my crash came, and my world was in ruins, it was my greatest fear that I would be dislodged from my Sabine farm. It even crossed my mind that Abbotsford had played the part of

Delilah, and that, in drawing so freely from the firms of Ballantyne and Constable, I had allowed her, as it were, to deprive me of my strength as the Philistine woman did Samson. But these were the cheating thoughts of delirium.

My ambition was, I think, a simple one, and not ignoble. I wanted to demonstrate, first to my own satisfaction, and then to the world's, that it was aye possible in this harsh mercantile age, when value is always to be measured – aye, and in pounds, shillings and pence – to make of life something finer, to gather around me family, friends and dependants, between whom relations should be measured in a different scale, not one of coinage, but rather of humanity and virtue. Without withdrawing from the world, which I could never have done and which would have been foolishness in one circumstanced as I was, I sought to make a different world around me, one in which men and women would be valued for what they were, and not for what they were deemed to be worth.

Now, in my decrepitude, I take a slow and painful turn around the place, and do not believe that in this, my chief endeavour, I have failed, though the world may think me a failure in other respects. I look on my trees, and believe my oaks will outlast the literary laurels with which I have been crowned; and find that thought good. There are few things to compare with the exquisite delight of the tree planter. He is like a painter laying his colours on the canvas; at every moment he sees his effects realized. There is no art or occupation that I know to be compared to it; it is full of past, present, and future enjoyment. I look back to when the land around me was a bare heath, and now I see thousands of trees, all of which I know as I knew the sheep on my grandfather's farm of Sandyknowe so long ago. There is no end to it, it goes on from day to day, year to year, and my trees will grow more beautiful and splendid long after I am in the grave. The planter is a little God, creating his private Eden. I have never cared for farming my land. The pleasure of seeing my cattle grow is cancelled out by the necessity of killing the poor beasts, which I hate to do. But with trees, you exercise such a benevolent command over nature; the writing of novels and poems is a shallow pleasure compared to that.

How Charlotte used to be bored by my rhapsodies on the subject! How I wish she was still here to reprove me!

The house itself grew almost insensibly. It was never a fully formed intention that it should be what it has become; and yet when my Grand Babylon was complete, it pleased me to think that I had made a sort of Romance in stone, built in the style of an old Scottish manor house; and yet with none of the chill and sense of foreboding that such houses often convey.

It pleased me too to throw my grounds open to the people of the neighbourhood. Nothing could have induced me to put up boards declaring them private and threatening prosecution. I saw to it only that some walks in the immediate vicinity of the house were reserved for the ladies, that they might not be alarmed by rude strangers. But for the rest, anyone who chose might wander over my land at will; I believe that was the good old way; and I often wonder how much of Burns's inspiration was due to his being able to ramble through the woods of Ballochmyle when he was but a ragged callant.

Perhaps because I passed so many hours alone, in solitary elaboration of my fancies, talking only to Jeannie Deans or the Laird of Monkbarns – listening to him, rather – or hearing Redgauntlet deplore the manners of the age and the death of loyalty – I delighted in the company of family and friends whenever I was free of my desk. Charlotte sometimes complained that we might as well keep an inn as Abbotsford, except, she said, that it is the hosts,

Scott, and not the guests that pay the reckoning. But she always managed. Once when we heard that Prince Leopold of Saxe-Coburg, the Regent's son-in-law, was passing through Selkirk, where it behoved me as Sheriff to greet him, it occurred to me that if he intended to pass on to Melrose as I suspected, it would be civil to invite him to call at Abbotsford. I mentioned this to Charlotte as she was lying in bed in the morning. She emitted a scream.

'What have we to give him?'

'Oh, wine and cake, nothing more, that will serve very well.'

'Cake! Where am I to get cake?'

So I pointed out that his visit was very improbable, and, that being so, he could not expect us to have made great provision for an invitation extended on the spur of the moment, and – I insisted – probably declined. So, somewhat mollified, she agreed to come into Selkirk with me to catch a glimpse of the Prince. As it happened, he said he could not see Melrose, but would very much like to call at Abbotsford. So Charlotte turned Merse forayer, until with a long face she said that the town could provide nothing but a bit of cold lamb. Yet, when the Prince arrived, she had ready for him a collation of salmon, blackcock and partridges – and I never learned how she contrived it.

The installation of my old friend William Laidlaw at Kaeside, and of my still older friend Colonel Adam Fergusson – still older for we had been school-fellows – at Tofthills, which was now re-named, at the request of his sisters, Huntly Burn, added to the pleasure of life at Abbotsford, for in the country there are few things more important than congenial neighbours. Adam had but recently retired from the army on half-pay after serving in the Peninsula. After a long intermission of friendship, owing to our being in different parts of the world, he had written to me to say how delighted his troop had been by a reading of *The Lady of the Lake*, which was gratifying, though to me improbable.

The greatest day of the year was when we held the Abbotsford Hunt. This was commonly celebrated on the 28th October, young Walter's birthday, and to it I invited all the lairds of the neighbourhood and my tenants, any other farmers or yeomen I esteemed, and indeed anyone I cared to have. We were never less than thirty in number, and I have known more than forty sit to the supper that succeeded the Hunt. The Hunt itself was followed either on the braes above Cauldshiels Loch, or on the moors of the Gala estate. In the old manner we chased the hare, and there were few years that we did not return with at least one hare for every cottager at Abbotsford. It makes me sigh to think of the joy of that bodily exertion, for I now have to be held on a fat old pony that cannot muster even a trot; and if we had a hunt I would be obliged to follow it in a carriage as best I could. But this good custom was intermitted, like so many others, on account of my financial misfortunes and declining health. Yet I can still enjoy it in retrospect, and as I do so, the songs that were sung of the evening rise up and sound again in my memory.

The dinner or rather supper, for there was nothing formal about it, was on a scale suited to men who had passed the day in the saddle. The auld dominie, George Thompson, who had been my sons' tutor before they went to school, and whom I had retained as a species of chaplain – for, poor man, his peculiarities were such that he could scarcely hope to hold a charge of souls, virtuous and honest man as he was, but with something simple and unformed to him – was commissioned to say the Grace. Though his wooden leg had prevented him from participating in the Hunt, you would not have thought so to hear the Grace he gave us – one 'as long as my arms' in Burns's phrase. He habitually began by offering thanks to the Almighty who out of his bountiful providence had given man dominion over all the beasts of the field and fowls of the air, and who maun therefore be muckle pleased to see with what zeal and consideration that dominion had been exercised the day. He then, casting an eye, from which the signs of a more than healthy appetite were not absent, proceeded to enumerate the dishes on the table, calling on us to witness how each one testified to the Lord's tender care for his creation. Next he expatiated on the blessings that individual members of the company had, to his certain knowledge, received at the Lord's hand since we were last gathered together. In short, as I said on one occasion, he gave us everything but the 'View Halloo', and indeed I am not certain that that was altogether lacking. The first year we held the Hunt, the dominie's long grace aroused a degree of impatience among some of those assembled; but, with each year that passed, it became established more and more firmly as an institution that was an integral part of the proceedings; until eventually, I believe, the regular attenders would have sacrificed one of their favourite dishes rather than have lost the Dominie's invocation; which offers testimony not only to the humour of mankind but to the effect of the dominie's essential goodness.

At last he desisted, and all were able to turn their attention to the viands. These were of the robust sort – none of your French sauces and kickshawses, no delicate fricassees or 'made dishes', such as a cook may produce to demonstrate his skill rather than to satisfy hungry appetites. There was aye a baron of beef at one end of the table and a noble piece of salted silverside or brisket at the other. There were tureens of hare soup, and hotch-potch, and an assortment of fowl – geese, turkeys, chicken and wild duck – both teal and mallard. There was a singed sheep's head, which I regard as a necessary feature of a country dinner, and which is in any case a dish that only a delicate-stomached fool would decline; and we could not omit the great chieftain o' the pudden race, the haggis. Then for the second course, blackcock and other moorfowl would make their appearance, supported by black puddings and mealy puddings, and great pyramids of pancakes. There was claret for those who wished it, but, in the rural manner, ale – brown, nutty, sweet and strong – was the favourite drink, supported, in the best fashion, by quaichs of Glenlivet. The port decanter made a formal but perfunctory circuit or two, but was soon supplanted by cries for hot punch, in the concoction of which, at my request, James Hogg took the lead, acting as manufacturer, taster, and master of ceremonies.

It does a man, now condemned to toast and soda water, good to recall such an occasion.

Then the hum of conversation was broken into by a call for music, and Adam Fergusson might give a lead with 'Hey, Johnnie Cope' or some other Jacobite song; my old friend Bob Shortreed would reply with the old ballad of 'Dick o' the Cow'. His son Thomas excelled in the macabre ballad of 'The Twa Corbies', while James Hogg set the company aroar and beating time with their spoons by his rendition of 'The Kye Come Hame'. At some point in the evening Willie Laidlaw would be persuaded to cast his modesty aside and sing his tender ballad 'Lucy's Flittin' which brought tears to many an eye unaccustomed to them. Johnnie Ballantyne, while he was yet with us, would cheer the company with his incomparable 'Cobbler of Kelso'. The Melrose doctor sang 'The Minstrel Boy', and sea-shanties jostled with Border ballads, while in the intervals my piper John of Skye sounded his warlike or melancholy notes. So the evening wore on, in the perfection of good fellowship – and indeed I do not recall a single quarrel breaking out at the dinner of the

Abbotsford Hunt, though several of the company might be men quick to take imagined offence on other such convivial nights. At last some farmer, who had perhaps twenty miles to travel, would begin to mutter that his wife and dochters would be getting 'sair anxious' about his crossing of the fords that lay between him and his home. So a *deoch-an-doruis* was called for of the best Glenlivet, and the party began to break up, though it was not uncommon for some of the guests to have several more stirrup-cups than they had stirrups; and on one occasion, James Hogg, having taken a wager that he could loup on to his horse's back without assistance from stirrups, louped so briskly that he went clean over his wall-eyed pony, and broke his nose on landing. Yet, *mirabile dictu*, I never heard of one who failed to find his way home.

And one of the greatest compliments I ever received came by way of a farmer's wife who told me that her husband on his return home said, even as he crossed the threshold, 'Ailie, my woman, I'm ready for my bed – and oh lass, I wish I could sleep for a towmont, for there's only ae thing in this warld that's worth living for, and that's the Abbotsford Hunt' – a tribute I would rather have had than all the eulogia bestowed upon my books.

It was my pleasure, as I conceived it also my duty, to keep all the traditional festivals of the year. So we aye had a 'kirn' or 'harvest home' at the end of November, when I gave a supper and a dance to all the peasantry, their friends and kindred, on the estate. There would come as many as the barn would hold, and they would dance the night away, with many a reel, and fortified by ale, hot toddy, and, for the more delicate of the ladies, copious pots of tea.

Christmas I liked to keep as a family occasion, which we celebrated with more gusto than this feast is commonly accorded in our dour Presbyterian Scotland. Nothing to my mind exhibits more clearly the narrow and chilly temper of the Reformers of the sixteenth century than their hostility to the old feasts of the Church. It seems to me that the refusal to celebrate Christmas, when the Son of God became flesh, and Easter, when he suffered that we might be redeemed, is to deny our religion that mystery which deepens our appreciation of the power and benevolence of the Almighty, and the sense of wonder which his works should arouse.

The end of the year, which in Scotland is known as 'the daft days', we celebrated in traditional style. I would have thought it uncanny not to welcome the New Year in the midst of my family, and among old friends, with the time-honoured *het pint*. But I derived even greater pleasure from the visit made to me by all the children on the estate on the last morning of the Old Year when:

> The cottage bairns syng blythe and gay
> At the ha' door for hogmanay

And I would reward them for their coming and their expression of good wishes by small gifts of cake and bannock and other sweetmeats, and a few coins a-piece – more, I daresay, than some of the poorest among them ever had in their hand on any other day of the year, though few, alas, for all that. The good sense and dignity they displayed on such occasions fortified me in my impression that the members of the Scotch labouring classes are, in their natural state, among the best, most intelligent, and kind-hearted of human beings.

There recurs to me now an odd thought that came to me one frosty New Year's morning when I was taking a turn around my grounds. It is said that the whole human frame in all its parts and divisions is gradually, but perpetually, in the act of decaying and being renewed. It would be a curious timepiece that could indicate to us the very moment when this slow and imperceptible change had been accomplished, so that no atom of the original person who had started out on life's journey now remained; but instead there existed a different person having apparently the same appearance, the same limbs and trunk, the same countenance (though bearing marks of age), even, in his own estimation, the same consciousness, but who was yet utterly changed. It seemed to me then to be a singular thought – a singular sensation to be at once another and the same.

Now it is less the singularity than the reality of this which strikes me. To the world no doubt, I still appear to be Walter Scott, Bart, of Abbotsford, the Author of *Waverley*, and all that; in my heart I know that that being is no more. He has vanished utterly, and the wreck that now waits, with an impatience he can sometimes scarce control, is another, and inferior, person.

I do not like that thought. There is an uncomfortable arrogance to it, and an evasiveness, as if I would escape judgement by pleading an alibi.

Yesterday, I had myself driven to Dryburgh Abbey to sit a half-hour by Charlotte's grave, and to wonder, tranquilly – with a tranquillity indeed that I have not often known in latter days – how long it would be before I too should find rest there. On the way to Dryburgh and on the way back we stopped at that high point of the road, where the view extends over the lovely winding river to the distant Cheviots. On the outward journey the beauty of the landscape pricked my heart, and I felt a deep and powerful reluctance ever to take leave of it. It is a scene I have known since boyhood, and I have found nothing more beautiful though I have travelled much. But on the return journey that reluctance had died away, for I perceived that this landscape had become part of me, and that even in the grave I could never be separated from it. This may seem fanciful to anyone who happens on this memoir; and yet all I can say is that it came to me with the conviction of utter certainty.

If I have done anything good in my life, Abbotsford is at the heart of it. My writings have, I am aware, given pleasure to many, and may continue to do so; it would be foolish to pretend otherwise. Yet this sort of pleasure is an easy business, and for my part, there has been no merit in the achievement. Writing has been as natural to me as breathing. But at Abbotsford I believe I have set an example.

Some politician – I now forget which – used to say that he would willingly bring in one bill to make poaching a felony, another to encourage the breed of foxes, and a third to revive the decayed – and to me repulsive – amusements of cock-fighting and bull-baiting, if by doing so, by thus sacrificing his own feelings to the humours and prejudices of country gentlemen, he could prevail upon them to dwell on their estates, among their tenantry, and care for them in the good old way. For my part I have required no such incentive. I have been fortunate to have had the opportunity to make of Abbotsford what I thought life should be.

We are all of us exiles from Eden, and it sometimes strikes me that the main object of our lives must be to find the route back. When I was but a bairn at Sandyknowe, I knew the reality of Eden; and it is the restoration of the sense of fitness which that knowledge insensibly secured for me that I have attempted in everything which I have done and made at Abbotsford. In doing so I have undoubtedly laid myself open to criticism, even mockery. It may be said – I jalouse that it is said – that in setting myself up as a laird in this fashion, I have gone clean against the spirit of the age. Then the waur for the spirit of the age is my response!

The paradox of man's condition is that we are each of us isolated individuals, activated frequently by mean and selfish impulse –

fear, resentment, hatred, greed. We are each conscious of our own uniqueness, and this feeling is intensified with the progress of civilization. Yet a man alone is but a paltry thing, for we are also tribal beings, and we flourish best in a community where we live in a state of reciprocal obligation towards our fellows. It was such a community that I tried to form at Abbotsford.

Now much is changed. The community is broken like Arthur's table: Charlotte, on whose good sense and vivacity I relied more for my own good spirits than any but our family and a handful of intimates ever knew, is gone. Tom Purdie is no longer on this earth to demonstrate with his every word and action the richest mould of humanity. The children are grown and have their own lives, only Anne, poor lass, remaining to undertake the ever less agreeable task of caring for me, as my temper grows uncertain and my spirits depressed. Even my favourite grand-child, little Johnny Lockhart, has but a slender hold on the thread of life.

As for me, I pray that I may go before my wits leave me. Well, I have been near death before, but never longed for it, as I do now, which is not, I trust, a grievous sin, considering my condition. I would be happy to slip away, with no fuss, and be laid by Charlotte.

When I was very ill ten years ago, and lying in our house in Castle Street, the old Earl of Buchan, as absurd a man as his brothers Thomas and Henry Erskine were intelligent, called to see me. Peter Mathieson, my honest coachman, whose evening psalm was one of my pleasures at Abbotsford when I took a walk by the bowling-green near his cottage, but who on this occasion was acting as a door-keeper, told the Earl that I was too ill to receive visitors. Since Peter's face could assume a lugubrious air that the greatest actor might envy, this would have convinced any man but the Earl, who however, insisting that he must see me, pushed past Peter and mounted the stairs. Peter followed him expostulating, and the noise drew my daughter Sophia from the sick-room. She supported Peter's opinion. In vain: the Earl would see me, and he would have pushed past Sophia had Peter not grabbed him by the coat-tails, spun him round, and shoved him down the stairs, not leaving off till the noble lord was back on the pavement. When I inquired the cause of the disturbance and was told, I was afraid lest Peter's forcefulness might have done the old man some injury. I therefore asked James Ballantyne who was sitting with me to follow the Earl home and explain that I really was so very ill and the family in such bewilderment that the ordinary rules of civility had been dispensed with, etc. James found the old man in his library in a high state of indignation, 'grumbling like a bubbly-jock'. However, James being a dab hand at the art of mollification – which it occurs to me now he had practised on many a creditor – at last appeased his Lordship, who therefore furnished him with an explanation for his extraordinary conduct.

'I wished', he said, 'to embrace Walter Scott before he died, and to relieve his mind by informing him that I had long considered it as a satisfactory circumstance that he and I were destined to rest together in the same place of burial at Dryburgh Abbey, he on account of his connection with the worthy family of Haliburton, I as the hereditary proprietor of the said lands. Moreover, to lay bare the principal purpose of my visit, so rudely forestalled – I wished to relieve his mind as to the arrangements for his funeral, and to show him a plan which I have prepared for the procession – in short, in one word, Mr Ballantyne, to assure him that I take upon myself the whole conduct of the ceremonial at Dryburgh, and the full responsibility. And this – had I been permitted to deliver my message – would have been of great comfort to him.'

Whereupon, for some half-hour, he treated James to a full account of the formal programme, which he had devised, and which existed in writing – 'ready to be sent to the printers instanter, in short, to you, Mr Ballantyne, if you so desire it' – in which programme there could be no doubt that the central figure was not Walter Scott, but David, Earl of Buchan.

Well, the hare-brained old man has beaten me to his resting-place at Dryburgh, and the worms have been at him these two years.

As to my own state, I had a nasty jar when I was in London last Spring. At some party a young lady called Miss Arkwright sang very charmingly. One song especially pleased me, and I whispered to Lockhart, 'Capital – but whose words are they? – Byron's, I suppose, but I cannot place them . . .' 'No,' said Lockhart, 'they are your own, from *The Pirate*.' I was much distressed. If memory goes, I thought, then all is gone, for that has ever been my strong point. And it is going.

Tom Purdie's death was the severest blow I have had since Charlotte passed away; he was my rock. While Tom watched over Abbotsford, for which he felt like all good servants a proprietorial interest that in his case extended even to my literary works, for he took early to referring to them as 'our buiks', it seemed a safe stronghold – '*ein festes burg*', as Luther puts it in his hymn. He came home from work in the woods one evening, laid his head on the table, and fell asleep, never to wake again. I was so shocked, and made wretched by this, that for the first time, I wished to be quit of Abbotsford, and back in the town. I cannot turn a corner in the place without expecting to encounter the comfort of Tom's presence. When I stood by his grave in Melrose, and let a handful of earth fall on his coffin, I knew that nothing, not even Abbotsford, would be the same again; and that my own created Eden was slipping from me like a dream from which I had wakened.

20

Last Days, 1831–2

It was determined I should go abroad for my health's sake – a sentence that discloses the shipwreck which is old age. For more than forty years I had made my own decisions in all important matters, as befitted one of the Black Hussars of Literature which I held myself to be. But now all was changed. It had become a case of 'Sir Walter, you must' and 'Sir Walter, you must not'. This was to be less than a man, less than myself, but in my enfeebled state I lacked the force or resolution to assert my own will. And indeed I did not know truly what that was, for I found myself thrown about like high branches in a big wind, and I was wild, changeable, and erratic as Lear.

> Warm-naked come we to the world, cold-naked take our
>   leave
> And King and Fool and Clown and Knave the grave gapes
>   to receive;
> In black night's wilderness of storm we all alike are tossed
> Like chuckie-stanes that bairns cast till a' distinction's lost.

Besides, my spirits were sore oppressed, and the agitation for parliamentary reform preyed on my weary mind. I scribbled some stuff anent the matter, for it was seldom long absent from my thoughts. But my friends persuaded me it would not do. My arguments, they said, were stale; I was too much 'out of things' to be aware of how the debate had proceeded. It was a further sadness that this mere political affair should be the cause of a coolness between me and James Ballantyne, the first time ever, I think, that a difference of opinion on such a matter divided us one from the other. Moreover, friends, on whom I relied, let it be known, in the kindest, and therefore most humiliating, manner, that they considered my attitude to this question wholly incomprehensible. They had forgotten what I could never forget – how the Revolution in France had begun with mild measures, widely approved, even welcomed with enthusiasm, by many men of sense and discrimination; but had then degenerated rapidly, proceeding to vile destruction for destruction's sake, and to acts of wanton, unspeakable, and unforgivable cruelty.

I endeavoured to make this argument at a meeting of the freeholders of Roxburghshire held at Jedburgh in March, but received an ill-hearing and was howled down. My hand trembled as I took my leave, the infirmity of the body betraying the spirit: '*moriturus, vos saluto*', I said; but believe my words were not heard, or, if heard, not understood.

Then, in April, I suffered yet another, and most severe, apoplectic seizure, which told me that my time on earth must be short. My medical men urged rest upon me. 'Abandon work for the time being, Sir Walter, and there is hope of recovery. We cannot answer for the consequences, however, if you continue to subject yourself to intellectual strain.' I would have none of it, and disregarded the interdict. Like Vespasian, I believed that an emperor should die standing on his feet. 'No,' I said, 'I must home to work while it is yet day; for the night cometh when no man can work. I had that text inscribed on my dial-stone, many a year ago; it has often preached to me in vain, in my idle moments; but now I must heed it.'

I struggled with *Count Robert of Paris*, dictating to my faithful and dear Willie Laidlaw, and, though discouraged by the dislike for the novel expressed by both James Ballantyne and Robert Cadell, yet persevered, for, as I said to Willie, 'we maun aye set a stoot hert tae a stey brae, and the waur the omens, the mair siccar it is we maun grind on,' or, as Addison has it:

> 'Tis not in Mortals to command success;
> But we'll do more, Sempronius, we'll deserve it . . .

It had been easy to preach the Stoic virtues when in health and afflicted only by financial calamity; difficult, but necessary to do so, when my dear Charlotte was taken from me; and I would have deemed it shameful to abandon them now that I was subject to both bodily and mental infirmity, as if a philosophy of Fortitude was not to be maintained when the weather was at its foulest.

The onset of the Elections in May necessarily interrupted me in my task. They tried – daughters, Lockhart, friends and doctors, all – to dissuade me from attending the hustings in Jedburgh, but the Tory candidate was my kinsman, Henry Scott, younger of Harden, to whose father I owed allegiance, and to whom personally I therefore felt loyalty and a due sense that I was obliged to offer my support; and I would not be thwarted.

Jedburgh was in a lively state, having been invaded by a throng of drunken and Radical weavers from Hawick – up to a thousand of the rogues, it was said, all hell-bent on disruption and intimidation of anyone bold enough to set himself against the proposed and pernicious reforms. Recognizing my coach, and being well acquaint with my sympathies, they gave us a rough reception. Stones were thrown, almost as numerous, and more dangerous, as insults. 'Ha,' said I, 'the Jacquerie are already on the march.'

We took breakfast with my old friends the Shortreeds in their house under the walls of the old abbey, and I made a fair go at the porridge and the kippered salmon, as if to feed my resolution; but I declined the proffered quaich of *usquebaugh*, lest in my uncertain and enfeebled condition it should have a visible effect upon me; then, thus refreshed, we made our way to the Court-House, exposed to insults, abuse, and threats, for which I cared not a docken. Young Harden was returned by 40 votes to 19, thus proving that the hearts of the freeholders were still sound; but the result incited the mob to still greater fury, so that some of the gentlemen of the other – that is, the Whig – party became concerned for our safety after we had made our way with some difficulty – but not, I think, actual danger – to the Spread Eagle inn. At any rate they came to us and entreated us not to think of bringing our coach to the front entrance, for they averred that, if we did so, no man could answer for our safety. I was for ignoring this advice, however kindly given, in order to display my contempt for the mob, but was persuaded to accede to it on account of the evident anxiety – for my safety, let it be said – of the other members of our party. Then a certain Whig gentleman, Captain Russell Elliott, recently retired from the Royal Navy, offered to guide us by a back route from the inn to his villa residence on the edge of the town. This was achieved without detection, though not without a degree of shame on my part, even while I naturally recognized the generous care for our safety displayed by a political opponent.

By and by my coachman, honest Peter Mathieson, whom no bullies could deter, brought our coach by a circuitous route to Captain Elliott's where we had meanwhile been refreshed with cakes and wine, of which however I partook but very moderately, mixing the wine with water, and sipping less than half a glass, only indeed accepting any on account of my natural desire to disguise my extreme weakness of health from our honest protector. We then left town, amidst more abuse and a shower of stones delivered to us at the bridge. A sadder set of blackguards I never encountered in any Border town. Lockhart said later that he believed there would have been a determined onset made on us at that point but for the stout-hearted defence offered by four or five of my tenants from Darnick, marshalled by the worthy Joseph Shillinglaw, carpenter. A sad day when such was necessary, but my gratitude to them all the greater. As it was, we left the town with the cries of 'Burke, Sir Walter' ringing in our ears, this referring to the method of murder employed by the villains of the West Port, Burke and Hare, who procured bodies for the Anatomy School of Doctor Knox in this efficient and callous manner.

Well, I suppose if the Bill for Reform is carried, young Harden will be outed next time – *Troia Fuit*, the brave days are done, and what will be the fate of my poor Scotland exposed to the ignorant passions of democracy? As it is, I am much obliged to the brave lads of Jeddart for their confirmation of the wisdom of my judgement as to the advisability of the measure. Their conduct made me think of what used to be called 'Jeddart Justice' – hang the knave and speir his guilt subsequently. But I believe the Hawick blackguards were more at fault; and no doubt drink had its part in enflaming the temper of the mob, as is generally the case in Scotland.

A few days later the Selkirkshire Election came on. This I was obliged to attend in my capacity as Sheriff, and was therefore able to disregard the fears expressed by my daughters, who dreaded a like occurrence, with less appearance of mere wilfulness on my part. But the good folk of Selkirk retained sufficient respect, and perhaps affection, for their Shirra, to behave in a seemly and decent fashion. I saw only one attempt to rabble or hustle a Tory voter, and took pleasure, as the Shirra, in clapping the delinquent in the gaol to cool his heels and teach him better manners.

In the summer I felt myself stronger, and was able to enforce my will, that I should bide at Abbotsford till the autumn. I set aside poor *Count Robert* to take up a tale that had long been in my mind, and to which I had animadverted in my *Essay on Chivalry* for the *Encyclopaedia Britannica*. It was to be called *Castle Dangerous*, and the setting was the Romantic and dramatic Douglas Castle in Lanarkshire, which now survives merely as a ruined tower, though the late Duke of Douglas commenced the building of a magnificent palace within sight of the old keep. I had written some sheets of this new romance, but, being anxious to refresh my memory of the Castle and its surroundings, which I had visited only once in my youth, prevailed upon Lockhart to accompany me on an expedition thither. I was especially eager to view again the tombs of the Douglas family in the old abbey kirk of St Bride, the saint to which that redoubtable clan of warriors paid particular reverence. We set off on a gloomy and heavy morning, with a hint of thunder in the air, but the journey up the Tweed past so many scenes that had delighted me so long – Yair, Ashiestiel itself, Innerleithen, and Traquair with its bear gates – awoke my spirits to a level which I had scarcely imagined they could attain again. I felt the years fall away, and when at last on the point of the ridge between Tweed and Clyde we came on the majestic ruin of Drochel Castle, raised by the Regent Morton, one of the murderers of Darnley, and a Douglas who displayed in the most extreme and sulphurous form the vast ambition which distinguished the family, it was all that Lockhart could do to restrain me from attempting the ascent of the hill to view the ruin more minutely. Then we pushed on to Biggar where we were detained towards sunset by the want of fresh horses, and where the people, informed of who I was, crowded round with respectful curiosity.

And here is an odd thing, in itself no doubt partly explicable by the infirmity of age. I have rarely been gratified by evidence of such public attention, feeling, rightly, I believe, that there is a proper distinction to be made between the author who excites it, and the mere mortal on whom it is imposed. But on this occasion I was aware of a softening of my heart, of a certain gratification. It puzzled me to feel thus; and it was not till I had retired to my bedchamber at the inn of Douglas Mill that it occurred to me that my changed temper must owe something to my memories of the rabbling to which I had been subjected at Jedburgh. This thought, it may well be imagined, was of little comfort, for I had supposed myself to have been but little affected by distress on account of that experience. I passed a wretched night, sleeping but ill, disturbed by the thought that, if I had arrived at a point when satisfaction might rest only in being lionized, I was indeed in a sorry state, my nerves frail, and my virtue fast departing.

> The wan moon is setting behind the white wave,
> And the wind tears the leaves from the trees, O;
> The pale moon of winter's last glimmer of light
> Dies ere the dawning is near, O.

Summer's without, but wan winter's within
A body that's long past repair, O;
The roses may bloom and the eglantine twine
In a morning that smells sweet and fair, O.

But the moon that is setting behind the white wave
Is the light that is dying for me, O;
And the sound that I hear from the black-veilèd barge
Is the raven of death calling me, O.

And the morning indeed brought, in a grey light, intimations of the mortality of man, the evanescence of splendour, the end to which earthly greatness must inevitably come. We descended into the crypt of the abbey kirk, long since itself deserted as a place of worship, though still displaying remnants of sculpture of rare quality, many however having been defaced and desecrated by Cromwell's soldiery who, after their barbarous fashion, used the holy place as a stable. And yet, as I remarked to Lockhart, that works of the sculptor's art equal to any of the fourteenth century to be seen in Westminster Abbey should be found, even in this condition, in so remote and indeed desolate a spot, testifies more surely than the witness of mere words to the grandeur and wealth of those haughty lords whose coronet so often counterpoised the crown. The effigy of the founder of the Douglas greatness, the Good Lord James, friend and companion-in-arms of the Bruce, was still visible, represented cross-legged in the manner of the Crusader who fell in battle against the Moors in Spain while carrying the heart of his king to Jerusalem.

The crypt itself which we surveyed by torchlight was full almost to overflowing of leaden coffins, piled one on top of the other, 'until the lower ones had been pressed flat as sheets of pasteboard', as Lockhart observed with pardonable exaggeration. Some indeed of more recent date stood vertical, there being no room to lay them flat, and, on these, inscriptions and coronets and other signs of heraldry could still be distinguished even in the dim light thrown by the flickering torches. Here, crowded in disorder and covered with the thick dust of long neglect, were to be found the pride and terror of Scotland, higgledy-piggledy in an airless den, a charnel-house where the brave note of chivalry and the fierce defiance of resented authority, which were the marks of this family, were no more to be heard.

'Well,' I said, 'so be it. So may it be for all. Foxes may sty and litter in St Paul's and owls roost in St Giles. *Troia Fuit*, and its windy plains are bare.'

When we emerged from the crypt a crowd had gathered, and a cheer was raised. An old man was presented to me as remembering the visit paid to Douglasdale by one to whom he referred as 'Duke Willie', and it was some little time before I established that this personage was none other than the Duke of Cumberland, the victor of Culloden – shameful and cruel in his hour of triumph, and yet in this westland moorland, which had sixty years earlier been the refuge of the persecuted Covenanters, recalled by this ancient with a degree of reverence which reminded me of the devotion to the graves of the so-called martyrs – and yet, I suppose, they were indeed in their fashion martyrs – which had been shewn by my own Old Mortality.

While I was conversing with the old man, who was proudly garrulous, but not the most coherent of narrators – a thing which could scarcely be wondered at since, at the lowest computation of his age, he must, from his own account, have been nigh on ninety

– while, as I say, we were conversing, a fiddler on the fringe of the crowd, whom I had not previously observed, struck up as if in mockery the old Jacobite ballad 'Kenmure's On and Awa', Willie', an old tune to which Robert Burns supplied new, or additional words. For a moment this pleased me, and I murmured the verses:

> There's a rose in Kenmure's cap, Willie,
>   A bright sword in his hand –
> A hundred Gordons at his side,
>   And hey for English land.

And then the fiddler looked me in the eye, and winked, and I knew him to be the fiddler of Hastie's Close, and I felt my heart chill and my mind in turmoil; for, no sooner did he mark my recognition, than he struck up a different song, which I had heard before. And as he did so, a girl detached herself from the crowd and with a soft swaying movement advanced into the centre of a ring that had been formed and began to dance. She, whom I also knew, from my night alarums, dreams, strange fancies, I knew not what, moved in languorous fashion, and, as she did so, crooned:

> And will ye come wi' me, cuddy,
>   Beyond the land and sea,
> And will ye tak the road, cuddy,
>   The road you ken, wi' me?

> And whatten a road is that, cuddy,
>   You hae nae need to speir;
> And whatten a road is that, cuddy?
>   The road that all men fear.

I felt Lockhart's arm sudden around me, as if I had stumbled and would have fallen.

'You look faint, Sir Walter,' he said, 'I fear the day's excursion and the pressure of the crowd have overtaxed your strength. I have sent to summon the carriage, and we shall take the descent to it by slow and gentle stages.'

'No,' I protested. 'It was but a moment's weakness.'

But, even as I spoke, I heard the cackle of an old woman from the crowd:

'Tak up your bonnie bridegroom while ye may, Ailsie, for his time is but short. His winding-sheet is up as high as his throat already, believe it wha list. His sand has but few grains to rin out, and nae wonder – they've been weel and brawly shaken. The leaves are withering fast on the trees, and he'll never see the Martinmas wind gar them dance round Tweeddale again in swirls like the fairy rings that enclosed and held fast the Young Tamlane.'

'Sir Walter,' Lockhart spoke now with an urgency which I could not mistake, and in which, tenderly, I heard love as well as anxiety, 'I am much concerned. Notwithstanding the force and merit of the interdict which your doctors have placed upon spirits, yet, desperate moments require desperate remedies, and such is your pallor and your shaken condition, that I am persuaded this is such a time'; and with that, he pressed a flask to my lips, murmuring, 'Drink it, pray, it is the finest Armagnac' I swallowed perhaps half a dram and felt the blood surge in my veins, and shuddered, and would have fallen, but for the firm hold on me which he maintained. Then the brandy commenced its recuperative work, and I felt myself steady.

'My head cloudy as the Eildon Hills, though no' sae firm,' I muttered. 'Yet time and I against any two ...'

'What was that, Sir Walter?' he inquired, not hearing, for I jalouse my speech was indistinct.

'Nothing,' I said, summoning up my strength, 'nothing of great matter. Thank you, Lockhart, thank you, my dear, I am myself again.'

But as we moved gently down the slope towards the waiting carriage, the singer's voice followed me, and I could not tell what note it held: mockery? menace? desire? regret? pity?

> And will ye come wi' me, cuddy,
>   To Elfland's fair estate?
> Far frae the strife of men, cuddy,
>   And troubles of the great.
>
> Now that you're auld and grey, cuddy,
>   A ragged lion poor,
> Oh what can haud ye back, cuddy,
>   Frae my enchanter's lure?

When we settled in the carriage, we were silent for a long time, and then, in a wondering tone, I found myself repeating the words that the old woman had pronounced.

'Did you not hear her?' I said. 'Did you not hear her, John?'

He looked at me as if he did not know how to answer, and would fain have remained wordless in his perplexity, but something urgent, something pleading in my eyes, must have told him that I required a response, for he then, after long pondering, said with the utmost gentleness:

'Sir Walter, I must tell you I heard no woman speak.'

'Nor any sing?'

'None.'

'Nor fiddler play?'

'None,' he said again, 'But these words you have recited, though in a broken and quavering voice that it pains me to hear, these words I recognize. They are your own, Sir Walter, taken with some modification and a change of person from *The Bride of Lammermoor*.'

Then we fell silent again, for we were both sair oppressed, I by the devilry it seemed that my mind played on me, and Lockhart by this evidence of my frailty; and there was no sound but the horses' hooves and the carriage wheels, and the sough of the wind as it played over the barren land.

Nine months have passed since that day of awful warning or presentiment, and I write this in Rome* where we are well lodged in the Casa Bernini; but the city is full of ghosts and my mind in a turmoil. On the one hand, I am happy, for I believe I have paid all my debts and am therefore at liberty to die free of all pecuniary encumbrances. Indeed, if my health, which is in general, or at least often feels, improved, since I abandoned the regime imposed upon me by my doctors, and have permitted myself to eat and drink what I fancy, permits me another year or two of life, I may yet purchase the adjoining estate of Faldonside from my old friend Mr Nicol Milne and so complete the accumulation which I have so

---

*   The chronology of the last months of Scott's life is somewhat confused in the manuscript; not surprisingly, considering his state of mind. He sailed from Portsmouth on 29 October 1831, accompanied by his daughter Anne and his elder son Walter, who had been given special leave by his regiment. They spent three weeks in Malta, and then left for Naples, where Scott's younger son Charles, who was attached to the British legation, met them. They remained in the city till mid-April 1832. Young Walter had returned to his regiment, and so it was with Charles and Anne that Scott set out for Rome. Here they stayed until 11 May, when the painful journey home was resumed. (A.M.)

long desired, and be master of a stretch of Tweed from its junction with the Ettrick to Melrose brig. That would be a fine thing indeed. On the other hand, I have cause for sadness. I long for Abbotsford and my poor dogs, and insensibly and foolishly expect, when my hand dangles from my chair, to feel one of them nuzzle it. Then there was the grief occasioned by the news of the death of my beloved grandson, little Johnny Lockhart, a pain too deep for words. The night we heard of his passing, when in Naples, I attended the opera, and I believe poor Anne was a little shocked and dismayed, for she loved the boy as if he had been her own, and her grief was such that she felt compelled to retire in tears to her bed. She did not understand that I attended the opera to staunch my wound. I could not have borne to sit at home and mope; it was that or the oblivion of the bottle, the refuge of Prince Charlie in his long years of exile here.

Here in Rome I am afflicted by a consciousness of certain presences, or rather absences. First, there is Charlotte. I cannot but remember that this of all cities was the one which she, who was normally content with her own domestic circle, most longed to see. 'I cannot say you why,' she would remark, 'for you know, Scott, I take no interest in history, which in general I find *verry* boring. But to visit Rome, that would be different. You will laugh at me, I know, who can scarce tell Brutus from Caesar, but there it is, I believe I should like Rome excessively, and I 'ope that one day you may take me there . . .'

And indeed I can picture too easily, and therefore sadly, how she would have delighted in the beauty of the city, and in taking a picnic or fête-champêtre among the flowery ruins of the Palatine . . . Thinking of this, I am conscious of her ghostly presence, and yet, waking in the cool morning, and stretching out my hand to touch her, I find nothing but the renewed pain of bereavement.

Then there is Byron. Wherever I move in Rome I see the city through his eyes and the verses of *Childe Harold* echo in my troubled mind:

A world is at our feet as fragile as our clay . . .

I have dreamed the last three nights again of Green-breeks, the young Goth of my far-distant youth, as he was in his boyish glory, and I can only account for the recurrence of this persistent memory of one who played so brief a part in my life by reflecting that I apply to him, and to his fall in our Causeway bicker, the lines Byron penned on the dying gladiator:

> . . . his manly brow
> Consents to death, but conquers agony,
> And his doomed head sinks gradually low.

But most of all I am conscious of the perpetual presence of the Stuart kings. I have visited the Cardinal of York's villa at Frascati, with its Romantic view over the serene Campagna so delightfully depicted by Poussin and Claude Lorraine. I have seen the monument in St Peter's which His Majesty George IV nobly had raised to his unfortunate cousins, and I have stood in the little courtyard of the Palazzo Muti where the piper played 'Lochaber No More' as the Prince lay dying; and I too heard that noble and melancholy music.

How true the note of exile rings!

> Oh, it's hame, hame, hame, fain wad I be,
> Hame ance mair in my ain countrie;

To the green braes of Yarrow and Newark's ruined tower,
Where the broom shines yalla and the whaups cry on the
  moor
  Hame, hame, hame, fain wad I be,
  Hame ance mair in my ain countrie.

The exiled sons of Albion have ilka ane a spot
That's dear to them as Paradise and canna be forgot;
Be it Appin or Lochaber or the bonnie braes o Mar,
Or the long moor of Rannoch, the song arises from afar:
  Hame, hame, hame, fain wad I be,
  Hame ance mair in my ain countrie.

In the cause of Prussia, the great Marshal Keith may die,
Honoured by its King, and yet expiring sigh:
'There's an eye that ever weeps and a fair face will be fain
When I ride through Ythan water wi' my bonnie bands
  again':
  Hame, hame, hame, fain wad I be,
  Hame ance mair in my ain countrie.

Oh the lands of France are lush and Italian flowers are braw
But the white rose o Scotland's the bonniest of a',
And my hert will no be healed, nor my spirit be restored,
Till Charlie has his right, and I'm back at my ain board.
  For it's hame, hame, hame, fain wad I be,
  Hame ance mair in my ain countrie.

Hame, hame, hame, fain wad I be,
Hame ance mair in my ain countrie;

Let me ride down Gala Water, let me satisfy my need
To hae one mair sight of Eildon and one hearing o the
   Tweed;
  For it's hame, hame, hame, fain wad I be,
  Hame ance mair in my ain countrie.

If I continue in this vein I shall unman myself.

That dark eerie day in Douglasdale was to my pleased surprise succeeded by a renewal of strength and spirit, and the absence of any strange or supernatural presentiment. Throughout the lave of summer at Abbotsford, I worked well, and to good purpose, contriving to finish both *Count Robert of Paris* and *Castle Dangerous*. Neither work, I was aware, was representative of my best – though the best I could then accomplish – but both served well enough. They were greeted with sufficient enthusiasm by the public, and the latter at least has scenes and moments of which I should not have been ashamed in the days of my full strength. Only in one respect was it affected by my own experiences at Douglas Castle, for the weather of the tale ensures that all events take place under hodden-grey skies, in bone-chilling mists, and driving rain.

That autumn, having also completed the introductions to the remaining novels to be published by Cadell in his Collected Edition, I prepared to obey my doctors and go abroad for my health's sake, sceptical though I was of the efficacy of the proposed remedy. Since, however, to give expression to my doubts would have pained those who loved me, I acceded to the proposed journey with such equanimity as I could muster. I believed death was close at hand, for I felt his cold breath on my cheek; and I was resolved to meet him with all the fortitude of which I was capable. I would indeed have welcomed greater pain if it could have been granted instead of the heartless muddiness of mind which too often oppressed me.

Lord Grey's Government, with a generosity of spirit not to have been expected by a political opponent, most kindly put the frigate *Barham* at my disposal for our trip to the Mediterranean.

'Come, Sir Walter,' said Lockhart, 'you are about to achieve what your admired Samuel Johnson declared to be the great object of travel: to see the shores of the Mediterranean – an ambition which he never gratified himself.'

I endeavoured to respond in the same spirit, for it was my determination to conceal from all, even my dearest, the misery occasioned by my departure and the fear that I might not see Abbotsford again. Indeed, I felt like Moses who was permitted to view the Promised Land only from the heights of Mount Pisgah, but forbidden by the Lord to cross over Jordan, because, as the Book of Deuteronomy says, 'ye trespassed against me among the children of Israel at the waters of Meribah-Kadesh, in the wilderness of Zin; because ye sanctified me not in the midst of the children of Israel.' Only, in my case, I had abided in the Promised Land, from which I was now driven into exile.

However the sea-voyage saw a restoration of both bodily and intellectual vigour – after we had passed through the Bay of Biscay where we were all confoundedly sea-sick; and I delighted in our passage of Cape St Vincent and Trafalgar, the scene of two of Nelson's great victories. We reached Malta on the 22nd November, less than four weeks after setting sail from Portsmouth. There we put up at Beverly's Hotel, where we were comfortably accommodated. I was pleased to meet certain old friends, particularly Mr John Hookham Frere, a notable antiquary who had retired to the island for his health's sake, and whose guidance around its historical sites was both instructive and stimulating. Indeed I was so refreshed that I set to work on a new novel, to be called *The Siege of Malta*, which I completed during our subsequent sojourn in Naples, and which I verily think as good a piece of work – of its type – as I have achieved since *Quentin Durward*. I also wrote a short story, garnered from a local legend, and began to feel that the expedition might be as productive of good as my doctors had assured me would be the case.

I should also say that the War Ministry with a kindness and tact, which I should wish to acknowledge, had granted my elder son Walter leave of absence from his regiment to accompany me on at least the first part of my journey; which was not only a source of great comfort to me, but of pleasure to poor Anne, who was not only thus relieved of responsibility for her ailing – and, I fear, too often crabbit – father, but delighted by the company of her favourite sibling.

The disconnections of my memory are such that I find I have forgot also to record the great kindness of my old friend Mr Wordsworth, the poet, in coming to Abbotsford with his daughter from his home in Westmorland, in order to wish me godspeed on my travels. I was the more sensible of this kindness because Wordsworth was himself in but indifferent health, being in particular afflicted by a malady which rendered his eyes peculiarly sensitive to light, so that throughout his visit he protected or shielded them with a deep green shade – a curious and picturesque addition to his costume. Of our conversation I recall little, though I do remember remarking that it was a singular circumstance that both Fielding and Smollett – who may in a sense be regarded as my precursors – should have been driven abroad by declining health, and had never returned. Mr Wordsworth generously expressed his confidence that such would not be my fate; I wish I could have shared it. Yet, in Naples, whither we travelled after our sojourn at Malta, I began to be more hopeful that he might be right, for I seemed the reverse of his idiot boy:

> For as my body's growing worse,
> My mind is growing better . . .

The first view of Naples filled me with delight; there can be few scenes more tenderly and beautifully Romantic than its bay. It is one of the finest things I ever saw. Vesuvius controls it on the opposite side of the town. My younger son, Charles, who is attached to our legation here, greeted us, to my great joy – so that but for the absence of Sophia and Lockhart and, of course, young Mrs Walter, the whole family was united. Charles, with his customary levity, amused me by assuring me that my arrival had been a signal for the greatest eruption from Vesuvius for many years. I could only reply as the Frenchman did when told of a comet supposed to portend his own death: 'Ah, Messieurs, la comète me fait trop d'honneur.'

Our time at Naples passed for the most part pleasantly. We were fortunate to find in the distinguished antiquary Sir William Gell an ideal *cicerone* – to employ the Italian term – who put himself at our service with the greatest kindness, arranging several expeditions for us, and ensuring by his profound knowledge and acute taste that we derived the greatest possible pleasure and instruction from them. Yet I confess that owing to my lack of Italian – though I could once read the language weel enough – I got as much pleasure from my conversation with Sir William's dog – a fine specimen of the large poodle type – as from my intercourse with even the most distinguished Neapolitans. 'Good boy,' I would say to him, 'I have got at home two favourite dogs of my own – so fine, large and handsome that I fear they look too grand and feudal for my diminished income and invalid state.' At this, the dog laid his head confidingly on my knee as if to intimate that he would do all in his power to compensate for their absence. It was therefore a great pleasure to be able to inform him – and Sir William – that I had received news from Cadell that poor *Count Robert* and sad *Castle Dangerous* had gone into a second edition, so that I was now certain that my debts could finally be cleared and I would be able to sleep straight in my coffin. 'Furthermore,' I told the dog, 'I shall have my house, and my estate round it, free, as long as I live, and may keep my dogs as big and many as I choose, without fear of reproach. But I shall be very pleased if you and your master deign to pay me a visit there . . .'

There is no foolishness in conversation with dogs, for they generally in my experience understand everything that is said to them – not necessarily the words – but the tone of voice conveys all the necessary significance and implications to them. And that is more than can be said for the exchange of compliments I enjoyed with the King of the Two Sicilies, as His Majesty is termed.

I was presented at the Royal Palace on the occasion of the King's birthday. I went with my sons and wore the uniform of a Brigadier-General in the Royal Company of Archers, and looked well enough, for a man of sixty, victim of at least three paralytic fits. I was somewhat afraid of a fall on the highly polished floor, but escaped that disgrace or indignity. The King spoke to me for five minutes, of which I scarcely understood five words – for apart from the lamentable rustiness of my Italian, he speaks habitually, I am told, in the Neapolitan dialect, which, Sir William assured me, Tuscans disdain – perhaps because they cannot understand it either. Had the subject been broached – or rather broachable – I would have repudiated their disdain, since I conceive Neapolitan to stand in the same relation to the Tuscan as our good Scots tongue does to the English. As it was, I answered His Majesty in a speech of somewhat the same length, and, I jalouse, equally unintelligible to him. The theme of my remarks was the beauty of his dominions and so on.

There is in Naples, I find, a general belief in the possession and efficacy of the evil eye. They call the possessor of such power a *jettatura*: well, we ken the phenomenon well enough in Scotland, and though I do not believe in such a power, yet, in recent years I have had moments when I have wondered whether I have myself been afflicted by an ill-wisher – moments of mental frailty certainly, yet sufficiently recurrent to cause me both to tremble and to reproach myself for doing so. They say the King is a firm believer – that would have been a subject to discuss with him. His father, too, is reputed to have been intensely superstitious. Once, in a fit of temper, he kicked a servant – having a frank old feudal way with him in such matters; then, panicking, since there was a portrait of the Madonna almost within sight of the deed, pressed a gold coin on the fellow and begged him on no account to tell the Mother of God of the episode; could anything be more ludicrous and yet more human?

We made expeditions to Pompeii – sad city of the dead – and to the remarkable temple of Paestum, built, Sir William believes, by the Sybarites – inconceivably grand; and to the dark Lake of Avernus, which reminded me, in the scenery, of Scotland, though Virgil makes it the point of entry to the Underworld: *'facilis descensus Averni. . .'* as, alas, I know all too well. I was recalling the noble

Scots version of the old Bishop of Dunkeld, Gavin Douglas: 'Throwout the waste dungeon of Pluto king,' when my attention was alerted by my three familiar figures whom I had not seen since that day in Douglasdale. The old woman sat by the water's edge, spinning, while the fiddler played a melancholy dirge, and the girl danced in a weaving manner as if she would lead me into the water. I knew by now that they were not visible to my companions, and therefore steeled myself to make no remark, but rather to stop my ears to the music, and pretend there was nothing to disturb me; but I fear I displayed some discomposure, for the other members of our party looked at me with concern, and made haste to curtail our inspection of the gloomy and yet sublime scene, and return to our carriage.

So we departed without incident, but with the music echoing insistently in my ears …

> Come, tak the bonnie road, cuddy,
>   That winds about the fernie brae;
> That is the road to Elfland, cuddy,
>   Where thou and I this night maun gae.
>
> And ye maun haud your tongue, cuddy,
>   Whatever you may hear or see;
> For speak ae word in Elfland, cuddy,
>   You'll ne'er get back to your ain countrie.

When we returned to Naples, they told me that Goethe, whom I had planned to visit in Weimar on my northward journey, was dead. I thought at once of *Faustus*, and of the great poet's serenity notwithstanding his comprehension of the possibility of man's voluntary surrender to evil. I thought of the airy beauty of his lyrics, of the terrible pathos of the scene before the *Mater Dolorosa*, and of the skilful and subtle handling of the characters of Mephistopheles and poor Margaret.

'Yet,' I said, as no doubt I had said before – for old men are doomed to repeat themselves, just as misfortune may make them rave with Lear – 'great artist as he was, Goethe was still a German, and none but a German would have had, I fancy, the audacity and arrogance to provoke, as he did in the Introduction, a comparison with the *Book of Job*, the grandest, most noble, and moving poem that ever was written . . .'

Then I said: 'But at least he died at home. We maun to Abbotsford . . .'

That night I fell stiffly to my knees and prayed. I prayed as perhaps Michael Scott, my reputed wizard forebear, may have prayed in Naples, when he realized, in terror and awe, the profound depths and dangers into which his knowledge of what passed then for the magical sciences had lured and exposed him; and I thought of how he, too, under Italian skies, might have longed for our cold and rugged Borderland, that is yet in other moods so gentle, and beneficent in its pastoral beauty, and, like me, have sighed to lay his bones there, within sound of Tweed.

And when I had prayed, I rose, a little unsteadily, to my feet, and turned to my desk, and began again to write:

> The Lord's my herd and in his bucht
>   He bields me siccar;
> He gars me ligg in a green mead
>   Aside still watter.

He wad my saul rejoice that has
   Kenn'd dule and shame;
He sets me on his straucht gude gait
   That leads me hame.

Tho' daith's mirk glen enshroudeth me
   And casts its shade,
Yet I maun dreid nor scaith nor de'il;
   His staff, my aid.

Thou'st breid and meat redd up for me
   In sicht o foes;
My heid with oil anointed, Lord;
   My quaich o'erflows.

Thy bounty and thy mercy, Lord
   My steps sall guide,
That I may in thy ain demesne
   Forever bide.

Afterword by Charles Scott, Esq.

My father died, at Abbotsford as he had wished, in the early afternoon of 21st September 1832. His last days had been painful for all, for his mind was increasingly disordered. Indeed, it is but just to say that there was a progressive deterioration, at least from the date of our departure from Rome on May 11th, and that this was rapid from the moment of his fourth paralytic seizure near Nimeguen on June 9th. His actual passing was tranquil, on one of those beautiful days of early autumn which so often favour Scotland with its most agreeable weather; the day was so warm that all the windows of the house were open, and, as he died in the dining-room on the ground floor, whither his bed had for convenience of all been moved, it may well be that the last sounds he heard were the rippling waters of his beloved Tweed.

He was buried, beside my mother, within the majestic ruins of Dryburgh Abbey. The day was overcast with a high wind, and the whole countryside followed his coffin to the grave.

Within a few days I was obliged to return to my post at the British Legation in Naples, and, passing through Rome, thought it proper to call at the Casa Bernini, where we had lodged, to acquaint the good people there with the circumstances of his death, and to thank them for the care which they had lavished upon us. I may be permitted to say that nothing, in my opinion, so clearly testifies to the virtue and nobility of my father's character as the affection and reverence which he habitually excited in those who served him, even if only briefly.

In the course of my visit I was informed that a manuscript had been discovered in my father's chamber. How it had been overlooked in our departure I cannot conceive; nor do I know whether he had abandoned it of intention, improbable as that must seem. What is certain, however, is that he never mentioned it, or the loss of it, either in the few weeks during which he retained the use of at least some part of his great faculties, or in the period of his more severe disorder.

I naturally thanked the good people for the care they had taken of it, and for restoring it to me, while they intimated that, had I not paused at Rome, they had intended to have it sent to me at Naples as soon as they had word of my return thither.

I carried it south with me in order to peruse it at leisure. The perusal itself was difficult, for towards the end of his life my father's physical infirmities rendered his hand-writing excessively hard to decipher. It may well be imagined that I read it with a mixture of interest, admiration, pain, and sorrow. On a personal or egotistical note, I felt a deep regret for my insouciance, and the demands I continued to make on him, at the time of his deep financial difficulties. It is little excuse to say that I was not fully aware of the extremities to which he was pushed; nor can I acquit myself on the grounds of youth, though I believe it is natural, or at least common, for those brought up to some degree of affluence, to assume unthinkingly a continuing paternal duty to provide for them.

The manuscript would appear to have been written over a period of years, for it certainly refers to events in 1826 as if they had just taken place, while the last pages were evidently written in Rome. If this is so, it may be considered to have been compiled in harness, as it were, with the *Journal* which he commenced in, I believe, the autumn of 1825. Yet I am not persuaded that this is entirely accurate an interpretation, for there are some odd errors of chronology which seem to contradict it. In particular, he would appear to place my mother's death somewhat earlier than it actually occurred, making it almost exactly contemporaneous with the pecuniary calamities that befell him. Furthermore, the hand-writing, though not uniform, is less well-shaped than it was in those earlier years.

This is a problem for my brother-in-law, John Gibson Lockhart, as his designated biographer, to solve. For my part, I incline to the possibility that the whole manuscript was composed during the last year of his life, and mostly during his sojourn in Italy; but that it was contrived in such a manner as to appear otherwise, and to be a disconnected, yet roughly chronological, record of what most occupied his mind in the last five or six years of his life. If this is so, it will be properly regarded, I believe, as a remarkable feat of intellectual and imaginative effort to have been performed by one as sorely afflicted as he was in these unhappy months. (I may add, in passing, that the sheets were unnumbered, and in some confusion of consecutive order, so that it is entirely possible that the manner in which I have been so bold as to arrange them is not that which he might himself have intended.)

Whether, however, it was meant for publication – at least within the lifetime of his immediate relatives – must be doubtful. There is much here that is bound to pain those who loved him; and indeed there have been moments in my reading when I regretted the discovery of the manuscript. Nevertheless, since there is so much of intrinsic interest – and indeed anything from the pen of such a man as my father *must* be of interest – I am arranging to have copies made, and shall send one to Lockhart, that he may make what use of it he will.

It is impossible to read the manuscript without being struck by the mixture of good sense and of what in his robuster moments my father would have dismissed as nonsense. Though he had a lively interest in superstition, and made good and discriminating use of the credulity which attaches itself to ideas of the supernatural, in both his poetry and his novels, no man, in the ordinary way of things, had his feet more securely planted on solid ground. Yet at times the more fantastic episodes, which can only be described by the epithet 'supernatural', which he recounts here, are offered as if they actually occurred, or at least as if he believed them to have done so. It is some small comfort that he seems, in his last weeks of general lucidity, to have realized that they were the product merely of his disordered and sadly perplexed fancy; and the very last page which he wrote appears to express his determination to banish them from his mind by a firm adherence to the Grace of God. At least that is how I read his rendering into Scots of the Twenty-third Psalm.

In his time in Italy my father's health and state of mind varied extremely. This was due partly to his neglect of the diet prescribed by his doctors, and his carelessness with regard to what he ate and drank. I may say that I never once in my life saw him intoxicated – no man indeed had a harder head than he in his prime. Yet in his last months even a small quantity of wine – a couple of glasses, no more – could cause him to talk wildly in an indistinct and incoherent manner.

In these moods he frequently spoke to me of his 'guilt'. I need hardly say that my father, being a man of the utmost virtue, generosity of spirit, and probity, had less occasion to feel guilt than any man I have known, or than almost any of whom I have read. Yet there is no necessary contradiction in this; indeed I believe that the more virtuous a man, the more like he is to be conscious of his deficiencies and failures. Dr Johnson, whom my father was accustomed to hold up as a model exemplar of true Christianity, was – it is well known – almost morbidly conscious of his own shortcomings.

There were three subjects to which he recurred. All surprised me. The first was whether, by making Abbotsford rather than his art the centre of his life, he had in some manner betrayed the gifts bestowed on him. I could scarcely believe he was asking this question – though in another manner of speaking I recalled that he had tackled it, or something like it, in the Introduction to *The Fortunes of Nigel*. When I assured him that it was not so, and that no one, who had given so much pleasure to so many, and been admired so greatly by the most distinguished of his contemporaries, instancing Wordsworth and Byron, could be floored by such an accusation, he looked at me for a long time, with the corners of his mouth drawn down, and then muttered: 'What about posterity? What will posterity say? Will it dismiss me as one who abused his gifts in order to gratify his folly and ambition?' I had never before known him to care for posterity, which I had heard him say was welcome to make any judgement that it chose; so I offered the light assurance that, if posterity was so foolish as to think in this manner, then the judgement of posterity would show itself much inferior to that of our own age. He fell silent again; but clearly the matter preyed on his mind, and is fully debated in the manuscript. I could argue the case, but shall content myself with saying that I consider his observation that Shakespeare may have cared more for his success as a theatre-manager than for his work as a poet and dramatist, but that this does not affect our reception of his plays, to have been a sound one.

His second matter of concern astonished me. He confessed one evening that he believed he had done my mother an injustice. 'It was damaged goods and a cracked heart I brought her,' he said. At the time I knew little of his earlier love for Miss Williamina Belsches – how many of us are interested in our parents' early life and loves, at least in our own youth? – so I was at a loss how to answer. After some pause for reflection, I could only assert that I was confident that my mother had been extremely happy in their marriage, that I was certain she had felt nothing lacking, and that, in any case, he had frequently advised me that mutual affection and esteem – which they certainly possessed for each other – formed a better and more secure basis for marital happiness than Romantic love. 'In general, yes,' he replied, 'but part of me was never with her; and she was never admitted to the secret world of my imagination.' 'Did she ever wish to be?' I responded; and again he fell silent, while I repeated my assurance of my mother's happiness. 'And yet I failed her,' he murmured.

Lockhart, I am sure, will judge otherwise; and so in all probability will any future reader – if there is one – of this work. All I can say myself – as one with no experience of the married state – is that I suspect that doubts of this sort are more likely to make a man a good and considerate husband than the certainty that he already is such a being.

If this astonished me, his third concern left me in a state of mystification. One night, in our last week in Rome, he recited the several stanzas in which Byron describes the gladiator slain in the Colosseum, three lines of which he quotes in the last chapter of this manuscript. Then he talked of the boy whom he called Green-breeks, 'the perfect specimen of the young Goth' – of whom indeed I had never previously heard him speak. He blamed himself severely for never having attempted to discover what had become of the lad, in order that he might have tried to be of some assistance to him in his passage through life, 'assistance such as I, from my superior position, could so easily and without discomfort to myself have afforded to provide'. Then he adjured me to make every effort myself to seek him out, and, if he had fallen into indigence, assist him to the best of our family's ability. 'I am incapable now,' he said. 'I have left undone too long that which I ought to have done; and there is no truth in me. But thou, O Lord, have mercy upon me, miserable offender . . .' then he paused and, collecting himself, said: 'if he is indigent, then Walter must give him a cottage at Abbotsford and provide for him with a pension. But you, Charles, must seek him out. You have the capacity to do so. Swear to me that you will . . .' What could I do but promise? I looked at his trembling hand, his eyes filled with tears, and his mouth twisted as a result of his successive seizures; it would have been too cruel to say that it would have overtaxed all the resources of the whole force of Bow Street Runners to have sought out an unknown boy who had inhabited a mean tenement in the Old Town of Edinburgh almost half a century earlier, and of whom all that was known was that he had once worn ragged green breeches. So I promised as he asked me to do, and I have indeed set enquiries in train; but, of course, they will come to nothing.

Why did he feel such guilt towards this boy? Again that is a matter for Lockhart to determine – though I jalouse he will prefer to ignore it, as an unfortunate aberration of my father's disturbed old age. Having read the sheets concerning him, several speculations present themselves –and, since I am all but certain that Lockhart will indeed let the matter go unremarked, I may as well set them down.

My first thought was that Green-breeks – and it seems absurd to name him so, indeed the designation seems more ridiculous each time I write it, but I know no other – well, yes, let me call him by the name of greater distinction which my father also applied – 'the young Goth' – well then, it occurred to me that the young Goth might have been my father's half-brother, a byblow of my grandfather's. This is of course possible, but improbable, for I do not see how my father could have had the means either of knowing or suspecting it. Moreover, my grandfather seems to have been a man of conspicuous virtue, who, had he fallen into temptation, as even the most godly and virtuous may do, would himself have provided for the child. One cannot be certain of this, of course; and yet the speculation appears to me too wild to be probable. Moreover, my grandfather's comment, when told in later years of the incident – that he wished he had known of it at the time, so that he might have been of some assistance to such a gallant lad – would seem to me to acquit him of responsibility for the young Goth's existence.

My second speculation was perhaps equally wild, and, I am afraid, unworthy. It occurred to me that the youth who seized the small hunting-knife, or hanger, and delivered the blow to the young Goth's head, might have been none other than my father himself. I find this hard to credit, for my father never in my experience told a lie – except – a fairly large exception, you may say – in his denial of the authorship of his novels. Yet I do not believe he would have concealed his responsibility at the time, and I am certain he would not have done so in an intimate memoir of this nature, wherein he reproaches himself for so many real, or imagined, failings. Yet I cannot entirely dismiss the possibility, if only because it is, I understand, well-established that the mind – that cunning instrument – is capable of blotting into oblivion the most unwelcome memories, which however, lurking below its conscious level, may rise to assail it in unexpected manner. If this may indeed have happened on this occasion, it would account for my father's strange agitation concerning the young Goth, even if his memory continued to deny the cause.

There is a third, and more probable, explanation. In concealing the injury the boy suffered, my father, who prized courage above all other things, was guilty for perhaps the sole time in his life of cowardice, of a failure of moral courage. That knowledge was certainly enough to prey on his increasingly uneasy mind; and I suspect this is the true and sufficient explanation of his belated interest in the young Goth's fortunes.

And yet – though this is the probable truth – I cannot stop there. It occurs to me that my father saw the young Goth as his *alter ego*, his Double. Their position in life might so easily have been exchanged – and if so, what of Sir Walter then? This makes a perfectly common-sensical explanation of his enduring, or perhaps revived, interest. This boy, so like himself in spirit and temper – noble, brave, generous – might naturally enough excite his imagination, especially in its infirmity, so that he came not only to wonder what had befallen him – as both he and his brother, Mr Thomas Scott, had wondered years earlier – but to feel a desire to assure himself that all was well with his former antagonist; and so assume responsibility for him in his old age.

Having advanced so far, let me plunge further. He may have come to see him as his *alter ego* in a darker, more macabre sense: the appearance of the young Goth in one of my poor father's fantasies, dancing with the girl who is the Temptress, the Enchantress, the Queen of Elfland, seems to offer two contradictory interpretations. On the one hand, in begging me to seek out his boyhood antagonist, my father may have wished for assurance that his *alter ego* had not in fact surrendered himself to the spirits of darkness; on the other hand, the vision itself seems expressive of a desire for that very surrender, on his part rather than on that of his *alter ego*.

(I could not write this to Lockhart, who would dismiss it as the veriest and most reprehensible nonsense.)

For one thing has been made clear to me by my reading of this, his last work and perhaps testament: that my father was a stranger, more uncanny, being than I had supposed. I never knew a man of more robust good sense, of greater intellectual capacity or sounder judgement; I have never known, nor expect to know, anyone more agreeable, sociable, hospitable, or, in the fullest sense of the word, virtuous. And yet, he was also, at heart, a solitary, living in the strange and secret world of the imagination much of the time. The Shirra – that model of good sense – also wanted to be True Thomas or the young Tamlane, carried away to Elfland. At the same time he wanted to be the great Montrose, or a Highlander assisting in the escape of the Prince, or a Jacobite exile mourning his lost Scotland. He brought all sides of his nature together in his work – at its best – and perhaps also at Abbotsford, for his conception of himself there, as Laird, re-creating a society of feudal obligation and dependence as the image of the good life, a society which was crumbling elsewhere, and which had indeed, I suppose, never existed in the ideal Paradisal form he attempted – that, too, may be judged a species of fantasy. Lastly, he also wished, while being a loving and considerate husband, father, and friend, to be the old magician Michael Scott, delving into the ultimate mysteries – matter which in company and the ordinary everyday life he resolutely shunned.

Of much of this he was well aware. I am persuaded that his conspicuous modesty derived from his consciousness of his own powers, and indeed his own strangeness. But then he knew the strangeness of other men too. When he remarks that it is just as well that while we are seated round the social table we should be unaware of the thoughts throbbing in the brains of our companions, that seems to me a recognition of his understanding of the complex and secret nature of a man. (I know very well I should be horrified if all my thoughts were known to others – especially since I took up my post here at the Naples Legation!)

Many things in this manuscript pained and dismayed me; yet I find its total effect exactly the contrary.

In his last months of lucidity, my father sometimes talked of turning back to poetry. The examples of verse here – often perhaps carelessly and perfunctorily thrown off – may not represent him at his finest, but they are sufficiently so, to suggest, to me at least, that he would not have made the return in vain.

I know Lockhart will disregard much here; but he may find some things of value to him. Then I suspect he will – out of a wish to protect my father's good name of which he is the very jealous guardian – a wish that, in my view, would be quite mistaken – destroy the copy I send him. But it will be only one copy. I am determined – and have grown more so the longer I write – that some day this revelation of how even in suffering and confusion my father remained triumphantly himself will be given to the world.

Ch Scott
Naples
March 1833

Glossary of Scots Words

agley	askew, awry	*cauld*	cold
ahint	behind	*channering*	fretting
aiblins	perhaps	*chiel*	fellow
ain	own	*chuckie-stanes*	pebbles
airt	direction	*collops*	slices of meat
ance	once	*corbie*	crow
ane	one	*crabbit*	crabbed
anent	concerning	*cratur*	creature
auld	old	*criwens*	expression of
awethegither	altogether		surprise/dismay
aye	always	*cuddy*	(*orig.*) donkey,
ayont	beyond		horse, pony; (*by*
			extension) term of
bairn	child		endearment
bannock	flat cake or		
	biscuit	*daith*	death
bield	shelter	*daw*	dawn
brow, brawly	fine, finely	*deeve*	to plague
breid	bread	*deil*	devil
bubbly-jock	turkey	*ding*	to strike
bucht	sheepfold	*docken*	a dock
		dominie	schoolmaster
callant	lad, youngman	*dule*	grief
caller	fresh	*dunk*	to dip
cantrip	piece of trickery,	*dunt*	a blow
	witch's spell		

ee, een	eye, eyes	*kelpie*	water-spirit/ water-horse
eek	also	*ken*	to know
eneuch	enough	*kirk*	church
		kirkyaird	churchyard
fain	eager	*kye*	cattle
feck	the bulk, the most		
flittin'	removal (of houses)	*landlouper*	a vagabond, vagrant
		lave	the rest, remainder
gangrel	wandering	*laverlock*	lark
gar	to compel	*lawin'*	the reckoning
gey	quite	*licht, lichtly*	light, lightly
gin	if	*ligg*	to lie
girny	complaining	*lily leven*	lily lawn
greeting	weeping	*loaning*	part of field used for milking
grilse	young salmon		
gude/guid	good	*loon*	a boy
gyte	mad	*loup*	to leap
		lug	ear
haar	mist, fog	*lum*	chimney
hae	have	*maun*	must
hairst	harvest	*merse*	marshland
hame	home	*mirk*	dark or half-dark
hinna	have not	*muckle*	much, large
hinny	honey		
hosen	stockings	*nane*	none
		neist	next
ilka	every	*nouther*	neither
ingle-neuk	fireside corner		
		quaich	drinking-cup
jalouse	to suspect		
		redd up	to prepare
keening	lamentation		

rickle	loose collection or pile (usually of stones)	*thole*	to endure
		tither	the other
		towmont	a twelve-month
roose	to praise	*tup*	ram
sair	sore	*unco*	excessively
saut-poke	salt-box	*usquebaugh*	whisky
shilpit	puny, sickly-looking	*wad, wadna*	would, would not
shirra	sheriff	*wae*	woe
siccar	certain, sure	*waur*	worse
sicht	sight	*whaur*	where
siller	silver, money	*whaup*	curlew
smoor	smother	*whilk*	which
snell	keen, sharp		
speir	to ask	*yalla*	yellow
stey	steep	*yare*	ready
syne	then, ago, since	*yeese*	use
		yin	one
thon	that	*yon*	that